EM  EAR

A NOVEL

MILTON GHIVIZZANI

Milt Ghivizzani (signature)

Colosseum Publishing
Seattle, Washington

Published by:
Colosseum Publishing
6000 South Eddy Street, P. O. Box 16483
Seattle, WA 98118

Map of Virginia Peninsula: Jo Gershman
Cover Photograph: Gregg Krogstad
Cover Design: Ryan Feasel
Website: Betsey White

ISBN 0-9753975-0-8

Printed in the U.S.A.

For Jean, with all my love

Acknowledgements

My appreciation to John Ferris and Duke Jenkins, my buddies from Virginia, for their technical advice and unflagging encouragement. To Harry Card, my buddy from California, for his editorial advice. To Glyn Copeland, Nancy Copeland and Gray Lynn who have always been in my corner. Special appreciation to my kids, Darling Fournier and Prof. Steven Ghivizzani, for their invaluable advice and generous support. And to Scot Ghivizzani, M.D. for his laser-like editorial guidance and his jumpstart at the beginning. To my brother, Ralph Ghivizzani, for his painstaking research. To Dave Johnson of the Richmond Public Defender Office for taking the time to advise me on Virginia law (any errors, however, are mine). To Cheryl Thompson, Rick Gillespie and all the gang at Seattle Office Furniture. To Jes and Kate at Lottie Motts Coffee Shop for keeping my coffee cup full and allowing me to use their shop as my office. To my wife, Jean, who tirelessly read and reread the manuscript. To Betsey White who performed wonders with both the website and the manuscript. To Henry Brown, Sr. for his many kindnesses. Finally, my most heartfelt thanks to author Deb Caletti who edited the manuscript and pulled me along with encouragement and kind words.

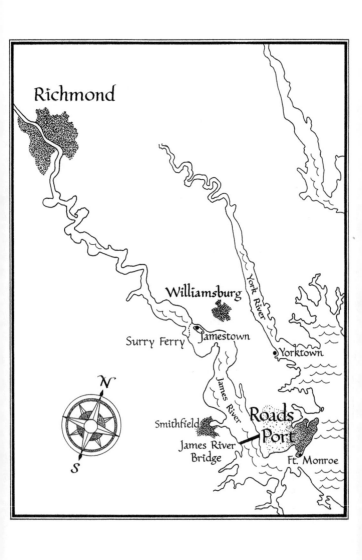

Richmond

Williamsburg

York River

Surry Ferry   Jamestown

Yorktown

N

S

James River

Smithfield   Roads
Port

James River
Bridge

Ft. Monroe

CHAPTER ONE

IF FEAR WAS THE YARDSTICK, this Monday morning was the most critical in Paul Feldman's life.

Desperate to get to the airport in time to make the 10:50 morning flight to Houston, Feldman felt sick as he fought murderous traffic for over an hour to the Richmond International Airport. Forcing down his roiling stomach, Feldman drove into the maw of the parking garage and punched the illuminated button for his parking ticket. He reached for the ticket just as a gut-wrenching wave of nausea hit.

Oh, God – not now!

Feldman raced to the first open space in the packed garage and threw up the second he stepped outside his car. After nearly ten minutes of vomiting, he managed to retrieve his cell phone from his briefcase and call his office– too sick to make the flight.

After more retching and heaving, he got behind the wheel of his car, weaved raggedly down the ramp to pay the cashier and leave.

"Sir, you all right?" the young cashier asked. "You don't look so good."

Feldman started to answer, but flung open his door and vomited again. The cashier jumped back to prevent the foul-smelling liquid from splashing on her shoes. Finally Feldman could only expel a small amount of spit.

"Sorry about the mess. I'll be okay," he said in a raspy voice. "I just need to get home and get to bed."

What the hell would his boss say now? After laboring in obscurity for seven long years, Paul Feldman's career finally looked as if it might take off like one of the solid fuel boosters manufactured by his company, Rocket Science, Inc.

For the very first time the company president himself had asked that Feldman fly to Texas and present the latest strategic plan to the Houston office. The company's travel office had booked Feldman on the morning flight. Only vice-presidents were ever sent to Houston. It looked to Feldman like he was definitely in line for a promotion.

On other business trips, Feldman had always asked his stunning wife, Marian, to accompany him. Thanks to indulgent parents, Marian was used to fine, expensive things, and Neiman Marcus in Houston was perfect for her up-scale brand of shopping. But there would be no time for shopping or sightseeing on this trip, he'd told her. This trip was going to be all business. It was *the* meeting, the pivotal point in his career.

Marian made a baroque show of disappointment, but in the end had wished him well. As he left, she pulled the blankets up around her and with a little girl smile sleepily kissed him goodbye. She was stretching and lazily reaching for the bedside phone as he backed out of the driveway. "All clear. Come on over."

After collecting his change and receipt, Feldman drove off toward home, wondering whether he should head for the nearest emergency room instead.

BY THIS TIME, Marian was entertaining Police Detective Arnold Carey in the Feldman marital bed.

Marian knelt on the edge of the bed doggie style . . . and the detective, wearing only his socks, assumed his position behind her, with his back to the bedroom door several feet away.

Marian moaned with pleasure. For her, anal sex was exactly what she craved. "You like it like this, don't you baby?" Carey asked her over and over.

"Yes, oh YES!" Marian shouted.   And in a low, thick voice, pleaded: "Deeper." Carey grabbed her hips and drew her toward him while he thrust forward roughly. "OH GOD YES! Like that." Neither of them heard the door quietly open.

The visitor stepped inside, took the detective's automatic from its holster hanging with his clothes on a chair near the door, aimed and squeezed the trigger.

The automatic's report filled the bedroom. The lead round hit the back of Carey's head, propelling him forward so that Marian was now face down on the bed, with Carey on top of her.

Marian couldn't hear her own screams as she struggled to get the detective's body off her. Nor, from her position, could she see the visitor's gloved hand slip the automatic back in its holster and exit the bedroom.

Adrenaline poured into Marian's system and she began to function well past her normal limits.   She shrugged off Carey's lifeless two hundred pounds and got herself free.

Marian's mind raced. She dragged Carey's body to the floor, then over toward the bedroom window. She struggled to keep the detective on his stomach as she moved him. She was aware of blood leaking from the wound. A trail of blood would tip investigators to her having moved the body.

With what seemed like superhuman strength, Marian

managed to dress the deceased detective. All the while she was reviewing in her mind TV crime shows and what criminals did to cover up evidence. Bleach, she remembered, was used to eradicate blood stains. Okay, she could do this . . . she had some bleach in the bathroom. Marian wiped up the blood, flushed the paper towels and reshelf the bleach. That done, she showered and called 911.

PAUL FELDMAN WOULD later tell homicide investigators that on his drive home from the airport he had stopped a couple of times so that he could vomit by the side of the road. And that when he tried to turn onto his street, both lanes were blocked by squad cars.

Still desperately nauseated, he had abandoned his car and staggered toward home. The place was alive with cops, firemen, and EMT people. Police cruisers, fire trucks and medic vans were parked all over the place, their intense blue and white overhead lights flashing while their radios crackled out unintelligible instructions. Shrill sirens in the distance announced the arrival of even more official vehicles.

When Feldman had walked up, a gurney carrying a covered body rolled to a waiting morgue hearse, and Marian was being escorted to an unmarked police car. Feldman called to his wife from behind the yellow crime scene tape, and, although she didn't respond, their eyes met for a second before she entered the back seat.

When questioned at the scene, Marian said that she had called Detective Carey about noises she heard outside her bedroom window the previous night. A uniformed cop wanted to know why she reported the noises to Detective Carey? Why not report them to police headquarters? She answered that she had met

Detective Carey socially and thought contacting him directly would speed up the investigation.

MARIAN AND PAUL Feldman were on their separate ways downtown to police headquarters when Homicide Detective Lieutenant Sammy Ditsel arrived at the scene. Behind his back, Detective Ditsel's subordinates called him "the weasel," which, with his pointed nose and receding chin, he uncannily resembled. The fact that he was good at his job made them like him even less, if that was possible.

After speaking with the uniformed cop who had briefly questioned Marian and Paul, Ditsel thought their stories implausible and unconvincing. In fact, in Ditsel's professional opinion, both Feldman stories were, as he put it, "unadulterated cow flop."

Ditsel had of course known of Carey's reputation for banging married women and had assumed that's what had happened here, except that in this case Carey finally got paid off, probably by the husband.

Ditsel was a percentage player. All U.S. domestic murder statistics pointed overwhelmingly to the husband in cases like this 50 to 1. Ditsel asked himself who the hell was he to buck those odds?

There was no question in Ditsel's mind that his late colleague had been redressed by someone after he died and that elaborate pains had been taken to wipe everything clean, but he said nothing to the other cops. Better to ask the Feldmans those questions back at the station.

It appeared to Ditsel that rigor mortis had begun by the time he entered the bedroom, which told him that Mrs. Feldman did not call 911 immediately. It was his experience that it took at least an hour, usually longer, for a body to become as rigid as Carey's. Also, the knot in Carey's tie was a four-in-hand, not the fat Ronald Reagan Windsor knot that Carey favored.

A forensic examination would later bear out Ditsel's discovery of blood on the heel of Carey's left sock and nothing on his left shoe, not even fingerprints. This would confirm what Ditsel had already surmised: except for his socks, Carey was naked when he was shot and then redressed afterward.

The ballistics report that followed stated unequivocally that Carey had been shot with his own gun, which was consistent with the husband's happening on the scene, becoming enraged, grabbing the convenient gun and shooting his wife's lover.

But Carey had been shot in the back of his head, and that was puzzling, because surely the enraged husband would have shouted something out before firing. If so, Carey would have turned to face the killer and gotten shot in the face, or at the very least, half-turned and taken it in the temple.

Then there was the husband's failing to take a scheduled business trip because of sickness and returning home just in time to see his wife leaving in a police car. To Ditsel's mind, that just had to be blatant bullshit. Yet, he was actually sick. Although Ditsel had seen first time murder perps throw up when they confessed, this apparently was different. According to a uniform at the scene, Feldman's shirt was soaked with sweat and he heaved every few minutes.

Something was off somewhere. Ditsel had gone over the room a dozen times, and it felt all wrong - and weird. *That Feldman woman knows something*, he thought. *The shower's dry, but the squeegee under the sink is wet. It has to be the husband, goddammit, and she's covering for him.*

The evidence against him so far was all circumstantial and on the thin side at that, but Ditsel had made up his mind to press the Commonwealth Attorney hard to charge Paul Feldman. He'd camp outside the CA's office day and night if he had to. If Feldman was charged with murder, something more would shake loose. Ditsel would bet his new Grand Cherokee on it.

In Ditsel's book, this was a classic domestic homicide: cheating wife diddles lover in the marital home; husband arrives unexpectedly; husband blows lover away.

In his long career, Ditsel had seen hundreds of these domestic killings play out. Absent a criminal history and evidence of premeditation, the husband would be charged with murder two, which would be pled down to voluntary manslaughter. The husband would be sentenced to three years, released in 24 months, over and out.

If, on the other hand, the judge wouldn't accept a manslaughter plea (and Ditsel had also seen this happen more than once), the husband was looking at serious time: from 5 to 40 years. And that meant a trial on a charge of murder two for sure.

Ditsel knew that the big difference in this case was that the husband had killed a *cop*, and no cop killer would ever be charged with anything as lenient as murder two. No, Paul Feldman would be charged with capital murder and the Commonwealth would demand the death penalty, and that made Ditsel smile.

PAUL AND MARIAN were questioned separately at the station and both requested lawyers when the interrogators started making accusations.

When Detective Ditsel returned to the station, he had come unglued when he heard that the Feldmans had lawyered up. Why, he railed, had the interrogators put them on the rack before they tested them for gunpowder residue? And why hadn't they waited for him in the first goddamm place? Now he'd never get a crack at them.

Suddenly Ditsel screamed, "SHIT PISS FUCK!" at the top of his lungs, shocking the squad room into silence. The other detectives stared at Ditsel like he'd lost the last of his little rodent mind, and the secretaries glowered at him sullenly, and not for the first time.

Ditsel didn't give a damn what they thought. How many goddamn times had he taught them that the classic method of interrogation was to start off nice as pie, and gradually apply gentle pressure? When that tactic had run its course, they should then say: "We'd like to run a routine test for gunpowder residue just to rule you out of the investigation."

Only after the residue test did you get tough. Ditsel discovered that the clowns doing the interrogation had jumped right in with the thumbscrews. "These fucking people aren't garbage off the street," he ranted. "Godammit, they're smart enough to know they don't have to answer jack after asking for a lawyer."

All it took was the mere mention of wanting to talk to a lawyer to stop further questioning on a dime. But Ditsel knew that the one thing lawyers couldn't prevent was a demand that their clients give nontestimonial evidence. For both Feldmans, this meant a test for gunpowder residue, which theoretically would prove that one of them had recently fired a gun. For Marian Feldman it also meant a request for a medical examination for rape, which she refused. "A man was murdered. I wasn't raped, you idiots!"

The harm was already done, but Ditsel still wanted to nail down his suspicion that Carey was banging the Feldman woman at the time of his death. After giving her a drooling once-over at the station, Ditsel knew he was right. In addition to Carey's reputation and Marian Feldman's lusciousness, Paul Feldman was several years older than his wife, and for Ditsel, who had a stormy May-December marriage of his own, that cinched it.

He threatened Marian with a court order if she continued to refuse his request for a rape kit. At that, Marian, obviously confident that no judge would issue such an order, simply turned and walked away from the seething detective and caught a cab home.

"WHAT HAPPENED, MARIAN?"

"I'm a wreck, Paul. I don't want to talk about it right now." Marian was pacing the room in a haze of cigarette smoke. She kept hearing the shot and smelling the burnt gun powder. Try as she might, she couldn't forget the dead weight of Carey's body when he collapsed on her. One second, he was very much alive; the next second, irretrievably, irrevocably dead. Christ!

"They think I shot that detective," said Paul. "They said I did it out of jealousy."

Marian stopped pacing momentarily and glanced at Paul. He looked sick and weak and desperately out of control.

"You have bigger balls than I thought."

"What? You think I did a thing like that?"

Okay, have it your way, she thought. *You didn't shoot him.*

Paul looked utterly confused and Marian could have kicked herself for mouthing off, but it never occurred to her until that moment that it could have been anyone but

Paul who had shot Carey. Yet, as she looked at him and thought for a moment, the idea of Paul as a killer was laughable. Whatever the truth, somehow she had to repair the damage her quick, sarcastic mouth had caused.

"No, of course not. You couldn't shoot a mosquito, but the cops don't know it." *And neither do I, for sure.* "All they know is that another cop was shot in your home while your wife was there with him, alone. They think that this was some kind of love triangle with you as the wronged husband who shot his wife's lover in a jealous rage. I told them what really happened."

"Is that the way it was, Marian? Was he your lover? Because if he was, then I think I'd better move into an apartment downtown."

"Emphatically not, you son of a bitch, and I'm insulted that you'd ask me a thing like that!"

Marian knew that if Paul were truly innocent, he'd be desperate to hear a lie, the balder the better. She also knew that there were going to be explosive repercussions. She had lied to the cops, which they had probably expected. But one of their own had been murdered, and they wouldn't give up without nailing somebody. They would dither for a while, with their thumbs firmly planted up their asses, then they would come after Paul with everything they had.

"As for your moving, right now I'd be happy as hell if you did move," said Marian, praying to God that Paul was buying her insulted act. Because if he wasn't, he'd divorce her and she'd lose everything. She'd lose her magnificent home and her lavish life, both of which were financed by Paul's inherited wealth and therefore not reachable by her in a divorce action. "But I think you'd better consult a lawyer before you do. Any lawyer will tell you to STAY-FUCKING-PUT!" she cried.

"Meanwhile, you can sleep in the guest bedroom."

PAUL HAD LEFT the house and walked out in the late winter cold to a small city park where he heaved into the bushes again and again, until there was nothing left in his stomach. He sat on a concrete bench and fought back the green waves of nausea. *My life with Marian and everything I've worked so hard for at Rocket Science are on the line. It will be a miracle if I don't lose it all. The police will arrest me, I know they will. Then I'll be tried and probably convicted. Game over, whether they execute me or not.*

Shivering and exhausted after standing on the curb in the freezing cold for what seemed like hours, Paul finally hailed a cab. He told the cabby to take him to a local motel, then sat with his head back, looking up at the headliner.

After he checked in, he stumbled to his room, fell into bed, and escaped the living nightmare for a few precious hours by slipping into oblivion.

CHAPTER TWO

FELDMAN KNEW A LAWYER HE would trust with his life. Joe Bari was an old college friend. The last he had heard, Bari was still practicing law in Roads Port, seventy miles east of Richmond, on the tip of the

Lower Peninsula.

"Mr. Bari's office."

"I'd like to speak to Mr. Bari. Tell him that Paul Feldman is calling."

Joseph Mahoney Bari, son of a second generation Italian businessman and a third generation Irish mother, was the star litigator in a small but influential law firm in Roads Port, Virginia.

Like many successful men, he had worked hard as a young man, in school and out. He had been obedient and respectful, and had harbored a secret, raging ambition. He also harbored the memory of a biting resentment at the prejudice he suffered as a youngster in the South. He was often shunned because of his Italian-Irish-Catholic heritage and his smooth olive complexion, but that was all in the past. This was the New South, and jokes based on ethnic background were déclassé and skin color was never mentioned in any company for any reason.

Bari had been good at sports and popular with the girls. Oddly, his buddies thought, he had become best friends with Paul Feldman, the gangly kid he sat next to in his college history class.

"Paul, is that you? How the hell are you, buddy? I've been meaning to call. How's Marian?"

"It's good to hear your voice, Joe. Listen, I'm in some trouble and I'd like to come down to Roads Port to talk to you about it."

"Sure, Paul. Come ahead. You stay with me while you're here, you understand?"

"I'll see you tomorrow morning, if you can fit me in."

"Of course I can fit you in, for Christ's sake. Where are you calling from, Paul?

"Richmond."

The two friends had decreasing contact over the years, not out of ill will or boredom, but simply due to the difficulties of living in different cities. Friends have to work at friendship when they are separated, and most simply don't have the time or the energy left over after work and family.

Joe tried to imagine what trouble was brewing in his friend's life - divorce, probably. Paul hadn't answered his question about Marian. That was it. Paul and Marian were splitting up and Paul wanted him to handle the divorce.

READING THE PAPER over breakfast next morning, Joe had discovered to his horror that it wasn't divorce his friend was coming to see him about, it was murder - of a cop.

Feldman got off the elevator and stopped at the receptionist's desk. "I'm Paul Feldman. I called yesterday . . ."

Joe Bari hurried from his office, a big grin on his face. "Paul! It's you!" He grabbed Feldman's hand in a crushing handshake. "How are you, buddy? I've been meaning to call - it's been what, a couple of years?"

As the two men entered Bari's office, Feldman, tears streaming down his cheeks, embraced him, "Yes, two years at least. It seems like twenty."

Bari was deeply touched, but he refused to give in to the moment. They had serious business to discuss and emotion would only get in the way. "How is that possible? How's Marian?"

"She's okay, I think. Listen Joe, there's going to be trouble, and I need to talk to you about it."

"That's what you said on the phone." Joe Bari gestured for Feldman to sit down on the sofa, rather than the client's chair in front of Joe's walnut desk, an antique given to him as a wedding present by his well-off in-laws. "Since you're down here on the Lower Peninsula, you stay with Ann and me. No argument, okay?"

Joe Bari went to his desk, fingered the intercom and asked that coffee and pastry be brought into the office.

"Joe, I'm a suspect in a murder that took place in my home."

"Yes, I know," Joe said as he sat down facing Feldman on the sofa. "There was a brief piece in this morning's paper and something on TV. Apparently, a police detective was shot in your home."

"I was at the airport when it happened, Joe. I couldn't have killed that man and I didn't."

"You weren't arrested, so that's good. Did you make a statement to the cops?"

"I gave some detective a stripped down account of the facts, and when he got pushy, I said I wanted to talk to a lawyer."

"Good going, Paul," said Bari, leaning over to give his shoulder a friendly punch.

"I remembered you gave that advice to the crowd at a party one night years ago. Everyone laughed. I never dreamed that one day I'd be following it."

Bari's secretary opened the door and set the silver tray service on the coffee table in front of the sofa. "Will there be anything else, Joe?"

"No, thank you, Helen. Just close the door if you will."

After the door clicked shut, Feldman said, "I'd like a drink if you have something here."

Bari went to a cabinet adjoining the bookshelves and took out a bottle of hundred proof brandy and a cut crystal tumbler. He put the setup on the coffee table and poured three fingers of brandy. Feldman quickly drank half of it, shuddered, and put down the glass.

"Hey, it's terrific to see you, Paul. Are you still reading Plato?"

Feldman laughed. "Oh, yes, just like in college. I'm still one of the 'Philosopher Kings of Agate Street.'"

"Damn, I haven't thought about our house on Agate Street in years," Bari said, pausing, his memories of those bygone days off campus seeping back into his mind.

"Those were great days, Joe," Feldman said, almost sadly. "The off-campus salon, students dropping over to discuss all kinds of stuff: everything from Aristotle to football; horse racing to sex."

Bari had always deeply valued his friendship with Paul Feldman because Feldman was the genuine article: a true intellectual, even at twenty. From their discussions, often continuing on late into the night, Joe Bari learned how to think. After that, the remainder of his academic life was a breeze.

Feldman polished off the glass of brandy, and shook his head when Bari offered more. "First, I want you to know that I had nothing to do with the murder. I was supposed to go on a business trip. . . ." Feldman gave his old friend a concise story of his illness at the airport and what he saw when he returned home.

"What's the story at work, Paul?"

"Tom Orbis, the company president called and offered his support. Anything I needed. When I told him that I might be charged with murder, he couldn't believe it. Good old Tom. In fact, he laughed. He told me to take paid leave until this thing was settled. Everyone should have such a boss."

Bari hadn't seen Paul Feldman in two years, but he

thought that his friend had aged more than that. "Listen carefully. Don't speak to anyone about this, except Marian, and be careful what you say to her. The paper said that Marian was present when it happened. Is that right?"

"Yes, but I'd rather not talk about Marian right at this moment, if you don't mind. Can we return to her later?"

Trouble. "Sure Paul. I'll represent you, you know that, but you've got to promise me something. You won't think it matters, but it's all important. You've got to take care of yourself while this is going on. You look like hell. Go see a doctor and get him to prescribe something to help you. You've got to eat right too. No missing meals even if you're not hungry. Do I have your promise you'll do that?" It was one thing to look owlish, which Paul did naturally. It was another thing to look like a scarecrow, particularly in front of a jury if, god forbid, it came to that.

Feldman smiled weakly, "Thanks Joe."

"What do you think happened? Take your time."

Bari knew the Richmond cops weren't about to let this case go into the unsolved pile along with hundreds before it. Richmond, Virginia wasn't the country's crime capital, but its murder rate was a respectable fifth, right after Detroit.

No, this was different: a cop killing. Tradition in police departments the world over held that you threw everything at the case until it was solved, and then you made sure the killer got the max, which, in Virginia, was death by lethal injection.

What this meant to Bari, was that his friend would be charged very soon, simply because the cop was killed in his house and his wife knew a lot more about it than she was telling. Bari's law stated that anytime a guy buys it in the presence of a 10 plus babe, which Marian was, indisputably, there was always a lot more.

"Marian had complained to me recently of hearing noises outside at night," said Feldman. "I told her to report it. The last time was two nights ago. She said the detective was there investigating the possibility of vandalism or attempted burglary.

"This was Carey?" Bari asked.

"Yes. She said he had been there only a few minutes when somebody shot him, probably from the bedroom door that opens onto the hallway. She didn't see the shooter. Apparently she and the detective were looking at the bedroom window and trying to get it open when the shot was fired. In that position, their backs would be to the door. After the shot was fired and she collected herself, she called 911, and that's all she knows."

"Were you tested for gun powder residue?" asked Bari.

"Yes, but they didn't tell me the results. Doesn't matter, because the results are negative; I've never fired a gun in my life."

"How about Marian . . . was she tested?"

Feldman tried to hide his reaction, Bari noticed. "I don't know. We've only spoken briefly since it happened and I didn't think to ask her."

Oh, shit, Bari thought. Paul suspected Marian of doing more than simply reporting an attempted burglary. "I'd like for you and Marian to stay with Ann and me for a couple of days. I want you to call Marian and tell her that you've talked to me and you want her to drive down and be our guest." They stood up together, and Bari put his hand on his friend's shoulder as they walked out and down the hall to the firm's reception area. "Drive over to the house when you leave here. Ann will be looking for you."

Bari knew that the tension between Paul and Marian Feldman would stick out like a herd of zebras. Something had to be done before the media spotted it and pounced.

THE RAIN AND snow took a breather, and, to mixed reviews, the sun made an appearance. It wasn't the decadent Florida sun that warmed bougainvilleas and magnolias; it was the puritanical Virginia sun that sent temperatures plummeting. Joe Bari hated the cold.

"Sonofabitch," he muttered, as he carefully negotiated the icy entry stairs. Bari called for coffee before hanging up his top coat and muffler.

"Helen, will you call the super and tell him to do something about all that goddamn ice on the entryway stairs? Then get in touch with Cammy and tell him to get over here. Thanks, Helen. And get that den mother look off your face. I look stupid in a hat."

His colleagues at the firm envied Bari his attractive, super-competent secretary. Helen Wythe had been his legal secretary since Bari graduated from law school and joined the firm. She was twenty years Bari's senior and she did cluck from time to time if he failed to wear a hat or go out without a top coat in cold weather.

"Cammy says he'll be right over if he doesn't slide into a ditch first," said Helen. "Personally, I hope he does crash into a ditch. I can't stand that ugly thing he drives."

"Cammy" was the nickname for Washington Sizemore Brown, Bari's private investigator. Cammy was short for chameleon. Fitting, because he was perfectly believable as a homeless drunk or a college professor, and he loved it when his assignments called on his acting talents.

Just as a great line makes a great quarterback, a great investigator makes a great lawyer; and no PI in the entire South could touch Washington Sizemore Brown, a.k.a., Cammy.

Cammy's father, now living an ill-gotten retirement in Smithfield, Virginia, had been a PI and a numbers banker, a bootlegger, a dealer in stolen merchandise, a pool/cards/dice hustler and a pimp. It's stretching the concept to the breaking point to say that he was a good father, but the fact was he always kept Cammy with him when Cammy wasn't supposed to be in school and many times when he was.

Cammy seemed to have absorbed everything he heard and saw, and when he decided to hang out a shingle, his dad's connections became his connections. He was on a first-name basis with judges, secretaries, scam artists, detectives and beat cops by the score all over the state - hell, they'd seen him come up - and there was no denying the value of such a Rolodex to a man in Cammy's line of work.

If a payoff was indicated, as it so frequently was, there was never a need to pussyfoot around to see who would take and who wouldn't. Cammy could walk right up to the man with the juice or the information, a man he would already know well, and with little preamble, grease him, and get what he wanted. Bing, bam, boom.

Cammy was also blessed with an impressive physical appearance. He was six-two, with Denzel Washington's good looks. And when he turned on the charm, panties dropped and doors opened.

When it came to appreciation, Joe Bari would have been first in line to praise the work Cammy did for him.

He would have been lost without him. Even so, Bari tried several times to get Cammy interested in show business. A career in TV or movies would have allowed his acting talents to bloom, and would have paid a lot more, although Cammy didn't do badly right where he was.

"You rang?"

"Yeah, come on in, Cammy, this could be a big one. A cop was killed in my client's home in Richmond yesterday morning. They haven't arrested him yet, but it's only a matter of time. A few days, maybe."

"Yeah, I saw it on channel ten an hour ago."

"It's more than just a straight up murder; Paul Feldman is a damn close friend. We were roommates in college. I was his best man, he was mine. He's innocent; I'd stake my life on it. How busy are you right now? Can you give this case some undivided attention?"

"I got a few things, nothing that Aaron can't see to till I'm done with this." Aaron was Cammy's sharp new assistant, a recent graduate of John Mason University's department of criminal justice. At first, Cammy had trouble getting used to Aaron's geeky enthusiasm, but he now seemed to be "working out," as Cammy told Bari a few months back.

"You've got contacts on the Richmond P.D." This was Joe Bari's educated assumption, because Cammy had never given up his sources to Bari or anyone else. "I want you to go to Richmond and see if you can get the police report and a copy of the lead detective's field notes," said Bari, pacing and reading from a yellow legal pad. "The investigation will more than likely be ongoing, so those notes won't be on file and they won't be easy to put your hands on."

"Amen to that," said Cammy.

"Also, find out what you can about the dead cop and my client's wife. And while you're at it, talk to some of Paul's neighbors. If they saw Paul or his car before the cops got there, we're dead. You'll need some expense money; I'll have Helen write you a check for five thousand."

"Better make it twenty." Cammy frowned at Bari's consistently unrealistic assessment of the market they dealt in. "The stuff you want won't come cheap. I hope Mr. Paul Feldman is loaded. I have the feeling that his defense is going to get very expensive very soon."

OVER THE NEXT two days, before Marian arrived, Ann Bari tried valiantly to lift Feldman's spirits. Difficult, because he mostly wanted to stay in the guest bedroom and read and watch television, but Ann, on her husband's instructions, insisted they spend the day in some distracting activity. Joe was right, of course. When his friend's attention was diverted, he was less likely to sink into the dismal swamp of depression.

To that end, they took the full tour of Colonial Williamsburg, thirty miles west of Roads Port, and had lunch at one of its many inns. They were served by College of William & Mary students who waited tables costumed in period garb.

They drove to Yorktown and saw where the French, the Colonial Army and the Virginia Militia hemmed in General Cornwallis two centuries ago and ended the Revolutionary War. Afterward they took a long walking tour of the battlefields between Yorktown and Williamsburg.

Before she and Bari were married, Ann worked as a docent for Colonial Williamsburg. She loved that job and was good at it, so she gave the preoccupied Feldman some lively lectures on Colonial history, which he enjoyed despite the strong undertow of anxiety and depression that threatened to overwhelm him at every turn.

They could see their breath as they walked along. All at once, Ann felt the need to reassure him. "Paul, I'm glad you have Joe. He's smart, and he'll fight harder for you than anyone else."

"Yes, I know. There's no one else I'd rather have on my side now."

IN THE EVENINGS, the two friends got caught up. "Tell me about Rocket Science. What's it like to work for a big outfit like that?" Bari asked.

"I've loved it," answered Feldman. "There's been quite a bit of resentment recently because I'm about to be made vice president in charge of development. Goes with the territory. I suppose we all love what we're good at, and I've made some significant contributions to the company." Feldman paused and looked at the embers in the library fireplace. "But I honestly don't know what effect the detective's death will have on my job. I wish to hell I knew what really happened at my home on February fifteenth."

"Paul, this is Joe you're talking to. If there's anything you want to tell me, go ahead. Your worries are my worries. Besides being your friend, I'm your lawyer, and I need to know everything."

Paul shook his head, "No, I'm utterly at sea. I have no idea what's happened to our lives in the last three days."

"JOE, THIS IS Cammy. I'm going to fax you the police and autopsy reports. I should be back in town with the rest tomorrow or the day after."

"Excellent, Cam." Good old Cammy, what in hell would I do without you? "Come by the office the minute you get in."

The police report and crime scene photographs gave all the usual information about the time of the 911 call, the position and condition of the body, the bloodstains, and statements given by the "subjects."

The autopsy report stated that Detective Carey was shot once with a 9mm lead slug from a distance of about ten feet. The shot entered the occipital lobe and lodged in the medulla, causing massive trauma to the brain and instantaneous death. The estimated time of death was ten a.m. The report went on to state that there had been recent sexual activity, and ballistics confirmed that the bullet in Carey's brain was fired from his own gun.

CAMMY RETURNED WITH a copy of Detective Ditsel's field notes on the morning of the fourth day. That afternoon Marian arrived at Bari's office and was ushered in immediately.

"Marian, what a vision you are," said Bari, all welcoming smiles and handshakes and pecks on the cheek. "How are you?"

"After all that buttering up, wary. How are you, Joe?"

Marian, who would look delectable in sackcloth, was dressed in anything but. She was elegant in a white Irish sweater, tailored tan wool slacks and medium heels, and Bari struggled to disguise the fact that she took his breath away.

"Marian, you know Paul asked me to represent him if he's indicted for Detective Carey's *homicide*." Bari chose his words carefully. It wasn't murder until somebody was charged with murder. "If you both are indicted, which is unlikely in my opinion, I could represent only one of you, because your interests would be in potential conflict, you understand."

Marian appeared more interested in Bari's desk than in his legal opinions. "Beautiful. Where did you get it?"

"Ann's parents gave it to me as a wedding present."

"Leave it to me in your will, Joe," said Marian with a small ironic laugh.

"Done," said Bari, sharing her laugh and pausing to shift gears. "I'd like you to tell me what happened at your home the morning of the fifteenth."

Marian gave her lustrous hair, black and shiny as a limousine, a small toss and turned her unblinking blue eyes directly on him. Her voice was strictly business. "My understanding is that even though you can't represent us both if we are charged, you can and do represent us both now. Correct?"

"Well, if you like, Marian, but . . ."

"And everything I say to you is privileged and confidential?"

"Yes, of course," said Bari, against his better judgment.

Marian told of being awakened and frightened by noises on successive nights and of waking her husband who had heard them too. "It wasn't a tree limb scratching against the side of the house. It was purposeful, like someone trying to get in. Paul said I should report it. May I smoke?"

Joe rose to come around his desk and light her cigarette with the desk set lighter he never used. Too late. Marian had retrieved a thin gold lighter from her purse and with one quick efficient motion lit her cigarette and put the lighter away.

"I called Detective Carey to investigate, because I had met him at a benefit once and he gave me his card. It seemed easier and a lot faster than reporting it to some bored desk sergeant at police headquarters." Marian inhaled deeply and resumed her story, and with each word the tendrils of smoke exhaled from her mouth rose up through her nose until finally she blew the remainder toward the ceiling. As Joe watched this performance, a kind of paralysis set in, as though he had been charmed by a cobra.

"As we were trying to open a window that had been painted shut, there was a deafening roar and Detective Carey dropped to the floor. Christ! He was dead! Someone had shot him. I could see the bullet hole in the back of his head." Marian had the barest hint of a lisp, which Joe would have considered a defect in other women. In Marian, it tripled her desirability.

"I was in shock and I was terrified. I thought maybe the shot was fired by the person who tried to break in the night before. If so, the bullet might have been meant for me. I was reeling, and here was this poor man on my bedroom floor, shot in the head. When I collected myself, I called 911." As if to punctuate the end of her story, Marian stubbed out the cigarette in the ashtray supplied by Bari.

"The medical examiner estimates the time of death at least an hour before your call to 911," he lied.

"No, that's all wrong. Ten minutes at the outside."

"Marian, I have to ask this." Bari made his tone as gentle as he could. "Were you and Detective Carey lovers?"

"Absurd."

"The detective investigating the case believes the victim was undressed when he died, and that someone -

you - redressed him. That would account for some of the time discrepancy."

"Bullshit."

Here Bari hesitated. He looked down and rearranged some items on his desk before going on.

"Actually, Marian, I know that you and Carey had been lovers once or twice a week for the past several months, and if I know it, the cops know it, or soon will."

Marian stiffened, but said nothing, and lit another cigarette.

"In fact, there was evidence of sexual activity discovered during the autopsy."

Marian leaned back in her seat and draped her arms over it carelessly. "And what the hell might that be?" she asked, dropping all pretense and clearly enjoying herself now.

"There was sperm in his urethra and traces of human feces on his penis," said Bari.

"He couldn't wipe his ass, so what?" asked Marian, with an infuriating smirk and another artful hair toss that would have buckled Bari's knees had he been standing.

"The feces weren't his," said Bari, showing his trump card at last.

"Fuck you, Joe."

CHAPTER THREE

CAMMY KNEW THAT THE INFORMATION he had given Bari about Marian Feldman's affair with Detective Carey was dynamite. It furnished Paul Feldman with a motive for murder. He also knew that it was unlikely that the cops would find out about the lovebirds, despite what Bari had told Marian.

While the cops stuffed themselves with Krispy Kremes and swilled coffee, Cammy's legwork had turned up the high end motel cum spa and gourmet restaurant where Carey and Marian met for fun and frolic.

The head desk clerk was a tall, elegant queen, and he had been highly reluctant to identify Marian and Carey even with the substantial encouragement of the fifteen hundred dollars that Cammy offered.

From what Cammy had gleaned from the motel's bartenders and maids, the staff was discreet, especially with cops. Their place of employment would be on everyone's blacklist if it became known that they blabbed about what went on. Then they would be out of work. This logic of self-preservation had been pounded into their heads again and again by their supervisors.

This particular motel, because of its amenities and reputation for secrecy, drew trysting V.I.P.s from as far away as Maryland and North Carolina. But let one breech of a guest's privacy become public, and that clientele would flee the motel like a covey of quail.

"Our guests' privacy is sacred," the desk clerk sniffed, "and I can see no reason to violate it."

"I can give you fifteen hundred reasons," said Cammy.

The fey desk clerk was discretion itself, but once he tucked the fifteen hundred away in his inside coat pocket, the floodgates opened, and he was magically transformed into the waspish gossip he obviously longed to be.

Unbidden, and with a cartoonish lift of one eyebrow, he also told Cammy that Marian wasn't the only woman that Carey brought to the motel. There were at least two others that he personally knew about, and, judging from their ages and their clothes and his own intuition, he'd bet all three were married. Of course, he was right.

ONE OF CAMMY'S contacts on the Richmond P.D. had corroborated the desk clerk's story. It seemed that Carey was an inveterate womanizer who specialized in married women. He hated the bother and expense of courting, and, after one catastrophic marriage years ago, he had absolutely no desire to try it again.

"No kids, which is a blessing, I suppose," said the cop, "but she buried him up to his fucking neck anyway. He hasn't been the same since she divorced him. I told him, 'Get over that broad. It happens to everybody.' Shit, I'm working on unhappy marriage number three myself. It didn't do any good. He told me to mind my own business."

Besides his divorce train wreck, there were other, darker reasons for Carey's habits with women.

Cammy talked to an ex-cop who had known Carey

since fourth grade. The ex-cop was now a Richmond PI who owed Cammy a big favor.

When this ex-cop was just starting out as a PI, Cammy gave him some information on a corporate defendant in a personal injury case that caused the case to settle successfully. So successfully that the ex-cop's reputation as a PI was made in Richmond.

"Yeah, his mother was a crazy bitch. Everything he did, even little things, she'd tattle to his prick of an old man, who would then beat the hell out of him. His girlfriend - another lulu, dizzy as they come - screwed everybody on the high school football team, except Carey."

By the time he had reached his teens, Carey distrusted and hated women. His quest, according to the PI, was to prove that they were phonies, all of them. This was a breeze to do, since his mind was made up in advance.

There had been another nugget about Carey that Cammy had uncovered from the PI. After much hemming and hawing and swearing Cammy to secrecy about where the information originated, the PI said that Carey had been crooked, and that he alone had known about it.

It seems that the PI and Carey had gotten drunk together soon after the PI had left the force, and Carey had unburdened himself about his underworld connections. Carey's secret was safe, of course, because the PI wanted to develop Carey as a source.

The story was that the number one mob enchilada in Richmond, the Lower Peninsula and Norfolk, had Carey on his payroll until Carey became part of a scheme to past-post one of the mobster's bookmakers by getting a bet down on a race that was over.

Carey's job was to furnish protection from the vice squad by giving the mobster's minions advance notice about raids, surveillance, wire taps and investigations, which Carey had done for years, until greed overwhelmed him.

The PI's information was a little sketchy; after all he was drunk when he had heard it. That was peachy with Cammy. Now that he had the outline, he knew where he could nail down the details.

NOTHING SO FAR had proved that Paul was innocent, but Carey had powerful enemies, and that was a promising beginning. As far as Bari was concerned, the more connected guys with hard-ons for Carey, the merrier. There was, however, a steep downside, and Bari had spotted it.

"Good start, Cammy," said Bari. "There's a hell of a lot more to do, but watch it, for Christ's sake. You're nosing around the territory of some very dangerous people. If you come to their attention, I'm afraid they'll want to take you out."

"I'll keep my eyes open," said Cammy, miming broadly.

AFTER MARIAN'S ARRIVAL in Roads Port and her interview at Joe's office, she moved into the guest bedroom with Paul at the Bari home. At dinner, Paul had been subdued, but polite, and he seemed grateful for the company. Marian was talkative and animated, lifting the burden of being a cheery hostess from Ann's shoulders.

Bari sat back in wonder. One would never guess in a thousand years at the conversation he had with Marian in his office mere hours ago.

"It must have been just horrible for you, Marian,

when that poor man was shot. My God, you were right there!" Ann had no clue, and Marian knew it.

"I didn't know what had happened. My hearing was gone, and then Detective Carey fell to the floor. I still didn't realize he'd been shot," said Marian, looking off as if trying to visualize the events that took place in her bedroom. "I knelt down beside him, and then I saw the gunshot wound. By then I was numb. My hearing began to return and I called 911. The next thing I remember is being questioned by the police." She finished brightly, as though she had been part of a terrible, yet thrilling adventure. Ann was as rapt as a child listening to *Hansel and Gretel.* Even Paul came to attention, this apparently being his first full hearing of Marian's account of the shooting.

Bari looked at Paul with affection and deep sympathy. What on earth was this brilliant Jewish intellectual doing in Richmond, Virginia, married to this conscienceless WASP bitch? He should have been teaching at Harvard's or Stanford's school of business. Instead, here he was, mixed up in a sordid mess that would affect the rest of his life, no matter how it came out.

BARI KNEW THAT the American public distrusted the legal system both civil and criminal, because the substance of an action often seemed to be ignored while the opponents engaged each other in childish games.

The thing that would astonish everyday people is that most judges and lawyers saw it the same way, except that they weren't repelled by the game aspect of the system. They reveled in it.

Bari had good days and bad. On bad days, he longed

to do something else. Maybe he should have been a carpenter. At least if you did a good job it would last, and you could stand back and admire your work.

But this Paul business was different. His friend, now client, was about to be in real trouble, and he, Bari, had the talent and the skills to protect him from the brutality of the state. No matter what the Commonwealth Attorney threw at Paul, Bari vowed he would protect him.

If Feldman was eventually charged with the Carey killing, the pretrial, trial and, God forbid, the appeal, would consume Bari's every waking hour for at least a year. Thanks to Virginia's "rocket docket," the trial could begin as soon as five months after arraignment; way too soon, in Bari's opinion.

He would have to turn over all pending matters in his practice to another partner or associate. He would allow nothing to interfere with his concentration. Nothing.

Then there was Ann. He would have to prepare her. All of her plans that included him would have to be put off or canceled. Joe knew that Ann planned to surprise him with a ten-day Mediterranean cruise for his birthday. She had connived with his secretary, Helen, to move all of his appointments and hearings around to accommodate those precious ten days. Ann would hate like hell to cancel that cruise, and she would hate him and Paul for causing her to cancel it.

Ann had wanted a new car for over a year. Maybe now was an excellent time to buy one for her. He wondered if that new Accord coupe she had gushed over at the fall car show in Norfolk would cool her out. Wearily, he thought not . . . it would probably take a Lexus.

There was also the unpleasant subject of a fee to

discuss with Paul. As a partner in his firm, Bari had to bill out at three hundred an hour. Perhaps his partners would allow two hundred, seeing as how the cash register would rarely sleep in this case. The fee would probably run between forty and fifty thousand a month not including Cammy's bill and office expenses. There was no bottom line - Bari would have to tell Paul that his total fee could go as high as a million dollars win or lose, maybe more.

If, on the other hand, Paul had hired a sole practitioner, the fee would be half what he would pay Bari. But if Paul couldn't raise the million, Bari wouldn't let him hire anyone else now even if he had to take a leave of absence from the firm in order to represent Paul.

Two weeks later it finally happened. The grand jury in Richmond had handed up an indictment. Paul was charged with capital murder and taken into custody.

NOW THAT SOMEONE had been charged with the Carey killing, the newspapers were filled with lurid stories backed with rumors and wild guesses. The stories were illustrated with the all-important pictures: pictures of the Feldman home, pictures of the bedroom, file pictures of Paul Feldman at company functions, and pictures of Marian's debut and wedding.

The responsible Richmond newspapers published the principals' biographies and Carey's obituary. Detective Carey had a distinguished career with the Richmond P.D. He had been awarded an impressive array of citations for valor, and he had been hospitalized on at least two occasions with gunshot wounds received while breaking up major drug operations.

Carey's sterling record would, alas, be trampled in a

trial, and Joe Bari couldn't wait. If he could get away with it, Bari would parade all Carey's enemies before the jury. He would expose all the seedy circumstances under which he had acquired those enemies, by way of demonstrating that any number of people might plausibly have killed him.

The prosecutors, for their part, would strive to give Marian the same treatment. Faithless wife had driven husband to the point of murder with her infidelities, the last of which was performed in her and her husband's home, *in their very bedroom, ladies and gentlemen of the jury.*

To avoid making the jury sympathetic to the defendant, the prosecutors would also point out the age difference aspect of the marriage, hinting that infidelity was part of the bargain when an older man marries a vital woman many years his junior, and that the defendant should have known better. Actually, there was only a ten year age difference between Paul and Marian, but the prosecutors would make it seem like forty.

"ART, THIS IS Joe. Can you give me some time this morning? Oh, I don't know, 'bout an hour. Yeah, I know. I wouldn't ask, but I really need your help. Thanks, Art."

Art Louis was the firm's motions expert and Bari's close friend. His princely office was on the corner diagonally opposite from Joe's corner office and, in Joe's opinion, had an arguably much better view of downtown because you could see a large slice of the marina.

"Well, what do you think?"

Louis hid his rotundity in expensive, bespoke suits, and then emphasized it with vests and watch chains. Nonetheless, he was living proof that weight never hurt a lawyer. In fact, it helped; it lent the air of gravity that clients loved.

"Let's see. You can file a notice of appearance on line," said Louis. "But I'd drive up to Richmond and pick up the discovery at the same time you file the notice. Court administration will have assigned a judge to this case. Take Cammy with you. He can ask around about the judge. If the judge is bad for us, maybe we can figure a way to get another one.

"Art, we need a change of venue above all. We're fucked good if the case is tried in Richmond. It's make or break. We've got to get the case out of Richmond," said Bari.

"Okay, I read you," said Louis. "Let the media kick the story around for a few more days, then argue a tainted jury pool. You know, that the prejudice against our client is so great that he can't get a fair trial. Virginia law is terrible on change of venue, but who knows? Maybe we'll get lucky."

"Will you draft it, Art?" asked Bari. "Paul's an old and dear friend."

Joe Bari knew all too well that trials were frequently won by thoroughly researched, well-crafted motions, such as the kind Louis filed.

In Bari's last drug case, the coke that was collected was suppressed. Louis helped out with a brief arguing that the cops had made an illegal search and seizure. The judge agreed and tossed the evidence, effectively ending the prosecution. No cocaine, no case.

The cops had seized coke from the defendant's VW camper. The nice point of law was whether the camper was the defendant's vehicle or his home. Different legal rules apply to each. Louis successfully argued that the camper was the defendant's home, which resulted in a dismissal.

As far as Bari could tell, there were no search and seizure issues in this case. But there would be other complicated issues - hence Art Louis.

"Sure," said Louis. "Aside from the baying media hounds virtually making your case for prejudice, there's something else we've got going for us." Bari said a silent prayer of thanks at Art's use of a plural pronoun. Even though he was a civil litigator, if Louis came on board in Paul's case, Joe would do back flips.

"Richmond's courts are flooded with criminal trials. Any Richmond judge would love to have a good reason to kick a trial down here to Roads Port," said Louis. "Naturally, the Commonwealth will scream that Roads Port is our home town, so we'll have to counter that argument with a slider."

ART LOUIS DID his best to be an attentive and loving husband and father, although he knew his best was well short of the mark. Oh well, no first-rate lawyer in the game was really much of a family man. Too damn much to do. He always managed to get home after the kids had gone to bed and he worked most Saturdays on top of it.

With his exhausted acquiescence, Louis's children shamelessly guilt-tripped him out of the presence of their mother. Sally, his wife, came down hard on them when she saw them bully their father.

Sally came from a poor family and now she was a wealthy Virginia matron thanks to her husband's hard work, and she had nothing but gratitude. For his part, Louis knew only one way to be a lawyer: work until he was finished, and then go home. There was an alternative. Cut back his practice, and he had been thinking for some time about doing that very thing. Then he'd remember Parkinson's law that work expands to fill the time allotted to it. Louis knew that if he cut his practice, he'd make half the money and still work evenings and Saturdays. At the end of these ruminations, he always faced the truth. Screw cutting back. He loved being just the kind of lawyer he was.

CHAPTER FOUR

CAMMY DISCOVERED THAT THE MOBSTER Carey had recently crossed was a Lebanese syndicate guy in Richmond named Manny Shilla. The Lebanese didn't have the hierarchical structure of the Mafia on purpose. What they had was more of a loose association of cooperating individuals. A conspiracy with no shape and no name was as hard to grasp as the smoke from their Cuban cigars. The feds tried to bust it up. There was nothing there, and eventually they shifted their efforts to the more glamorous rock-star Mafia criminals who crazily thrived on media attention.

Shilla owned a wholesale house that sold new and used restaurant equipment. His warehouse was as cavernous as a Wal-Mart and Shilla made a legitimate profit from stock pots and deep fryers.

He was careful never to make any sort of splash. His house and his car were modest, and he had no apparent vices. On paper, Shilla looked like nothing more than a successful businessman, but he had another face and Cammy knew it.

As far back as he could remember neither his father's activities nor his own ever brought Cammy face-to-face with Shilla, who was a master at keeping his hands clean. Oh sure, Cammy ran into Shilla's associates all the time, and he had a pretty good idea how extensive his operation was. But what he didn't know was whether Shilla would clip a guy who crossed him.

THE METROPOLITAN RING and Turf Club was a throwback, an old time greasy spoon and bar in downtown Richmond with three pool tables in the back and yellowing photographs of winners posed in front of some racetrack's tote board with the owner, jockey and trainer. There were also a dozen or so photos of sluggers long since forgotten and living out their punch-drunk existences in grimy state-supported nursing homes reeking of Pine Sol and piss.

The Metro was one of those Richmond institutions not worth anyone's effort to change, and so it remained as always: a smelly haven for old white men who made up stories about past glories and drank port wine by the shot.

An elderly tipster called Buzz because of the flat top he'd worn since high school, haunted the Metro day and night, playing nine ball and cadging free drinks from the pensioners on the first and fifteenth of the month. Cammy dropped in the Metro looking for him, because in addition to his prodigious memory, Buzz knew everything happening in Richmond.

It wasn't all that many years ago that Cammy would have been tossed out of the Metro for stepping up to the bar. No longer. Richmond, like Atlanta, was a black man's town now, with a black mayor, a black police chief and a mostly black city council. Thanks to the Voting Rights Act, the black majority simply went to the polls and took over.

Buzz was shooting one-pocket for wine when Cammy spotted him.

"What it is, Buzz?"

"Still looking for the best of it, Cammy. You?"

"Keeping afloat," answered Cammy. Buzz was drinking Photo Finish, a much loved fortified wine served at the Metro. "Put down that poison and let me buy you a real drink."

Cammy picked up a double Jack Daniels for Buzz and a Seven-up for himself at the bar. He paid the bartender and took the drinks to a high-backed wooden booth you could camp out in and no one would know you were there.

"Talk is not cheap, Cammy."

"Maybe this will get you started," said Cammy, putting a hundred dollar bill in Buzz's palm with a handshake. "What can you tell me about Detective Arnold Carey?"

"You're not interested in his good points, I don't suppose."

"No. The lawyer I'm working for represents Feldman, the guy they arrested."

Buzz took a sip of his Jack Daniels and lit a cigarette, exhaling off to the side to avoid offending Cammy who had quit.

"The esteemed Detective Carey had the kind of enemies nobody wants." You got a lot more out of Buzz if you just let him talk.

Buzz tossed back the rest of his drink and signaled

the bartender for another. "Carey was Manny Shilla's man at the police department until about four months ago. Seems Carey became friendly with a D.C. hustler who had the bright idea of past-posting one of Shilla's bookies right at the racetrack. You know the guy, Stubby Minetti," said Buzz.

"Yeah, I worked for him one summer," said Cammy.

"The way it worked," said Buzz, "was that Carey would sometimes tag along with Stubby and his buddies when they went to the track for pleasure. Well, not entirely pleasure. Stubby would take the betting action of his entourage on the races they watched. It's illegal, of course, and if you're caught doing it, they'll rule you off for good." Buzz held up his empty shot glass for the bartender to see.

Tell me about it, Cammy reflected. *I was with my daddy when he got caught at the Fairgrounds in New Orleans. They kicked us both out and told us never to come back. I was nine years old.*

"Occasionally, someone in the entourage would place a bet with Stubby on a horse running at a different track," said Buzz. "As you know, dope on all the races in the country is listed in the *Racing Form*, and everybody had one.

"The scam, involving electronic signals, let Carey place a bet on a horse running at an out of state track after the race had run, or at least after the race had begun and the outcome was no longer in doubt.

"Until then, Carey had been a hundred dollar hunch player. All of a sudden he bets a grand to win on a forty-to-one shot. Stubby took the bet. The horse won by fifteen open lengths and paid eighty-two fifty!"

Christ! That's a bundle, thought Cammy. *And a motive.*

"Stubby didn't have that kind of money on him, and he smelled a rat besides. When they got back to Richmond, Stubby called Shilla who gave instructions to pay Carey the amount he had coming: forty-one thousand, two hundred and fifty dollars. But that tore it, and Carey's association with Shilla was over."

The ancient bartender, sporting a stained ankle length apron, brought over the refill for Buzz and Cammy paid him.

"Did Shilla do anything? I mean, surely he wasn't about to sit still for a hit that large," asked Cammy, raising a skeptical eyebrow.

"Shilla's harder than Japanese arithmetic, no question about it," Buzz replied. "I heard about some very bad stuff he did when he was in the corn whiskey business in Carolina years ago, but I hear his philosophy now is to hurt a guy in the pocketbook. I guess in Carey's case that meant firing him. Now, if Carey had turned around and tried to get even, then I imagine that would have been a different matter, but I ain't heard nothing like that yet. I gotta tell you, jealous husband or no jealous husband, that shooting is suspicious."

Cammy passed Buzz another hundred. "Why?"

"Because no ordinary husband is going to clip a guy fucking his wife, slip out of the house, wait for the cops to come, and then walk up and pretend he just arrived.

"Granted, Carey got scratched with his own gun, and that would argue that the husband did it. I mean Carey's undressed and the husband comes home, sees Carey and his wife going at it, grabs the gun and fires. And by the way, Cam, the gun only had Carey's prints on it.

"On the other hand, the wife swears she saw nothing, and the cops believe her. Not because they trust her, but because they think Carey was fucking her when he got hit, in which case she couldn't have seen who did it.

"Here's the part that gets me. Instead of cursing his wife and maybe taking a shot at her too, the husband coolly slips the gun back in its holster and books, unseen. Naw, I don't buy it, too pat. It was pro, I'd bet my life on it," said Buzz, pausing to light a cigarette.

"Okay, Buzz, give me your version."

"Here's how it went down," said Buzz, relishing the opportunity to exercise his smarts. "The hitter knows that Carey is fucking Feldman's wife. He follows Carey to the house, waits till he thinks they're going at it, enters, climbs the stairs, and when he opens the bedroom door, he can't believe his luck. Instead of having to use his own piece, he uses Carey's which is hanging right there. Boom. Puts the gun back and leaves. Maybe he's dressed as a mailman or UPS guy.

"The only problem is, by using the gun of opportunity, the husband, returning home unexpected, gets blamed, and the whole point of the hit is lost."

"What point?" inquired Cammy, knowing the answer, but wanting confirmation from Buzz.

"To make a statement, Cam. Fuck with Manny Shilla and you pay."

Cammy sat back, nodding in agreement. "I like it. I like it. What else?"

"Cost you another C. Word is that Carey was a ladies man, aside from the Feldman broad. There was never a day when he didn't have two or three on the line at the same time, all married. I don't have names for you right at the moment, but I can get them if you're interested."

Cammy put his business card on top of a folded hundred dollar bill and slid both over. "I am indeed, Buzz, I am indeed."

"A MILLION DOLLARS! Christ Almighty, Paul. How did you raise it?" asked Joe.

"I put the house up as security," Feldman replied. He sounded elated, despite the cell phone, which was breaking up.

Defendants charged with murder might be released in some jurisdictions, but Virginia wasn't among them. Joe Bari figured that the court had released Paul because the case against him was circumstantial and weak and the Commonwealth knew it.

Bari knew how those cynical pricks in the Commonwealth Attorney's Office would see it. They wouldn't much care if Paul skipped. *Let him run, our cops will get him sooner or later, meanwhile, the Commonwealth of Virginia gets a nonrefundable million-dollar gift.*

BARI AND ART Louis drove to Richmond on Interstate 64's treacherous icy glaze to argue the motion for a change of venue.

The law was against them on a change of venue, Bari knew, regardless how piercing Louis's motion. In fact, the law was against them on just about everything. Virginia is a law-and-order state and proud of it. If you are a defendant accused of a serious crime in Virginia, you're in a lot more trouble than you would be in any other southern state, except Florida.

But law or no law, Bari and Louis simply had to get this case transferred to a venue where no one had heard of Carey. If they didn't, they would lose and Paul would be finished. With Carey's glowing reputation - a reputation that included absolutely no brutality or civil-rights accusations - all Richmond would want to avenge his death.

The matter would rest in the motion judge's hands alone. There was no appeal from the decision regardless what it was. And a judge who doesn't have to worry about being overturned on appeal is a frightening prospect for both defense and prosecution alike.

The courtroom was as big as an auditorium and so cold you could see your breath. The judge's secretary, his clerk and his bailiff - the so-called lower bench - all looked like Bob Cratchits, wearing mufflers and blowing into their hands. But the cause of their misery wasn't an autocratic Scrooge; it was the forced-air heating system, which went on the blink every time the temperature dipped into the twenties.

"It's kinda like the song, isn't it? 'You left me just when I needed you most,'" the bailiff said to the assembled.

The fifty or so clients and their lawyers who gathered to argue motions of their own responded to the bailiff's joke about the disloyal furnace with a brooding silence.

Paul Feldman rushed in and joined them at the defense table, smiling and shaking their hands. "Good to see you out, Paul, even in this weather," said Louis, rapidly rubbing his hands together. Bari seated Feldman between him and Louis, and saw Marian taking a seat in the spectators' pew behind them.

"All rise," cried the bailiff, as the judge exited his chambers and climbed to the bench.

"Mr. Louis, you're first up," said the clerk.

Oh shit, thought Bari, sitting back down at the defense table next to Feldman and trying to keep from freezing. *Here we fucking go. Please, Art, put your heart and soul into this.*

"Your Honor, this case is *Commonwealth v. Feldman.* Art Louis for the defense," said Louis, standing to face the judge. "We have served the Commonwealth and this court with copies of our motion for a change of venue in this case."

The old judge, wearing a heavy white turtleneck sweater under his black robe, looked like a merchant sea captain. He reared back in his tall leather chair behind the bench, looking bored, which was a signal to all the lawyers to keep it short.

Bari, for the first time in thirty years, began saying Hail Marys quietly to himself.

"Because of the welter of pre-trial publicity," Louis continued, "it will be impossible for Mr. Feldman to receive a fair trial in this jurisdiction. Already, the newspapers and television have convicted Mr. Feldman, and the prejudice will grow as the trial date approaches."

Bari had a death grip on his copy of the motion. *Good, Art. Keep it brief and right on point.*

"Remind me, what is the trial date, Counsel?" the judge asked.

"August 6. That's about five months from now."

"I'll hear from the Commonwealth," said the judge.

The Deputy Commonwealth Attorney assigned to oppose the motion was a jowly porker who looked like he would explode with indignation.

"If it please the court," he whined in a soprano voice. "The defense argument is ridiculous. If a change of venue was granted in every trial in which there was publicity, all trials would be moved. The crime occurred in this district. The evidence and the witnesses are all here, and it would be extremely inconvenient and disruptive for them to appear elsewhere."

"Mr. Louis?"

"Your Honor, my client is prominent in his community," Louis answered. "He is charged with a capital offense because the victim was a police detective, and a popular detective at that. Those facts and the lurid speculation in the media that the officer was having an affair with my client's wife are driving the publicity."

That's right, Art, take it to this whiner.

"Where a defendant's very life is on the line, it is incumbent on this court to take care that his Sixth Amendment rights are protected, and Mr. Feldman's rights are best protected by a change of venue," said Louis, picking up steam. "With respect to the Commonwealth's suggestion that the trial would be more convenient to witnesses if held here in Richmond, the defense will be calling at least three expert witnesses who teach at the University of Roads Port. Witnesses will inevitably be inconvenienced wherever the case is tried."

Bari immediately recognized that this was Art's slider. Get some important witnesses for the defense that live and work in Roads Port to even things up. Art hasn't a clue who these witnesses are at the moment; but he'll find them in a damn big hurry if we win this fucking motion.

"As Your Honor knows," Louis continued, "Roads Port is at the tip of the Virginia Peninsula, sixty-five miles away. Those sixty-five miles will act as quarantine against the prejudicial publicity and insure that Mr. Feldman receives a fair trial."

"Has the Commonwealth anything further to add?"

"Your Honor . . . I, I, I . . ." pleaded the porker, perspiring despite the frigid temperature.

Bari chuckled to himself. The porker had completely overlooked the fact that he and Louis lived and practiced in Roads Port. The one aspect of the change of venue motion that had worried them most never became an issue.

"Very well, motion granted. The trial will be moved to Roads Port. You'll have to arrange a new trial date there, Counsel."

Joe Bari slumped in his chair, "Thank God."

Louis turned and congratulated Feldman with a bear hug, and then reached over and punched Bari's arm. "Thanks Art. You did a masterful job," said Bari.

Just as Bari had expected, there was a big fat purple elephant in the courtroom during the hearing that everyone saw but no one dared mention. Juries in Richmond tend to be heavily black, and Paul was a Jew. Thanks to affirmative action, quotas, and the Reverend Jackson, former black and Jewish friends who had worked together during the civil rights struggles were now hated enemies.

If the Commonwealth were successful in loading the jury with black jurors, defense counsel would cry foul, and then the media would be joyously full of a nice juicy race issue, which would increase local tensions and influence the trial in ways difficult to predict.

The Deputy Commonwealth Attorney didn't care about increasing racial hatred so long as his office got a conviction, but the judge didn't want any part of it in his jurisdiction.

"Thank you, Your Honor," said Louis with audible relief.

It was Bari's turn to hug Paul. "This was huge, Paul," he said. Feldman turned and smiled and reached for his wife right behind him in the first row of the spectator benches. Bari looked on as Marian took her husband's hand in both of hers in a moving display of wifely solidarity.

THINGS WERE GOING well, which made Joe Bari worry. Paul had been released from custody, which was a godsend. He would have deteriorated quickly or died of shank wounds in the insane, medieval pit of horrors known as the Chesterfield County jail. And Louis had prevailed on his venue motion. Two victories the jury would never hear of had vastly improved their chances of winning an acquittal. That was all to the good.

But years of tormenting experience had taught Bari that criminal trials were a rollercoaster. And they were now at the top of the very first hill in a long, harrowing ride.

MEANWHILE, MARIAN WAS living her story so thoroughly that she was beginning to believe it herself. This wasn't an exercise in self-deception - Marian didn't deceive herself about anything - this was essential if she was to reclaim the plush life that she had stomped on with both feet.

Her main concern was neither the cops nor Bari, but Paul. In her estimation, Paul bought her story, and he understood that in cases such as this, the statistical bad guy is almost always the husband. Bari and the cops didn't matter. She had made very sure that she was Bari's client at the time of their discussion so that attorney-client privilege would keep his mouth shut, and she was positive that the cops couldn't prove a damn thing about her and Carey.

Paul's exquisitely boring friend and Rocket Science mentor, Harry Ames, was tapped by his department head to be the bearer of mixed tidings: working for the company with a murder charge pending was impossible.

But a return to the company after acquittal? Certainly. There was no way, Harry had told them, that the company would deny its most valuable employee his rightful place once he was cleared. Yeah right, Harry. And pigs roost in the trees, Marian had thought.

Marian was relieved that Paul's boss had offered him paid leave, which, Paul being Paul, he had reluctantly accepted. Anyway, loss of income was one less thing to feel guilty about when she looked at Paul bravely bearing up and playing the role of martyr to a fare-thee-well.

The print and TV wolves had set up camp on the sidewalk and street in front of their Richmond home, and rather than allow the media to keep them prisoners, Marian insisted they take an apartment in Roads Port for the duration.

"OKAY, WHAT DO we know?" Bari asked to open the meeting. The defense team so far was Joe Bari, Art Louis and Cammy Brown. The three of them met in Louis's sumptuous office to see where they were.

"We know that Paul was going on a long-scheduled business trip on the morning in question. We know he made it to long-term parking at the airport, because he's got a time-stamped receipt. We know he called his office from the airport to say he was sick and couldn't make the meeting in Houston," said Bari.

"Also," he continued, "the gal who gave him the receipt remembers Paul, because it was an in and out trip and she saw him get sick when he paid her on his way out."

"Be a hard thing to forget," added Louis.

"Right," said Bari. "Paul pulled in, hit the button and the machine printed out a ticket. He parked, immediately got sick and threw up outside his car. He cell-phoned his office. Then he got back in his car and left the terminal after paying the gal in the box.

"The exit parking receipt was stamped 9:55 a.m. Paul drives back home, stopping twice to vomit. He arrives at approximately 11:45 a.m., as Carey's body is being put in the morgue's hearse. The business trip was legit. Cammy, you checked with Paul's secretary, right?" Bari asked.

"Yeah, I checked with his secretary and his boss. The company travel office made Feldman's flight arrangements. He was booked on Delta flight eighteen sixty-one to Houston. The flight left on time at 11:40 a.m."

"Okay, so far so good," said Joe, rubbing his hands together and pacing soundlessly on Art's deep Aubusson. "The medical examiner makes the time of death sometime between ten and eleven. Question number one is, naturally, could Paul have driven home from the airport in time to park his car somewhere, walk to the house, climb the stairs, and shoot Carey by 11:00 a.m.?" Bari paused to check if they were in agreement.

"Question number two is could he then leave the house without being seen and reappear as Carey's body was being put in the meat wagon at 11:45 a.m.?"

"Let me stop you there, Joe. There are two important neighbors yet to interview," said Cammy. "They both live directly across the street. If anyone saw another car, or another person for that matter, it most likely would be one of them."

"Okay Cam, get on that right away.

"Let me trim your analysis a bit, Joe," said Louis from his perch on the edge of his ping pong table-sized desk. "The only real question is, could Paul have arrived home from the airport sometime between ten and eleven, and the answer is probably not, unless he was driving on rails. The airport is an hour away.

"I mean we all realize that if it were physically possible to get from the airport to Feldman's home between ten and eleven, no matter what the conveyance, we'd get creamed at trial. Am I right?" asked Louis.

Bari, looking less cheerful, said "On the stand, the medical examiner will testify that he can't be a hundred percent sure; that time of death is inexact; blah, blah, blah."

"The other time on record is Marian Feldman's phone call to 911, which is key," said Cammy, checking his notes. "Mrs. Feldman called 911 at ten-fifty."

"Then that's it," said Louis. "There's no way in hell that Paul could have driven home from the airport in time to shoot Carey, not that the Commonwealth won't try to manipulate the times."

"You're right, Art," said Bari. "They will want to push the time of death forward as far as possible, and we want to push it back. The farther back the actual time of death, the less time Paul would have had to drive home and pull the trigger. But since Marian called 911 at 10:50, there is no way the time of death can be later than 10:45 a.m. Well, there it is," Bari hooted. "Paul's innocent."

Cammy got up impatiently and went to the window where he stood looking out with his hands clasped behind his back.

Bari looked over at him. "Is there something you want to add, Cam?"

"What if Feldman didn't stop to throw up?" Cammy asked, turning from the window. "What if he came straight home from the airport? The traffic is lighter at ten, and with a little fancy driving, he's home by 10:45.

As far as Marian Feldman's call to 911 at ten-fifty, that could be fucked up too. I've checked the 911 clocks on other cases. Every one was off."

"Holy shit, Cammy. Why didn't you say so?" asked Bari.

"It's on my list, Joe. I'll let you know how it checks out."

Bari, glancing at his wrist watch, ended the meeting. After they left Louis's office, Cammy passed a small object to Bari in the hallway. "Happy birthday. You are now in possession of the world's most expensive shell casing."

"From the crime scene?"

"From the crime scene."

CHAPTER FIVE

THE ROADS PORT CIRCUIT COURT informed Bari that *Commonwealth v. Feldman* had been duly transferred from Richmond, and that the case was now assigned to Judge Harley Jones. The new trial date was September first.

Bari had known Jones before he had been appointed to the bench two years ago. Jones had been in private practice for fifteen years before that. Bari knew that the courthouse gossip was that Jones sought the appointment because he couldn't make it as a lawyer, but courthouse wags always said that about judges.

It was incomprehensible to that crowd that anyone would take a drastic cut in income to sit on the bench. The suggestion that a lawyer might consider an appointment to the bench a high honor well worth the difference in money was blown off as nonsense.

The legal gossips were all wrong about Harley Jones, though. Bari knew Harley Jones well enough to know that Jones considered a judge's duty just as sacred as the president's.

After his appointment to the bench, Bari didn't see Jones around town anymore. Bari suspected that Jones had separated himself from all his friendships with colleagues. After all, how it would look for a judge to be personally friendly with those who appeared before him in court? That was nothing against Harley. Bari understood perfectly well that appearances were important to all savvy judges.

"Let's stick with Harley; what do you say?" asked Louis.

"I agree, Art. Harley, it is."

THE VIRGINIA WINTER slogged on, and Bari for one, was sick of it. One day: five degrees, the next day: fifty. Snow, then rain, then more snow. Steel wool skies were dully reflected in the Chesapeake Bay, obliterating the horizon. Sullen gray everywhere, like the missile ships and carriers that silently moved in and out of Hampton Roads.

Bari thought it was fitting in all that wintry gloom that the Richmond prosecutor assigned to this case was the angel of death herself, Assistant Commonwealth Attorney Harriet Atkins.

If you met Harriet at a social function, as Bari had

done last year at a bar dinner, you'd never guess that she had sent more men to the death house than any prosecutor on the eastern seaboard.

In social settings, no Sweetbriar debutante was more gracious or flirty than Harriet. In court, well, that was a different story. No woman back to Eve was trickier, as Bari had discovered by calling around to public defenders and other criminal defense lawyers in Richmond who dealt with her daily.

The lawyer who headed up the public defenders told Bari that over the years, Harriet had acquired an impressive number of bar complaints, at least two of which led to brief suspensions. Bari wryly reflected that Harriet's suspensions were quite an accomplishment in Virginia, where judges and the bar association treated prosecutors like royalty.

Harriet's first appearance before Judge Jones was to argue a motion to revoke Paul's bond, a perfectly bitchy thing to do, in Bari's opinion.

The judge told her that Paul's release was granted in Richmond and that unless she could cite some violation of the conditions of his release, he would deny the motion. Since Paul had followed every condition to the letter - such as calling the probation office daily - Harriet could cite no violation and her motion was denied.

Like many of her brother and sister prosecutors, Harriet pouted and became surly when her motions were denied. But apparently sensing that Judge Jones wouldn't stand for such theatrics, she bit off: "Thank you, Your Honor," and grimly packed up her brief case.

"She's not bad looking," said Louis to Bari on their way out of court.

"Harriet? She goes a little heavy on the makeup and

hairspray, but she must have been a fox when she was younger. Lucky for us, she dresses about fifteen years younger than she is. That'll piss off the women jurors."

WITH THINGS STILL tense, Marian knew they couldn't stay cooped up in their eight hundred square-foot apartment. The pantry in their home back in Richmond was larger than that, for God's sake!

"As long as we're stuck here, honey, why don't we see some of the sights around?" she asked Paul.

"Sure, Marian, whatever you say." Marian had used all the imagination that she could muster thinking of ways to ingratiate herself to Paul.

No more belittling him or dismissing his suggestions. Marian knew that she couldn't get away with her appalling past behavior now.

The circumstances of Carey's death, the cops' insinuating questions, and Paul's indictment had caused Marian to take a second look at her marriage and her prospects. And when she did, she recoiled.

Just as soon as the trial is over - win or lose - he's going to throw my booty out in the street, she thought. *I'll wind up broke and with a shitty reputation. I'll have to leave the state!*

Though he said nothing, Paul still had lingering suspicions; Marian could sense them. She had overheard him call Joe's office after they moved into the apartment. Joe had told him of Carey's former mob connections and of the enemies who would want Carey's hide, which gave Paul a boost.

Bari's news gave Marian a boost too. It just might turn out that Carey's death had nothing to do with her.

For the purposes of a trial, it was to the defense's benefit that she and Paul appeared to be lovebirds.

Marian required no persuading on that score. Any hint of discord would help the Commonwealth of Virginia, in the person of the ever-watchful Harriet Atkins, prove its theory that Paul had killed Carey in a jealous rage.

"Let's go through the casemates at Fort Monroe. It's just a few miles from here," said Marian.

"Yeah, let's go. I've got to get out of here.

And so off they went to submerge the present in the violent history of the past.

"CAMMY! I HAVEN'T seen you since Christ knows when."

"Hi, Stub. Let me have a Coke."

Stubby's hole in the wall carried a dozen newspapers, cigars, pipes, every known brand of tobacco and soft drinks from an abbreviated soda fountain.

"What can you tell me about that cop who was shot last week?"

"Carey?"

"Yeah, I heard about that stunt he pulled at the track."

"What's your interest, Cammy?"

"I'm working for the lawyer in Roads Port who represents Paul Feldman, the guy they charged."

"What's his angle?"

Lying to Stubby would be a mistake. There would be other cases, and Cammy knew that if he got a reputation for lying to guys on the inside like Stubby, all his sources would dry up.

"He wants to know about Carey's enemies."

"I don't want to be called to testify, Cammy. If I am, I'll refuse, and if I'm cited with contempt, I'll never forgive you or him. *Capisce*?"

"I follow, Stub. I'll tell him."

Cammy had known Stubby for years and years. One summer when his daddy was in jail doing ninety days for pandering, Cammy had run errands for Stubby. He had also swept and mopped up. In exchange, Stubby gave him pocket money and let him sleep in the back room. That was after the troubles.

Anthony "Stubby" Minetti was a small trim man in his sixties, always nattily dressed as many small men are. He had beautiful corn silk hair that he kept carefully barbered. Women, perfect strangers, were moved to touch his hair to see if it was as fine and silky as it looked. Cammy had seen it happen two or three times that summer when he worked for Stubby, and he still talked about it.

Stubby got his nickname as the result of a childhood accident with an ice shaving machine out back of his old man's soda fountain, which was a front for a bookmaking operation. The accident left him with only the thumb and index finger on his right hand. Stubby could nevertheless count money faster than the fastest bank teller.

He loved to regale Cammy with stories of his youth. As a kid, whenever Stubby's arithmetic teacher called for an answer to a calculation, Stubby's hand shot up. It got so bad that eventually he was no longer called on. "All right, class, who can give me the sum of this column of figures: six hundred thirty-five, nine hundred sixty-two, eight hundred fifteen and three hundred ninety-six? Put your hand down, Anthony. Class?"

Stubby was an indifferent student in his other subjects and it showed on his report card. Under the arithmetic column, it was a different story - straight "A"s.

His dad had operated a soda fountain and sports

book until he died of a heart attack during Stubby's second year of high school. Stubby dropped out of school immediately and took over the business.

Everything went well until January 12, 1969 and Super Bowl III, when the N.Y. Jets, who were a seventeen point underdog, beat the Baltimore Colts straight up 16-7. The biggest overlay in pro football history, and Stubby was on the wrong side of it. The outcome was local legend. All the gamblers in Richmond and the Peninsula knew "The Story" by heart.

Smart bettors from everywhere had realized the seventeen point spread was a gift from The Almighty and pounded in the money on the Jets, which put Stubby's books way out of balance. He called all over the country, but he couldn't lay it off, so he was stuck. He lost his home, his savings, everything.

Since then, he had moved to a smaller location and had elected to work on a percentage basis. As he told young Cammy: "Let somebody else take all the goddamn risks for a change." Stubby's current employer was Manny Shilla.

"What's the shyster's name?"

"Joe Bari."

"I heard of him. Well, this Carey is a greedy, lying S.O.B. The most I ever seen him bet was a hundred. I never would have taken a thousand dollar bet from him in a million years, but Manny told me to treat him good.

"Anyway, his horse comes in and pays off in telephone numbers. Manny says pay him, so I paid him. Later on, Manny says this Carey is 'no price.' I never seen him so pissed off."

Cammy knew that when a sports event is "no price," it means the bookmaker won't touch it no matter how inviting the betting line. When a mobster like Manny

Shilla says a *guy* is no price, that guy should maybe think about blowing town.

"I heard Carey tried to pay the money back in installments," continued Stubby, "but Manny refused. He told Carey they were quits. That's the last I heard of it."

"So you don't think Shilla was mad enough at Carey to zero him out?"

"A cop? Over a lousy forty grand? Hell no. Manny was steamed, no doubt about it, but he ain't gonna commit suicide over it, which is what killing a cop would be."

It looked to Cammy like Stubby was working overtime to throw him off the scent. He had his reasons. His financial security rested with Shilla, and if he mentioned Shilla's name in court, his bookmaking days, as well as his life, were over.

"Just for the sake of argument, who would he get to do it if he was pissed off enough?"

"Oh shit, Cammy. We're in Never-Never Land, now, because I just told you he wouldn't, but Lolly, probably."

Lolly Ruggiero, also known as "Last Rites" Ruggiero, was a contract hitter from Norfolk by way of Baltimore. Last Rites was a gorilla in a shiny silk suit. He was dark and had black hair coming out from under his shirt collar, all over the backs of his meaty hands, out of his ears and nose, everywhere.

"On the other hand," said Stubby, "this fucking thing went down in the morning up in that snooty neighborhood, am I right? Lolly don't operate in broad daylight. Christ, he'd be spotted at a hundred yards. Believe me. Lolly didn't have nothing to do with the Carey shooting."

"I figured as much, Stub, but I wanted to talk to you about it anyway."

"JOE, DAVID AND Rachel Feldman are here to see you. They're a half hour early for their appointment."

"That's all right, Helen," said Bari. Put them on ice for ten minutes while I finish reading this brief, then show them in."

David and Rachel Feldman were a handsome couple, well into their seventies and expensively and tastefully dressed like many well-to-do men and women of their generation. You would never pick them as Paul Feldman's parents. Paul cared little about his own appearance, and without Marian to finance, he could have lived entirely on his parents' clothing expenses.

Bari greeted them, helped them off with their coats and seated them on the sofa as he had done with their son.

"Now, how can I be of assistance?"

"We are here about our son, Paul, Mr. Bari," said Mr. Feldman. He reached over and grasped his wife's hand, which was fingering rosary beads.

"I'm sure that you appreciate that I can't discuss his case with you," Bari explained, "beyond saying that he has been charged in the shooting death of a police detective. Paul was taken into custody and released on bond, but you probably know all that."

"We have been sick with worry, Mr. Bari," implored Mrs. Feldman, concern and sorrow etched deeply on her face. "We are seeking reassurance. Something, anything."

"I can tell you without violating attorney-client confidentiality that I believe Paul was hastily charged because the victim was a police detective. There was pressure to charge someone."

"This has been a nightmare. Paul is innocent of this terrible accusation," continued Mrs. Feldman brokenly, her eyes filling with tears. "What will happen to our son, Mr. Bari?"

Bari was in a quandary. In ordinary nonlegal circumstances, the humane thing to do would be to come to the aid of this elderly, beseeching couple and murmur reassurances such as, "I'm certain that everything will turn out well and that Paul will be vindicated completely and soon."

As their son's attorney, knowing from bitter experience how badly and unexpectedly things can go in a criminal case even prior to trial, he was bound to say nothing about outcomes.

"As much as I'd like to, Mrs. Feldman, I cannot discuss Paul's case with you beyond what I have already. However, I would like to ask some questions of you individually. The reason for that is your collective memory might differ from your individual memories, and it is your individual memories that I am interested in."

Mr. Feldman gave Bari a knowing look signaling that he knew they were being *handled*. No offense taken. This intelligent and elegant couple realized that they had no choice but to trust Joe Bari and his methods.

Joe asked his secretary, Helen, to make Mrs. Feldman comfortable for a short time. Helen gently took her arm and Joe returned to Mr. Feldman.

"Sir, we met when Paul and I were students together and again at his wedding."

"Yes, I remember you quite clearly, Mr. Bari."

"Please call me

Joe, sir. I'd like to have your thoughts about what

happened at Paul and Marian's that morning."

Feldman removed his eyeglasses, closed his eyes, and massaged the bridge of his nose. Out of his wife's presence, he let his worry and exhaustion show.

"My wife has reached a time in her life where she forgets. It's a blessing, really. But then sometimes, like today, she's lucid and seems to remember everything, although I'm sure you noticed the rosary beads. That's something new. Rachel is Jewish. The doctor says her condition will probably worsen as time goes by."

"I have no intention of questioning her, Mr. Feldman," said Bari softly. "I understand that . . . according to Marian . . . Detective Carey was in their home to investigate noises that were heard on the two previous nights."

"Yes, I heard the same."

"And that while the detective and Marian were trying to raise the bedroom window above the spot from where the noises had seemed to come, someone came into the bedroom and shot him."

"Yes, I heard the very same story," said Mr. Feldman wearily.

Bari paused briefly before continuing. "But, since the police have arrested Paul, I imagine that they have reason to think that the detective and Marian were having an affair, and that Paul either knew about it or that he discovered it when he came home unexpectedly."

Bari could see that this was an ordeal for this old man and he hated to put him through it. "I know that you have resources, Mr. Feldman. Please tell me what your informed opinion is of what happened."

If Feldman was surprised by this line of questioning, he didn't betray it by so much as a hesitation before answering. "First, let me say that I know my son well,

Joseph, and there is no possibility that he had anything to do with that killing."

"I agree, sir," said Bari.

"According to my investigator, Detective Carey had a reputation as a sexual predator; he preyed upon married women" Mr. Feldman continued. "He was caught once, but nothing came of it. Apparently, the couple involved was at the point of divorce anyway, and the husband was only too happy that Carey and his wife had inadvertently given him the upper hand in the divorce negotiations."

"I would like to have that pair's names," said Bari.

"You shall have them. You want to know if Carey was having an affair with my daughter-in-law. I don't know. Please don't tell my wife any of this. She loves Marian. It would be the end of her if she knew my feelings. But based on Carey's reputation, Marian's considerable allure, and the improbability of her story, I do believe that she and Carey were having an affair."

Suggesting that it had been a long day, what with their driving all the way down from Richmond, Bari told Mrs. Feldman that perhaps the two of them could have their chat some other time. Mrs. Feldman looked deeply relieved.

Bari got the impression that she relied upon her husband to shield her from life's squalor. A private conversation with her about so sensitive a subject would have been more than she could bear, and for nothing.

Before leaving, Mr. Feldman, out of his wife's hearing, promised to have his investigator send his report to Joe's office.

As he had many times, Joe Bari wondered at the selfishness of people who started a downhill snowball like the Carey shooting. He, or possibly she, didn't give a damn about all the innocent people whose lives would be blighted by it. This damn thing might kill the elder Feldmans before it was over.

Bari had learned that Paul's grandfather made a fortune in prefabricated housing right after World War II. Vets coming home wanted the normalcy of a home and family, and with the G.I. Bill, they had the means to achieve the American Dream, or at least make a down payment on it.

Upon his death in 1962, grandpa Feldman left his only son, David, an estate valued at over twenty million dollars. The old man also left a million dollars in trust for his infant grandson, Paul.

David Feldman left real estate development and went into the road building business and acquired a reputation for bringing in state contracts on time at or below the contract price. The state legislators loved him for that, and soon he had a virtual monopoly on road building throughout the state, allowing him to add considerably to his inherited wealth.

Rachel Feldman had been a concert pianist in her youth. She still played her Bosendorfer concert grand at home for her own enjoyment. Rachel loved music. No, she adored music, and she worshiped the composers who had given the world such divine enrichment. To this day, her repertoire numbered in the hundreds, although she frequently couldn't remember why she had left one room and gone into another.

No matter, to save her beloved son, she would willingly light a match to every musical composition on earth, if that's what it would take.

CHAPTER SIX

"SID, YOU HEARD ABOUT THAT schmuck, Carey?"

Word had come to Manny Shilla that some lawyer was trying to make a connection between him and the Carey killing. After debating with himself about making any kind of move, he met with his own lawyer.

"Yeah, I've been following it in the news,"

"The lawyer who represents the husband is trying to tie me to it. I think you should have a talk with him. What do you think?" asked Shilla.

"Might not be necessary. I think he'll have zero success if he tries to introduce your dealings with Carey at trial. That is, unless the prosecutor drops the ball and opens the door," answered Sidney.

Sidney Foxe, Esq. spent his formative legal years defending drug clients. He came to Manny Shilla's attention after he had graduated to white collar crime. Foxe was perfect for Manny Shilla, because despite his successes, he stayed out of the limelight. He got his clients from the word-of-mouth referrals of other satisfied clients who undeservedly breathed the air of freedom because of Sidney Foxe.

"What the hell are you talking about?" asked Shilla,

his eyes narrowing with menace.

"The judge won't let far-out defense theories come into evidence, unless the prosecutor says something like 'The defendant is the one and only person who had a motive to kill Detective Carey.'"

"What's that have to do with the fucking price of beans?" asked Shilla.

"A statement like that might open the door to rebuttal by the defendant to show that others also had a motive," replied Foxe, who, as Shilla knew, despised explaining trial tactics to clients.

"What a load of crap," said Shilla, shaking his head.

"I know the prosecutor assigned to the case, gal named Harriet Atkins, a real S.O.B., but too smart to make a mistake like that," said Foxe. "Even if she gets overheated and says something foolish, she still has an objection that the rebuttal evidence will confuse the issues and mislead the jury."

"Then I'm safe."

"Not completely."

"Make up your fucking mind, Sid."

"It's strictly up to the trial judge's discretion," said Foxe. "Tell you what: call this Joe Bari who represents the husband, and say you'd like to talk to him privately, off the record. Let him pick the place, but not at his office. You don't want to be seen going in or coming out of his office."

Shilla stood with his head down, absorbing Wolfe's instructions. "Yeah, what's next?"

"Then when you meet him, just tell him you had nothing to do with Carey's death. You know, tell him you fired him and that was that. Carey never retaliated and you had no further dealings with him. Impress upon him that you're no murderer, but that even if you were, there is no way you'd harm a cop, dirty or no." said Sidney.

"Tell me again why it's better for me to talk to him. I pay you a bundle to do shit like this for me," said Shilla.

"It's a bit risky, but here's what you can accomplish: he meets you, he sees that you're sincere and that you're clean. Now, if he's an ethical lawyer, he won't drag you into the case unless he has a good faith basis to believe you're implicated."

"Ethical lawyer. Don't make me fucking laugh," said Shilla with contempt aimed directly at Sidney Foxe.

"Some of us are," said Foxe through clenched teeth. "Getting back to the matter at hand; you make a good impression. I've seen you. I trust that you will be calm and convincing even if he tries to goad you. Remember, say what you came to say, shake hands and leave. Answer clarifying questions if he doesn't understand something you said. Don't answer any probing questions, and you'll be fine."

"Yeah, fine. Fine is what I would be if that fucking guinea shyster and his Jew client dropped dead. Then I would be fine," said Shilla.

Shilla knew that Foxe feared him too much to give ill-conceived legal advice. His fear was well founded, because Shilla was already planning a punishment for Foxe if this backfired.

"CAMMY SPEAKING."

"This is Buzz, Cammy. I've got some news for you. Something different and hot."

"Shoot."

"Not over the phone. Can you get up here?"

"I don't want to waste a day, Buzz, unless it's

absolutely necessary."

"We have to meet right away."

Cammy wasn't exaggerating. It would be a full day. Two and a half hours to drive up, find a parking garage with space, and walk to the Metro Ring & Turf. After talking with Buzz for however long that would take, he'd face the same thing returning to Roads Port in knock-off traffic. By that time, the day would be pretty well shot.

The next day, when Cammy walked into the Metro, Buzz got up from his seat at the bar and pulled him back to the high backed booth secluded in gloom.

Cammy went into his handshake routine to pass Buzz a hundred dollar bill, and Buzz recoiled. "It's going to take a more than a hundred this time, Cam. Make it five."

"Okay, Buzz, but I hope for the sake of our ongoing relationship that you're not jerking me off," said Cammy quietly, as he added four more bills to the one in his right hand and passed them to Buzz.

"I said I'd get the names of those other broads Carey was fucking. I got 'em, but I got something else, too," said Buzz. "Maid Marian was making it with someone else besides Carey. Gunner by the name of Richard Kingman. Yeah, and she told him to go fuck his self just before she started with Carey last summer.

"That's dynamite, Buzz," said Cammy, breaking into a wide smile.

"Seems this Kingman blabbed that he had something going with her. Yeah, and she found out about it. The next time he called her, she told him to fuck off, that she had somebody else - meaning Carey. Can't say as I blame her."

"Me neither," said Cammy.

"Anyway, he took it hard. Got drunk in some joint

up town and started talking crazy about killing the son of a bitch who stole his woman. *His* woman, can you beat that?" asked Buzz.

"Yeah, but . . ."

"Loose talk. Sure, we've all popped off when we were drunk, but this clown's got a heavy record," said Buzz. "He beat an assault-with-a-deadly-weapon charge in Carolina. He had another felony assault here in Richmond dismissed a year and a half ago, when the poor fuck he pummeled failed to appear. So he's capable, you know what I mean?"

BARI RECEIVED HARRIET Atkins's witness list by messenger and the surprise of his life by phone.

"Morning Counselor. Got an offer for you. Tell your client that in return for a guilty plea, we'll reduce his capital murder to murder one. Carries a statutory twenty to life, but we won't oppose your motion for a sentence reduction."

"He won't go for it, Harriet; he's innocent."

"Well, you never know. He's facing death right now. He pleads, and maybe he's out in fifteen, a middle aged man. Tell him to think about it. With a dead cop victim, it's a gift."

Bari laughed to himself. Harriet would give sand to the Saudis, so either she's spotted the weakness in her case or she's trying to play with my mind. Better call Art.

"Hey Art, are you free? Good, I'm on my way to your office."

Still smiling, Bari opened Art's office door. "Guess what? Harriet offered to let Paul plead to murder one."

"SHE WHAT?!" Art shouted.

"I think maybe it's because she knows fucking well

she can't get a death penalty instruction out of Judge Jones if she argues that Carey was making it with Marian."

"Why the hell not?" asked Art, his cherubic face blank with incomprehension.

"You get the death penalty for killing a cop if the killing is for the purpose of interfering with the performance of his official duties, not while he's banging your wife."

Harriet's witness list contained the names, professional addresses and phone numbers of the cops who investigated Carey's murder, the pathologist who performed the autopsy and the ballistics expert. There was no one on the list that Bari hadn't anticipated.

"Unless Harriet argues that Carey was killed in the line of duty, she doesn't have capital murder. But, if she does argue he was killed in the line of duty, she throws out her lead detective's testimony and her case along with it. Man, she must have eaten her liver when it hit her," said Bari, in full gloat. "Hell, she doesn't even have murder one."

"Because no premeditation," said Louis.

"Bingo!"

They went over the raft of people who didn't appear on Harriet's witness list. These were people with solid motives to kill Carey: a jilted lover with a record for violence and the husbands of Carey's other married girlfriends. But as valuable as those witnesses might be, Bari couldn't figure out how to use them.

"We can't use Richard Kingman, that's for sure," said Bari.

"Why not? He's a prime suspect," said Louis. "Christ, he even said he was going to kill Carey for taking Marian away from him."

"Yeah, but his testimony trashes Marian's character, and we can't have that. Marian is sticking to her story that Carey was upstairs investigating a prowler, and we can't undermine her."

"No, of course not," said Louis, downcast. "It's a shame though. We've got the names of great witnesses and we can't use them. If we could use them, we could spread reasonable doubt all over the place."

"Oh, I didn't say we couldn't use them," said Bari. "We just can't use them in court."

Louis eyed him suspiciously, "I'm afraid to ask."

"You worry too much, Art," said Bari, hugging Louis's shoulder. "Then, of course, we've got the mob boss Carey screwed. Won't the jury eat that up: the crooked cop and the Mafia?"

"CAMMY, HAVE YOU got any police department forms? You know, the kind they use for witness narratives?"

"I can print some up, Joe."

"Okay, do that. We're going to give Harriet our cuckolded husbands."

"After all the trouble and expense it took to scare them up, you're going to give them away?" asked Cammy, rolling his eyes.

"She won't know we gave them to her. Think for a minute. If we try to deflect suspicion onto the cuckolds, we concede that Carey was a womanizer. Sure, the husbands had a motive to ice Carey - jealousy - but then so did Paul. See what I'm saying?" asked Bari.

"Yeah, but why give them to Harriet? Won't she use them for the very same purpose?"

"No. From Harriet's standpoint, all those husbands do is dilute her argument that Paul was the one with the motive and the one who pulled the trigger. In other words, the husbands are bad for us *and* bad for Harriet."

"Then why bother giving them to her in the first place?"

"Because she'll find the information in her box at the Commonwealth Attorney's office and think it came from the cops investigating Carey's killing," replied Bari. "Her first impulse will be to sit on it. If she does sit on it, we've got a *Brady* motion."

"What about Richard Kingman?" asked Cammy.

"No, definitely not. I don't want Harriet to know Kingman exists."

"Go slowly, Joe. You're beginning to sound like my daddy," said Cammy.

"We'll say that a little bird told us that Harriet has failed to turn over information tending to show that Paul is innocent," explained Bari. "That's *Brady* material. Harriet will deny that the information about the jilted husbands shows Paul's innocence. Judge Jones will insist on seeing the material, and then he'll rule. If Jones denies our motion, it's an automatic reversal on appeal."

"You have a devious mind, Joe."

"On the other hand, Cammy, if she turns the information - that you will have planted - over to us, she's in the clear. Look at it as a test of Harriet's honesty."

"Yeah, I sure don't want to look at it as a test of my own . . . or yours, for that matter."

"Cam, look. Paul's my dearest friend in the world. If he goes down, it's for life, and you know it. I can't let that happen. I won't let it happen."

"MR. BARI, THIS is Manny Shilla calling. I'd like to talk to you about that Carey business at some place of your choosing, but not at your office, if you don't mind."

Bari's mind was doing end-overs. Why not his office? Did this sonofabitch want to get him somewhere and kill him? Do I need to talk to this man? What was there to talk about? What if he threatened me? Calm down, he had told himself, this was no gangster movie.

"Why don't you want to come here, sir?"

"I just don't want to be seen going in or out. Some reporter might see me and make something of it."

"I see," said Bari. "Well, there's a small lunch place near Jamestown off of 31, called The Spot. It's got a big fish on the sign."

"Yeah, I know the place."

"If we meet there after the lunch hour, say about one thirty, it should be empty."

"Sounds good. Can you make it tomorrow?"

The more Bari thought about it, the more confused he became. But at the very least, meeting face-to-face would be an opportunity to assess for himself whether Shilla was implicated.

Still, it was a puzzle. If Shilla was involved in any way, even if he had five cutouts between himself and the shooter, it made sense he'd lay low.

If Shilla's invitation to meet was for the purpose of demonstrating that he had nothing to do with Carey's death, then it was either clever or reckless, and, so far as Bari could determine, Manny Shilla was not reckless.

ON THE WAY home from the office that evening, a nondescript car had passed Bari and then immediately slowed down in front of him. Why pass, asshole, if all you're going to do is slow down once you get in front of me? Bari muttered. No wonder road rage was rampant.

He was going to pass the guy and let him know how

he felt when another car pulled up beside him on his left. Now he was boxed in. He looked over at the driver who held up a badge and signaled him to follow the car in front of him. The lead car gave a right hand signal and pulled into a mall parking lot.

Bari would have worried that he was about to be robbed or taken out, except that these two had "cop" written all over them.

They parked so that Bari's Porsche Carrera was sandwiched between them. The two cops got out of their cars and motioned for Bari to do the same.

"Mr. Bari, we're with the Commonwealth Criminal Investigation Unit. We know that you're meeting with Manny Shilla tomorrow and the Attorney General's Office wanted us to speak to you about it," said the taller of the two. Both wore sport coats, not dark blue suits, but it didn't matter. They still looked like cops.

"May I ask how you know about my schedule?"

"The AG has a tap on Shilla's phone," said the runt. "It's court ordered, so don't worry about the legalities."

"I'm in the middle of a pre-trial investigation," said Bari. "I can't imagine what that has to do with the AG's office."

"If we can get Shilla to cop to organized gambling, we can break up his operation and maybe others along with it," said the tall string bean.

"And how do you propose to do that?" asked Bari, knowing full well what their pitch was going to be. "Let me answer my own question. You want me to wear a wire. Am I right?"

"That's right, Mr. Bari. The AG will appreciate it. In fact, he can make the trouble that Mr. Feldman is in go away."

"Christ Almighty! The AG can make a capital

murder charge go away?" asked Bari, stunned at the string bean's brazen candor.

"Yeah, and a lot more."

This was more temptation than anyone should have to endure. If he went along with them, the case against Paul would evaporate, never to return? That of course was the rub. There was no statute of limitations on murder. If the AG could make the case disappear, he could also make it reappear down the road if you didn't do exactly as he said. These tactics would be familiar to Shilla and other mob guys who created them in the first place.

"Fellows, I'd like to help you, I really would, but I can't. For one thing, secretly taping a witness statement for the benefit of the police is an ethical violation. I'd lose my license to practice law. And even if I could somehow get past the ethics, cooperating with you would put my life and my wife's life in danger. I mean, you do intend to use the tape in court, right? Shilla and everyone else would know I was a part of it."

"We might find a way to use your tape to get a confession from others," said the shorter, more sinister of the two. "They would hear Shilla talking about them. They wouldn't hear your voice. And the beauty part is that Shilla tells you what we want as a natural part of your conversation. You won't have to ask any questions. Well maybe one or two, you know, to get his story straight."

These cocksuckers take the cake. "I'm sorry fellas," said Bari. "I really would like to cooperate with the AG to stamp out organized crime, but I can't." They had offered the carrot: Paul. Bari held his breath and waited for the stick.

"If you flat refuse to help the Commonwealth on so

important a matter, I'm afraid the AG won't forget it, Mr. Bari," said the runt, with a vindictive smile oozing venom.

"And just what does that mean?" asked Bari, afraid to imagine what it meant.

"There isn't a lawyer alive who doesn't fuck up sometime, somehow," said the string bean. "Cut a corner here, shade the truth there. And when you do, we'll be waiting, Mr. Bari."

The short one again: "Yeah, and if you're thinking of telling Shilla about our little meeting here, forget it. The tap on Shilla's phone was sanctioned by the court, and you are an officer of that court . . . for the time being. So keep your mouth shut about it."

"Fuck you and your threats. So long as your tap doesn't involve me or a client, I have no obligation to reveal it to Shilla or anyone else."

"That's the ticket. See you around, Counselor."

WHEN JOE BARI drove into the Spot's parking lot the following afternoon, he had it all to himself. The lunch crowd had come and gone. He picked a table with a clear view of the entry and placed his briefcase in plain sight to identify himself. He had no sooner ordered than a man in work clothes shambled through the door.

"Mr. Bari? Glad to meet you," said Manny Shilla with a handshake.

He stood when Shilla called his name, and now they both were seated. Shilla got back up when he remembered he was still wearing his hat, an old, beat-up fedora. He hung it on a hook and sat back down.

Shilla was mid fifties, paunchy and indifferent to his clothes and his appearance. He wore a two-day growth of gray beard and the tops of his shoes were coming loose from the soles.

"I ordered a Smithfield ham sandwich apiece and coffee. I hope that suits you."

"I love Smithfield ham, but it don't love me. Too salty. The doctor says I have to watch my salt. I'm not hungry anyway."

Shilla wasted no words. "Mr. Bari, I heard that your investigator was asking questions about a falling out between me and Detective Carey. We did have a falling out, it's true. Detective Carey was dishonest . . . with *me*, and we were supposed to be friends." It looked like Shilla was going to do the talking. Like all powerful men, when they call the meeting, they set the agenda.

"I ended our friendship after that, and wanted nothing further to do with him. He came to see me and wanted to make it right, but I refused. When I heard on TV that someone killed him, I was sorry, because he used to joke with me and make me laugh. I enjoyed his company." Shilla paused, apparently thinking back. "Oh, I called him names after he stole from me. I was angry. But the truth is, he hurt my feelings."

A cheery, older waitress with a hair-sprayed helmet of red hair and big rolling hips came with the sandwiches and coffee. "Here you are boys." Bari nearly laughed out loud at the remark. Here was one of the most fearsome men in the state, and he'd just been called "boy."

"People who know me know that I am a careful businessman. I have many valued associations going back to the year I was first in business. I have this other business that you know about."

It was at this point or one like it Bari supposed, that the AG would have wanted him to ask Shilla for some clarification. What business is that, Mr. Shilla? What a fucking laugh. Shilla would have instantly smelled a rat.

"I'm retiring from my wholesale business and the other thing also," Shilla continued. "I made up my mind yesterday. Me and my wife are going to spend more time together, you know, traveling and visiting family." Shilla's shrewd eyes and large beaked nose evoked millennia of Levantine cunning, and Bari had begun to wonder if this meeting wasn't an act.

"I have never taken a human life," said Shilla. "I would never take a life, unless in self defense. When I found out about Carey stealing from me, I thought 'you ungrateful bastard.' But it never occurred to me to do him physical harm."

In the end, Bari was forced to concede that Shilla's story rang true for the most part. If he had wanted Carey dead, there were a million ways to get rid of him. He would never send a hitter to Paul's house; it was too complicated and messy. Why draw unnecessary attention?

Bari had to introduce evidence that Carey had enemies, and that these enemies had a motive to kill him. And much as he wanted to bring in the possibility and the drama of an underworld assassination, he couldn't.

If he tried now to make the trial about a corrupt cop who was murdered by his former criminal associates, he'd blow it, because even he didn't believe it.

More importantly, it would also be dangerous, now more than ever. He didn't care about himself. In a trial, you do what you have to do to defend your client. But there were Art and Cammy and especially Ann to think about. If he brought Shilla's name into the trial now, feeling as he did about Shilla's noninvolvement, and somebody got hurt, he'd never forgive himself.

"This case is troubling to me," said Bari, "because

Paul Feldman, the accused, and I have been close friends since we were young guys. There is simply no chance that he could kill anybody. But Detective Carey is dead and someone killed him, so my investigator has been trying to uncover people who might have had a motive."

After listening to Shilla, Bari didn't believe he had a motive to kill Carey. Forty thousand dollars might be a motive to kill for some people, but not for Shilla.

For spite, Bari handed him a handwritten message, because he was afraid that the Attorney General's goons had a directional microphone pointed at them.

After Shilla had read the message, Bari retrieved it. The message said: "Be careful what you say on your phone. It's tapped."

DRIVING BACK TO the office, Bari had felt a palpitation followed by shortness of breath, and he pulled into a strip mall and parked. He cut the engine, and his heart quickly jumped back into rhythm and he began to breathe regularly. He recognized these symptoms, and he knew all too well what they betokened.

Tiny butterflies in the stomach would grow into hummingbirds and then into California Condors, and then he would have a fainting spell or two out of nowhere. The drink before bed to help him sleep would become a pint, and he would toss and turn nonetheless.

Early in his practice, a giant class action for millions in damages began to go sour. Reputations were made or lost on such cases. He was helpless to improve the case, until he caught a series of surprising breaks that turned it around. Some crucial documents magically turned up, and they in turn caused a key witness to recant his damaging testimony.

It was during that time before the turnaround that he

began feeling what he felt now and it grew and grew. The feeling was fear.

"GODAMMIT ART, ON top of everything else, the AG's office sent a couple of their special gorillas to talk to me about wearing a wire when I talked to Shilla. They said that the AG would make Paul's case go away if I wore one. When I refused, they threatened to get something on me. Can you believe those arrogant S.O.B.s?"

"I think we should complain directly to the governor. I can't stand it when the government throws its fucking weight around." said Louis.

"I agree, but we'll wait until this case is over."

"How in hell could the AG get Paul's case dismissed?" asked Louis.

"He could just call the Commonwealth Attorney and tell him to withdraw the charges because of, I don't know, mistake," said Bari. "He would tell him to say that the investigation into Carey's death would continue, but that all the evidence now pointed away from Paul. The press would have some questions, but in the end, the Commonwealth Attorney would look good for admitting a mistake and removing the cloud over Paul."

THERE HAD BEEN a succession of motion skirmishes before Judge Jones. Harriet Atkins had correctly assumed that there would be a time issue at trial. There was the medical examiner's estimate of time of death and Feldman's time of arrival home from the airport. She had requested notice of an alibi defense, arguing that the Commonwealth needed time to question any and all alibi witnesses.

Art Louis, with Bari by his side at the defense table,

responded that the defense wasn't ready at that point to declare its defense, alibi or otherwise. Judge Jones admonished that the defense was now obliged to inform the Commonwealth of an alibi, if indeed one existed, within sixty days, or forfeit that defense.

Louis countered with a motion that the Commonwealth disclose all exculpatory evidence, evidence tending to show that the defendant was innocent.

"Your Honor, the Commonwealth has a pile of evidence that the defendant is guilty, but not a scintilla of evidence showing, or tending to show, that the defendant is innocent," said Harriet in a sing song, affecting boredom. "These defense motions about nonexistent evidence are a waste of the court's time,"

"Do you have a basis for your motion, Mr. Louis?" asked the judge.

"Rumors, Your Honor," Louis replied. "Nothing concrete at this point."

Harriet's bored denial was a lie. Cammy's associate, Aaron, had stuffed a manila envelope with the dope on the cuckolded husbands in Harriet's box ten days ago. Aaron had also gotten a time-dated receipt for it from a clueless office clerk who thought he was a cop.

Louis, who kept himself in semidarkness about Cammy's role, reserved the right to bring the motion again at a later date. "Next time, have something more than rumors, Mr. Louis," said the judge.

What appeared to be typical pretrial wrangling aimed at gaining some advantage over the opposition at trial - or a later appeal should the worst happen - was in fact a bear trap that Louis had laid. Now, with Harriet's lie, it was set.

"For chrissakes, Art, why don't you just admit you

want to make Harriet scream like a panther?" asked Bari.

Louis and Harriet were beginning to respect each other's strengths by now. As their mutual respect grew, so did a corresponding and complicated hatred. Bari, watching these developments, looked on amused. Art and Harriet remained civil in court, but with clenched jaws and stares that could freeze the James River.

"Are you kidding? I wouldn't fuck her with your dick," said Louis packing up his briefcase.

"Yeah, sure. I hear you, Art. I think you're in denial," said Bari, laughing.

"Go to blazes, Joe. I can't stand that goddamm woman." Art's earlobes had turned a precarious purple.

Thus warned, Bari gave him a pat on the back. "Just kidding, Art. Damn good job on that motion, by the way."

CHAPTER SEVEN

"JOE, THIS IS CAMMY. I'M afraid we've hit an iceberg. Her name is Bernice Early."

Cammy had interviewed two neighbors directly across the street from Paul and Marian Feldman. One was out of town on February fifteenth; the other was Bernice Early, great granddaughter of Confederate General Jubal Early, she was proud to tell Cammy.

On the morning of the murder, Miss Early had seen a

big black car parked beside Carey's unmarked blue Chevrolet Caprice. Ten minutes later when she looked out, the black car was gone.

"I know what I saw, young man," said the elderly spinster dressed in tweed and a stylish light tan cardigan that came down past her hips. "I didn't see it arrive, but I had looked out my front window only minutes before and it wasn't there. After taking notice of it, I went to the kitchen to get a cup of coffee and when I returned, it was gone. So it couldn't have been over there more than fifteen minutes, but closer to ten, I'd judge. I didn't think anything of it; I thought it was Paul's car at first. But later, I decided it wasn't, because Paul's car is maroon."

"Actually, ma'am, I believe Mr. Feldman's car is black." suggested Cammy.

"Don't contradict me, young man. Paul's car is maroon, but even if it isn't maroon, it isn't that big either."

"*Big*, ma'am?"

"Pay attention, young man: not nearly as big as the black car that was parked there briefly on the morning of February fifteenth."

"May I ask if you have spoken with anyone else about what you saw?"

"Yes. I spoke to some city detective that very day. I have his card around somewhere."

Very tricky, thought Cammy, Miss Early's name doesn't appear on the prosecution's witness list.

"Did you happen to see a delivery truck, like UPS or FedEx stop at Paul's, Miss Early?"

"No, but there was one in the neighborhood that morning, now that you mention it. It was one of those brown UPS trucks."

"I'd like to ask a favor of you Miss Early, ma'am. I wonder if you would allow me to videotape your statement."

BARI WAS SICK. He agreed that Bernice Early was indeed the iceberg that could sink this case. Harriet would have a picnic with this witness. Maroon, black, big, not as big - Fuck! With no prompting at all from Harriet, the goddamm jury would justifiably believe that Miss Early saw Paul's car parked in front of his house for ten minutes on the morning of February 15, and that would be the ball game. And Harriet, that underhanded slut, was keeping her a secret until right before trial.

"HEY BUDDY, YOU play tennis, or is that just a great looking tie?" asked Richard Kingman, who was also dressed to kill. Cammy's tie was a rich silver blue with crossed tennis rackets in hand-stitched navy at the tip.

"I play intermediate," Cammy answered. "You?" The tie trick always worked with tennis players, but it had worked particularly well with Kingman who was sitting alone at the bar.

"Yeah, I've played all my life. I was on the tennis team at UVa, until the administration asked me to leave," Kingman laughed.

"Well they kicked Poe out too, but that hurt their reputation a hell of a lot more than it did Poe's," said Cammy, scoring big points with Kingman.

"We'll have to play sometime."

"Sure, if you think I'd give you a game. What are you drinking?" asked Cammy.

Richard Kingman had been Marian's other lover, the one she dumped because he couldn't keep his mouth shut. Kingman was the kind of guy women go goofy over and men despise. He was handsome with a voluptuous mouth that hinted at a cruel streak.

Cammy's digging had uncovered some interesting facts. Women hung all over him, yet he remained a dissatisfied, complaining asshole. Guys that knew him asked each other, "I mean, what is his problem? If I had as much going for me, I'd be as happy as a sissy in jail."

Kingman didn't care what people thought. Women, beginning with his mother and other female family members, spoiled him from infancy to the present day, and it stuck. He now sincerely believed that he looked down upon the rest of humanity from a great height.

No surprise that he had taken it hard when Marian dumped him. Richard Kingman, like infants the world over, flew into a rage when he was denied his toys.

Cammy's tactic was to run into Kingman early and stay with him until he got good and sloshed. He knew that it was going to be a long tedious evening drinking with Kingman. He wanted to find out whether Kingman had what it took to kill Carey.

Bars in Richmond don't come any slicker than Stonewall's, with its art deco furnishings and its well-dressed, sophisticated clientele. It was evidently considered chichi to name the joint after a Confederate war hero, conjuring up all the swirls and bowing etiquette of the time - then decorate it in an ironic, mocking style.

With a little extra poking around, Cammy had discovered that Stonewall's, or "Stoney's," as the gang called it, was Kingman's favorite base of operations. It was in Stoney's that he had met Marian more than a year ago.

According to a former bartender, Kingman thought

of himself as Stoney's most popular patron. After all, he spent a lot of money and caused a lot to be spent by the women who courted him there. In fact, the help tolerated him. Barely.

Cammy had gotten dressed in his best suit and his tennis tie. He had let Kingman arrive first and five minutes later walked in, unbuttoned his suit jacket, and took a seat near him at the bar.

Cammy kept the drinks coming. Within two hours, Kingman had his shirt collar unbuttoned and, with nudging from Cammy, was deep into lamentations for the lost Marian. It was duck soup for Cammy to steer the conversation toward the topic that egotists like Kingman love most - themselves.

"I mean, how in the hell did I know she would take it like that? I slipped up and said something to this fucking lawyer who represents me. I'm gonna sue his ass. Anyway, he turns around and starts playing position on her himself by telling her what I said. The bitch came unglued. Next thing I know, she's kissing me off for some fucking cop. Believe that - a cop?!"

Kingman gestured with his drink and soon he began to spill as much as he drank. When some of it spilled on Cammy, Kingman apologized profusely, spilling more, and patted down the spots with a paper napkin. Cammy instantly absolved him and ordered a refill.

"It could be that after she cools off a little, she'll let you back in. Why not wait a week and then call her?"

Kingman's face went from hopeless gloom to conspiratorial snickering mirth. "Come here, Cammy," motioning him closer. If there are two things drunks can't do, it's ride a bicycle and whisper. Kingman made a stab at the latter: "Here's the funny part. Did you read about that cop that got killed in that rich guy's home a month ago? That's her. That's was her home and that cop was her boyfriend, my replacement. Somebody took the sonofabitch out. Can you fucking believe that?" At this, Kingman slapped Cammy's back by way of getting him to join in the fun, which of course Cammy did.

"Who do you think shot him?"

"Who the fuck knows. I'd like to kiss him, I'll tell you that."

In his most jocular, we're-just-guys fashion, Cammy said, "You're the one with the motive, you know," and laughed raising his glass in an exaggerated toast.

"No. I've done some nutty things in my life, but I never fought over a woman, let alone killed anybody over one," said Kingman with boozy solemnity. "Oh, I thought about it a couple of times, but I'd never give a broad the satisfaction of knowing she had my nose open."

That's it. This guy didn't do it, thought Cammy. He was a self-pitying, egotistical, loudmouth asshole and he was a drunk, but his false pride would never let him kill a rival.

EL NINO HAD caused the jet stream to drop down to Southern California before heading cross country and inundating the East Coast with week after week of steady spring rain.

Joe, Art Louis and Cammy hunkered again in Louis's office for what had become their regularly-scheduled meeting.

"I've had it with this rain," said Cammy. "It's depressing. I have to force myself to work."

"Wait till you have kids," said Louis. "They go nuts around the house when it rains and they can't go out. Sally's tearing her hair out."

Bari's mood was just a notch or two from suicidal. "Well, I don't think Shilla had anything to do with Carey's death and Cammy doesn't think Casanova Kingman did it. Our two most promising suspects and we've ruled them out," he said pacing in a large oval, hands behind his back. "And now the Commonwealth has Bernice Early, and God only knows what she'll say on the stand."

"Yeah, and you have to be damn careful when you put her through cross. Try to confuse that old lady, and the jury will never forgive you for it," said Louis. "I hate to say this, Joe, but . . ."

Bari cut Louis off, "Well don't say it. Paul's innocent, and that's final. If we go soft, we'll stop looking, and then Paul will be cooked, because the cops are damn sure not looking for anyone else."

"You can say that again. The grand jury handed up an indictment. The cops made an arrest and put this one over in the win column. Case closed," said Cammy. "Why keep looking?"

TWO MONTHS HAD sped by. After a three-week 24/7 blitz after the killing, the Richmond media had lost most of its interest in Paul and Marian. One reporter discovered their new address in Roads Port. He and his colleagues made nuisances of themselves for a few days, until Paul and Marian moved into one of Louis's small Grand View vacation cottages that he rented out by the week in the summer.

There was a two mile-long string of beach homes on stilts along a spit at Grand View beach facing the Chesapeake Bay. On the back side of the spit were wetlands full of feeding aquatic birds. Paul and Marian walked along the wetlands side of the spit on early mornings when the air was still cool.

With little else to do but read, Marian had discovered that the large fresh water rivers that emptied into the salt water of the Chesapeake Bay diluted the Bay's salinity, creating an ideal nursery for a hundred thriving species of marine life before the young animals matured and made their way out to the Atlantic Ocean.

In the past, a recitation of such facts would have driven her to a double martini in a hurry, but not now. Maybe it was living so close to it that piqued her interest. Maybe it was self-defense. With little provocation, Paul would dash off a minilecture about the local ecology.

They had finally escaped the pitiless media magnifying glass. Their story had been eclipsed by an outbreak of flu in Richmond that had spread to hundreds, prompting historical pieces in the press and TV, resurrecting the infamous 1918 Spanish flu epidemic that killed over six hundred thousand people in the U.S. alone.

There had also been a spectacular bank robbery in downtown Richmond in which three were killed and four were wounded, the actual perpetrators having escaped to parts unknown.

Shortly thereafter, the Richmond press misreported a solitary case of West Nile disease as a case of Mad Cow disease, scaring the hell out of every stock-raising farmer in five states. Later, even the case of West Nile disease turned out to be something innocuous, which led to a week of journalistic soul-searching about the duty to check and recheck a story before filing it.

Paul and Marian had established a pleasant routine of long walks on the beach, followed by warm lovemaking. When the rains came, they read books and rented movies.

They shopped for groceries and other items, tentatively at first, and then, when they weren't recognized, more boldly, but always in disguise. Marian would wear baggy clothes and no makeup. Instead of his beloved tweed sport coat, Paul wore a windbreaker, as well as sunglasses and a ball cap.

Marian, before any of this and before meeting Paul, had always found her path at the chilly intersection of pragmatism and self-interest. Reflecting on her marriage and especially the events leading to Paul's indictment, she had to admit that she had been self-destructive, not self-interested. And instead of pragmatic, she had been impulsive and harebrained.

Marian had never seen real strength before. She'd heard plenty of tough-guy bullshit. She had seen through her father's bragging and she couldn't stomach it. Now, when she thought about it, all the guys she had slept with were weakling losers. Why, Marian asked herself, did she ever screw around with men she despised?

Here was Paul, under indictment for murder, calmly bearing up, living his life, extending himself to her as if he had no problems whatever. Marian realized that she had badly underestimated Paul, and it called her judgment about everything else into question. Maybe now it was too late to rescue her marriage, she thought. Maybe the shit she had brought into their lives was too deep.

"MR. BARI, THIS is Ruby Shilla calling. My husband would like you to go to a public telephone at noon and call the number I'm going to give you. Will you do that?"

Joe knew at once that the number Ruby Shilla had given him was also a pay phone number. Manny Shilla didn't want this call to appear on Bari's phone records or his own; neither did he want it overheard by the tap.

Shilla's caution was catching. Bari got into his Porsche and drove a quick two miles to the old Viceroy Hotel at Ft. Monroe. There was a bank of phone booths in its sumptuous lobby. "Hello, this is Joe Bari speaking."

"Mr. Bari, the hitter was an independent contractor outta Miami, name of Lupo, Jackie Lupo. That's all I heard. You take it from there."

"I will. Thank you sir." Joe's last phrase was spoken into a dead phone. Shilla had already hung up.

If Bari hadn't feared arrest for disorderly conduct, he would have skipped back to the firm. He was on fire with optimism, and he danced around his office with an imaginary partner. He sang, he shouted, until Helen poked her head in asking if anything was wrong.

"No Helen, everything is right!" She blanched when Bari grabbed her around the waist for a spin down the hall.

Bari had believed him when Shilla said he had nothing to do with Carey's death. Both he and Shilla knew that meant that he would not drag Shilla's association with Carey into the trial. And the heads-up from Bari about the phone tap would spare him untold grief. The phone call naming Carey's killer was a big fat "thank you" from Manny Shilla.

He yelled down the hall for Louis, and asked Helen to find Cammy wherever he was and get him to the office now.

"I never heard of the guy, Joe," said Cammy. "At any rate, knowing the hitter's name doesn't do us much good. This Jackie Lupo isn't likely to give up the name of the guy that hired him to a PI."

"He might if the approach and the price were right," said Louis, ever the negotiator.

"I catch your drift, Art," said Cammy. "Well, if I don't make it back from Florida, you've got my will and insurance policies in your safe."

"Hell, if you feel that way, Cam, I'll go myself."

"Yeah, right, Joe. You'd wind up on a slab in the Miami Beach morgue in forty-eight hours. I'll go first thing tomorrow morning if Helen can get me tickets. Anything to get away from this fucking rain."

HARRIET ATKINS FILED a motion to restrain any disposal of "property subject to forfeiture." She apparently had her eye on Paul and Marian Feldman's million-dollar-plus home, which would make a nice prize for the Commonwealth. It would also burnish Harriet's nefarious reputation for snatching property from unsuspecting defendants.

Bari had been completely baffled. "First off, Art, 'property subject to forfeiture' is usually property gained from or used in criminal activity, like a million dollars in cash from the sale of drugs or a home with a drug lab in the basement."

Harriet's motion asserted that Paul had used his home to facilitate the murder of Detective Carey, and now the issue would be before Judge Jones.

"RESPONSE, MR. LOUIS?"

"Your Honor, my client is free on a property bond. The deed to Mr. Feldman's home is currently held by court administration to secure his release. In other words, his interest is already frozen."

Harriet was inspecting her shoes while Louis spoke.

"Furthermore," Louis continued, "the forfeiture

statute was intended to deprive perpetrators of ill-gotten gains and deprive them of property closely associated with the crime of which they are accused.

"Detective Carey was murdered in my client's home, *as it happened*," said Louis. "He could have been murdered anywhere. It is pointless to move for forfeiture in this case."

"I agree. Nice try, Ms. Atkins. Motion denied."

"Harriet's motion was bullshit, Art," said Bari.

"It's the typical harassment I've come to expect from that harridan. The Commonwealth didn't have a chance in hell of winning that motion and she knew it."

Louis braced her in front of Bari on the way out of court. "What the fuck are you trying to pull, Harriet?"

"That was a legitimate motion," she spat. "I don't give a good goddamn if you and that liberal ass judge don't agree."

"Oh come off it, Atkins," said Bari, chuckling. "Benito Scalia wouldn't have granted that motion."

"Asshole!" With that, Harriet Atkins was off down the hall tossing her auburn mane and clicking her heels loudly against the marble floor.

Louis knew that all the criminal defense attorneys badmouthed Harriet behind her back. She never showed for a second that she gave a damn, and for that Louis gave her credit. His pet theory about Harriet - one that he did not share with Bari, who no doubt would have howled - was that she drew strength from her certain knowledge that every lawyer and judge in the courthouse wanted to fuck her into submission.

CHAPTER EIGHT

BEFORE LEAVING ROADS PORT, CAMMY checked with other PIs he knew. Could they refer him to a PI in Miami? He got three names, the most promising of which was Causeway Investigators, located appropriately near a causeway over Biscayne Bay.

The flight out of Norfolk had taken off in rain and unseasonable cold and had landed thirty minutes later in Charlotte in the same conditions. After the plane crossed the Florida state line, however, it was straight sunshine.

Cammy's commuter flight didn't pull up to a gate. It disgorged its passengers a hundred feet from the terminal. As he left the plane and started down the ramp, a blast of hot air nearly laid him out.

After collecting his bag from the carousel at baggage claim, he found the shuttle that took him to the rental car that Helen had reserved for him.

"You can have your choice today, sir," said the Alamo babe behind the counter. "For an inexpensive upgrade, we can give you anything up to a silver S 500 Mercedes with all the trimmings."

"With air?"

"Of course with air. This is Florida, sir."

This could be the last ride I ever take, thought

Cammy. Might as well get the best. "I'll take the big Merc."

"Here's a map. As you leave our lot, take a left, then two rights to go downtown. If you want to go to the Beach, look for the signs just after you make your second right. You'll go across a bridge and through Coconut Grove. Look here on the map. This is Little Havana, and it's safe. Don't go through here. That's Little Haiti, and it's very dangerous," she said with a fetching little frown. "If you see a car broken down on the side of the road, it's a scam. Don't stop." The Alamo babe looked up from the map, and broke into a radiant smile. "The company makes us tell that to all our customers."

Cammy had FedExed his piece to the motel Helen got for him on line, but that wouldn't help him now if some crazy boat person who decided he wanted a Mercedes ran him off the road. Cammy had never flown armed, and now because of airport security, he couldn't if he wanted to.

CAUSEWAY'S LARGE OUTER office and waiting room was pretentiously stylish, and Cammy felt a pang of envy. It wasn't the slick Miami furnishings; he didn't like those anyway. It was the spaciousness and the feeling you got when you walked through the front door of an efficient, well-run operation. It was not the same feeling Cammy got when he walked through the front door of *W. S. Brown, Investigator.*

"My name is Cammy Brown. I have an appointment with Mr. Harrow."

"Mr. Harrow is expecting you, Mr. Brown. I'll show you to his office," the trim, fortyish receptionist said smoothly. Her professionalism further dismayed Cammy.

Clyde Harrow was the chief investigator and owner of Causeway Investigators. Tall, rail thin, and sixty, he wore ivory linen slacks and a Sno-cone lime short sleeve shirt open at the collar that revealed gray hair sprouting from a concave chest. Harrow's deeply tanned skin had turned to leather years ago. When he gestured, the loose skin beneath his triceps flapped disconcertingly.

"Cammy Brown, come on in and take a seat," said Harrow, reaching across his glass free-form desk and shaking Cammy's hand. "After you called me yesterday, I talked to some of your friends in Virginia. All I can say is wow! You come very highly recommended."

"Thank you, sir. You do as well. I'll come right to the point. I want to talk to a guy called Jackie Lupo. I'm not the cops, as you know, and I'm not working for the cops directly or indirectly. I will consider Lupo a source and will protect him as I would any source. In accord with our code, there is no court order or contempt citation that could cause me to reveal his name to anyone, even if it cost my license. Let me add that I don't expect your help as a professional courtesy. I am prepared to pay a fee for your services."

Harrow let a few moments go by as he considered Cammy's offer. He picked up a pencil and tapped it on the glass desk top before he answered.

"I've heard of Lupo, of course," he said carefully. "He's dangerous. He probably won't talk to you. That's just a guess, Cammy. I never met the man, but I know his kind. What, if anything, is in it for him?"

"I want information that I believe he has," Cammy replied. "I'm prepared to pay him for it. After he knows what I'm after, he can set the price."

Cammy gave Harrow the number of his motel room located in one of the countless pastel palaces in Miami

Beach.

"There's a jazz joint on the Beach, right off Collins Avenue, called Pococurante," said Harrow. "It was Jake Lamotta's joint in the fifties. It's been there since forever. Every dope smuggler, funny money artist, and button man on the East Coast makes it in there sometime."

Harrow's brow was knitted in thought as he stood and walked around his desk. Cammy rose to meet him.

"You might try there, but be very, very careful. The clientele at Poco are bad people, and one offbeat move will land you in the bay in more than one piece."

Harrow was concluding the interview and he hooked his arm in Cammy's as they walked toward his office door. He stopped at the door and took Cammy's hand in collegial friendship, one pro to another.

"The bartender's name is Johnny. I'll give him a call when he comes on shift and tell him to look for you. I don't know as he'll help you out on this Lupo thing, but he'll get you oriented and maybe tell you who the players are."

Cammy left Harrow's office on a cloud. It was pure gold to get inside information in a place as complicated as Miami Beach. It was called being "aced-in" in the trade.

Cammy knew from experience that an out-of-state investigator could fiddly fart around for months trying to get connected, and still come up dry.

Unlike New Orleans or Las Vegas, every big hustle at the Beach was federal. Major coke deals that had been negotiated in Martinique went down in Miami Beach and the Keys. Nothing new about that, but nothing straightforward either. Offshore politics were woven through everything. Money from dope deals financed dissident Haitians and Cubans, and loyalties shifted like the sand at high tide.

As a consequence, the Beach was crawling with Cuban and Haitian counterintelligence operatives as well as CIA and DEA agents. On a packed weekend night at Pococurante, it would have been impossible for an outsider to know the players without a program.

Cammy returned to the motel and checked with the desk clerk. As he expected, it was too soon for his FedEx delivery. He climbed the outside stairs to his room, took a shower and prepared to wait until dark when Pococurante would begin to cook.

WAITING WAS THE part of an investigator's gig that Cammy hated. Waiting in Miami was a special hell heretofore unknown to Cammy; an air conditioned hell with daytime soaps - in Spanish.

In the cool, sleep came like a benediction. When Cammy awoke, it was after eight and still daylight. He figured that by the time he brushed up, dressed and ate something, it would be time.

The largest, gaudiest hotels in Miami Beach are located on the beach side of route A1A, otherwise known as Collins Avenue - an eight-mile strip that once was the coveted vacation address of New Yorkers from the first of December through the middle of March. The Avenue still had cachet, even though its biggest and most outlandish hotels had been built in the mid fifties and had long since undergone condo conversions.

Cammy drove past Pococurante, circled the block and pulled into the valet parking lot and gave the attendant the car keys.

The lot attendant dog-eyed Cammy sullenly and screeched his rental Mercedes into a slot, guaranteeing a zero tip. As Cammy took his ticket and headed toward the front entrance, he caught the lot attendant's reflection in the rear view mirror of a parked car. The attendant was making a call on his cell phone.

The blinking and sputtering neon sign on the front was in script that spelled out the bar's name. Just as he reached for one of the bass clef-shaped chrome bars to open the door, an androgynous couple in rose colored shades walked out permitting the hip beat of "Well You Needn't" to escape.

There were banquettes against the wall and forty or so small tables with tiny lamps on them. At the back of the room, there was a raised stage where a quartet was doing its thing and doing it well. Along the rear half of the right wall, unsmiling, anorexic waitresses made their ways like wraiths, carrying drinks from the bar to the tables.

A bartender came over and pointed his index finger at him in a small gesture asking for his drink order. "Scotch rocks," said Cammy. "Make it a double on me," the bartender replied. Seconds later, he set a generous drink in a squat rocks glass in front of Cammy. *My man, Johnny.*

The sounds were cool and Cammy half turned on his stool to go over the crowd and watch as the quartet traded fours. The crowd was everything - black, white, Spanish and Arab. Most of them wore shades and spoke in each other's ear. It was probably just to make themselves heard over the music, but it looked instead like a giant conspiracy.

"Tonight's spy vs. spy night. Do not fuck with any of these people," said the bartender in a low, confidential voice as he leaned forward to wipe the bar in front of Cammy. "Your boy comes in about once a week, has a drink and looks around, then leaves. Every now and then, he makes a night of it, but I haven't seen him in a couple weeks. Try Tortugas in Lauderdale." And he darted away to serve another customer. Soon he was back, quickly emptying ash trays and wiping the bar top, "He's a swarthy, tough-looking fucker: low forehead, straight black hair, looks like he works out. That's about it. Another?"

"No man. Thanks, you're all right," said Cammy putting a hundred wrapped in a five under the corner of his glass.

The night air was lovely after the smoke and air conditioning of Pococurante. It had been a good first night. Word would get to Lupo fast now and he would either put Cammy's lights out or he would talk.

The lot attendant sprawled in a wooden chair propped back against the side of the building. Cammy handed him the ticket. "Twenty," he said, without moving, and flipped Cammy the keys. For two cents I'd kick your ass, and then violate you to your probation officer, thought Cammy, crunching through the gravel toward his rental.

As he punched the remote door opener on the key ring, two hulks appeared from the shadows, one black, one white. "Well, well. What's a brother doing down here in this territory? Looking to get a tan?" asked the black one. Despite the heat, he was wearing shades, a black beret, and a hip-length leather coat that barely contained a fifty-inch chest.

"Speak up, my brother," he said, giving Cammy a quick pat down and retrieving his wallet. "Says here he's a PI from Virginia," he said to his ugly white partner. And then to Cammy, "My advice to you is go back to Norfolk, or wherever the hell you come from, and don't come down here no more. Am I coming through?"

"Five by five, but tell me something. Who the fuck are you?" asked Cammy, scared, but obeying the unwritten PI code section that dictated: never take any unnecessary shit off nobody.

"Never you mind who I am, my brother," he said, giving Cammy back his wallet. "Just slide your ass in your rental here and get the fuck off the Beach."

Cammy sprayed the lot attendant with gravel as he gunned the big Mercedes out of the lot. When he checked the rear view mirror, he could see the attendant giving him the finger.

Things had been going so well before those two Neanderthal D.E.A. types had shown up and ruined his mood.

THE FOLLOWING DAY, Cammy took a dip in the motel pool. He had the day to kill, so he dressed in his lightest weight clothes and drove south through Homestead, which still looked like a war zone thanks to Hurricane Andrew. He continued farther south to Plantation Key and then back to Miami Beach.

Another dip in the pool and another shower and it was time to head north to Ft. Lauderdale on the edge of Florida's gold coast. Fifty years ago, some developer had a brilliant idea. Quintuple the amount of waterfront property by dredging canals in from the Atlantic Ocean. Each canal finger was a peninsula with a street down its spine. Million-dollar homes, each with its own dock and million dollar boat, lined both sides and the tip of each finger. Unspeakable luxury? Or merely a collection of huge dwellings, with no privacy, and scarcely used boat toys in the back yard? Whichever, but certainly not

Lupo territory, at least not that part of town.

Lauderdale's tenderloin was near the oceanfront where old U.S. 1 and A1A are nothing more these days than one traffic light after another the length of Florida, with bars, car lots and fast food joints in between.

Tortugas was a gray clapboard seafood restaurant and bar at the end of a street that ran into the beach. The entryway was a weathered duckboard ramp on sand that was decoratively littered with driftwood and rusting marine hardware.

Cammy pulled into Tortugas's parking lot and parked his car, since there was no surly lot attendant to contend with. The place was busy but not packed and "Moon Over Miami" came out of the ceiling speakers. "Are you expecting someone, sir, or will you be dining alone?" asked the hostess, holding menus the size of a 747 tail fin.

"I think I'll just have a drink at the bar."

The scene was so different from Pococurante, and Cammy couldn't figure it out.

"What'll it be?"

"Scotch rocks."

The bartender served four drinks at the cocktail waitress's station and returned with Cammy's drink.

"Say, I'm looking for Jackie. Is he around?"

The bartender's look turned hard, "No, man. He don't come in here no more. Drink's five dollars."

Cammy finished his drink, left a tip and was about to head back to his motel in Miami. Judging from Tortugas's frosty bartender, Lupo had worn out his welcome in this joint.

"Excuse me, Pal. You looking for Jackie?"

Cammy turned around to confront the guy in the electric pumpkin dinner jacket who had been taking reservations on the phone when he walked in. *Another fucking meatball torpedo,* thought Cammy. *Where do they all come from?*

"Yes sir, I was."

"Will you step this way?"

The "host" led him to an office in the back. When he opened the door, two more Soprano fugitives were waiting. "We are related to Jackie. What do you want to see him about?"

Cammy produced his business card. "My name is Cammy Brown. I'm a private investigator from Virginia. I am not with any police department, state or federal. I believe that Mr. Lupo has some information that my client needs. I'm sorry; I'm not at liberty to tell you the nature of the information."

"Where you staying, Mr. Brown?" asked the older, fatter thug behind the desk.

"I'm at the Blue Flamingo in Miami Beach, room 204."

"We'll deliver the message, and then it will be up to Jackie whether he calls or not, but I'm going to ask you not to come here again."

"I understand," said Cammy, who understood only that he might lose the use of his legs if he did come back.

CHAPTER NINE

NEXT MORNING, WHEN CAMMY WENT out to the motel pool to do some laps, there were a few late middle-aged walruses lying on deck chairs reading the paper. A youngish woman with a cap of close-cropped blond hair was already in the water.

As Cammy eased into the water at the shallow end, the blond woman at the deep end effortlessly pulled herself out of the pool to a standing position and walked over to the table next to her deck chair and polished off a small glass of orange juice.

Cammy tried his best to be inconspicuous, but this was a little bombshell in a string bikini, a miniature Venus about five feet even. She punctured his nonchalance like a child's balloon. Just as Cammy was thinking that she should be arrested for disturbing the peace, she dove back in and swam down the pool to where Cammy crouched hoping the water disguised his erection.

"Hi. Where are you from?" she asked, flashing a set of perfect teeth.

"Virginia. You?"

"Savannah, Georgia." She stood cupping water and patting it on breasts that looked to Cammy as if they were plotting an escape. "It's beginning to get hot, don'cha think?"

Double or nothing, Cammy thought. "I'm in 204. Let's go up and cool off in the A/C. I'd like to get to know you."

"Okay. I'll be right up."

Cammy raced to his room and, leaving the door ajar, jumped in the shower and was out drying himself in less than five minutes. He hid behind the door and peeked out to see if his tiny pool companion was on her way.

"Close the door, why don't you?"

Cammy looked behind him and there she was lying on his bed minus the string bikini.

"WHAT DO YOU hear from Cammy?"

"Nothing yet, Art. He's supposed to check in with me sometime today," said Bari.

"I've got a bad feeling about that Miami trip. We should never put anybody in that kind of danger."

Bari felt the same way, but he refused to chime in with Art and start a panic. "Cammy's a big boy, Art. If things get dicey, he'll get the hell out. I know him."

"I don't know him as well as you, but I know he has a lot of professional pride. He won't want to come back empty-handed."

"You have a point, Art, but somebody had to do this job. We gotta know who hired Lupo. After we find out, we can decide what to do next. I'm betting the case against Paul falls apart after we get that goddamm name."

"It's your call, Joe. I just hope Cammy isn't lying at the bottom of Biscayne Bay."

CAMMY WALKED OVER to the bed, the bath towel knotted around his waist. "What's your name?"

"Kiki. What's yours?"

"Cammy, with a Y."

Kiki stood on the bed and put her arms around his neck and kissed him like she meant it and then licked his eyelids.

Cammy put his arms around her legs and lifted her to the floor, carefully placing her where he could see her back in the mirror.

Kiki reached over and grabbed a pillow, put it at Cammy's feet, and knelt down as she undid the knotted towel.

"My oh my - what they say is true," said Kiki, running her tongue up and down Cammy's erect member. "Your cock is gorgeous, and your balls are enormous." After a few tries, she took his pulsing cock in her mouth. She held his cock in one hand and massaged his balls with the other as she sucked hungrily.

Some time passed – one minute? Fifteen minutes? There was no telling. Cammy couldn't stand much more, and he lifted her up so that her legs were over his shoulders, and he buried his tongue in her sweet wetness while she continued to suck his cock.

"Now, baby . . . now," she murmured, and Cammy put her on the bed and was about to mount her.

Kiki put her tongue in his ear and said, "Baby, you're so big . . . please go easy at first."

It took a quarter hour of careful in and out . . . then penetrate . . . "OH! Not so much!" she begged. Then more gentle in and out . . . then penetrate a little more. "Okay, okay, yeah that's delicious." After Cammy was all the way in, they got a rhythm and he became drunk with the movement, the feel, the sweat, the smell, and the noise of smacking together - and the sounds of begging and cursing. Suddenly Cammy withdrew! But not entirely, and stopped.

"Oh baby, what are you doing?!"   There was growing panic in Kiki's voice. "Don't STOP, PLEASE DON'T STOP! FUCK ME, FUCK ME HARD!"

Then it began. The apocalyptic fuck. Slowly at first,   then faster and harder and deeper, faster and harder and deeper, faster and harder and deeper, faster andharderanddeeperfasterharderdeeperfasterharderdeeper fasterharderdeeperfasterharderdeeperfasterharderdeeper . . . up to the summit of Everest, and then . . . and then . . . escape velocity! OH CHRIST YES! And all at once Cammy felt like a 1,000 hp Shop-Vac was attached to his cock sucking him dry, spine and all. Floating on an iridescent bubble of nothingness, he thought: This is as close to heaven as I'll ever get, but this is close enough.

Cammy and Kiki pulled a sheet around them and fell asleep in each other's arms. When they awoke, they lay there silent for a long time.

Kiki rose up on an elbow, "Darlin, they want to know why you're really here. They want to know why you want to talk to Jackie."

Shit!   Cammy was looking at the ceiling and breathing evenly. "Lupo did some work down in Roads Port for somebody. I want to know the name of that somebody."

"Why on earth would he tell you that?"

"Money. His price, within reason."

"You're the best I've ever had, baby, that's why I'm being straight with you" said Kiki. "If you fuck with these people, they will kill you. They might kill you even if you don't fuck with them. The point is, they're stupid and crazy."

"I'm a PI from Roads Port, Virginia. I work for a lawyer who represents Paul Feldman.   Feldman is charged with murder," Cammy said, still looking at the ceiling. "I have reason to believe that the real assassin was Jackie Lupo. The lawyer isn't interested in Lupo. He wants to know who hired him, period. Lupo's name stays out of the case whether or not he tells me who hired him."

Kiki began drawing slow figure eights on his chest around his pectorals. Cammy continued: "I know the kind of people I'm dealing with and so does the lawyer. Neither of us would do anything to make Lupo and his people retaliate. That's it. I want to meet with Lupo and make an offer. He takes it or he doesn't. Either way, I'm back on the plane to Roads Port. And by the way, you're the best I've ever had too, and I mean that."

The fact was that Cammy had lurking suspicions of Kiki from the first. Their meeting the way they did, and the sex that followed, were too sublime to be completely legit. Life was sweet sometimes, but not that sweet. He had thought maybe she was a working girl, but he tossed that out when there was no mention of money up-front. He was heartsick to discover that she belonged to the Lupos.

Cammy could barely admit to himself that sex with Kiki was so good that he would have taken her home to Roads Port and who knows . . . but now, knowing that she was a mob gal . . . well the sex was terrific, but under the circumstances, it had to end here.

Cammy heard the water running in the shower and he joined her and soaped her down and Kiki reciprocated, raising Lazarus. "I'd like to stay, darlin, but I can't," said Kiki on her toes to kiss him. "I'll tell them you're on the level. Don't cross me up. They'll throw me in an acid bath if you do."

AFTER ANOTHER DAY and a half, Harrow called to say he had put out feelers, but nothing yet. Two days later, Cammy had enough. He had booked a night flight to Norfolk and called Harrow to thank him and ask him to send the bill to his office in Roads Port.

He packed his bags and opened the door of his rental car. "Don't move, motherfucker," said a voice at his back. Cammy could feel the muzzle of a large caliber pistol in the small of his back. A gloved hand moved quickly over his clothes and came up empty. Cammy had FedExed his piece back to Roads Port that morning after he had made up his mind to leave.

"Get in the driver's seat," ordered the voice.

Cammy got in the driver's seat and heard the back door open and someone get in directly behind him.

"I heard a spook PI was looking for me. That's you. What do you want?"

Cammy felt a white hot spear of hatred go through him. *Can't afford to let it bug me now. This cocksucker will blow me away.* "I'd like some sensitive information, information that only you can provide. If you choose not to tell me, I leave, and we never had this conversation. If, on the other hand, you do choose to tell me, I pay you and leave, and we never had this conversation."

"What do you want to know?" said the voice, with a scant hint of amusement.

Cammy took a deep breath and said a short prayer. The question he was about to ask might be the last question he asked anybody. "Who hired you to do the work on Detective Arnold Carey?"

"What is this, some kind of fucking joke?"

"No, I . . ."

"Dig, Motherfucker. I'll blow your fucking black

head off right here."

Cammy felt the sweat break out in his arm pits and trickle down his sides. "I work for the lawyer who represents the accused. Naturally, he wants to get him off. He can do that without mentioning you. In fact, he couldn't mention you anyway after negotiating with you for information. Lawyer-client confidentiality covers you."

Cammy hadn't an idea in hell whether this was in fact true. But, he reasoned correctly, if he didn't know, neither would Lupo.

"Where did you and that fucking lawyer get my name, Nigger?"

Cammy's investigative fee meter began to spin. *If I have to sit here and listen to this psychopath reel off slur after slur, somebody's going to pay a packet. Too bad it can't be fucking Lupo. I'd like to cripple this dago cocksucker.*

"Anonymous phone call. Don't have any idea who it was."

"I hear that you or that fucking shyster ever mention my name in any connection, and I'll come after you. Understood?"

"Perfectly."

"Then get the fuck outta Miami, and don't come back."

It was beyond belief that an assassin for hire would pass up serious money merely to tell the name of his latest client. After all, Cammy wasn't the FBI squeezing him for his testimony. And Lupo wasn't the type to honor some weird assassin's code.

In any case, this zero was a time bomb, and Cammy knew that one word, if it was the wrong word, would set him off. He took a shot. "About the money . . ."

"Fuck the money. I got money."

Cammy figured that now was the time to sit there and be quiet. Nut case here would either get out of the car with another warning, shoot him in the head, or stay and talk more about the money. He was literally betting his life that it would be the latter. Joe, Art and Paul Feldman would pay through the nose for this . . . if he survived.

"Okay, let's talk about the money," said Lupo. "First, what are you going to do with the name if I sell it to you?"

"Depends who it is. Maybe nothing. Maybe guilt trip him. We can also warn him for you that if he mentions your name, he's a dead man in prison or out. He'll know it isn't an idle threat," said Cammy, praying to God that he hadn't overreached.

"Fifty K."

"I think I can probably get half that."

"Tell the shyster, it's fifty K or nothing. Tell him it's worth it. Call me at Sun Stroke Billiards in Miami before ten-thirty tomorrow morning. Ask for Jackie L."

LUPO SLAMMED THE back door shut and was gone. Cammy figured if he checked back into the same motel for the night, it would only make the desk clerk remember him for certain. With all the motels around, it was simpler to drive a half mile up the street and check into yet another Art Deco extravaganza.

After stopping at an all night liquor store, Cammy checked in to a motel that was a carbon copy of last night's, except it was a washed-out pastel pink instead of blue. The shakes hit him hard as he was unzipping his luggage, and he stopped, reached for the bottle of Scotch and sat down on the bed.

He took a couple of long pulls from the bottle, held the back of his left hand out in front of him and watched the shakes subside. That lunatic had scared him like no one or nothing before. Lupo was a snarling dog that might lunge for your throat at any second. You just prayed you could keep him in snarling mode, because once he went for you, only a bullet could stop him, and Cammy wasn't armed.

It was after midnight when Bari's home phone rang. "Sorry to wake you Joe. I met with the man, and I'll tell you all about that when I get back. He wants fifty thousand. Says it's worth it."

"Christ, Cammy, couldn't you talk him down?"

"No dice. I'm afraid it's gotta be fifty thousand or nothing."

"Okay. I'll make arrangements with my bank for a wire transfer to a Miami bank tomorrow morning."

"That's cool."

"But I'll have to see Paul first. I don't have that kind of money . . ."

A part of Cammy hoped that Bari couldn't raise the money. He devoutly wanted to be away from south Florida and Lupo and his fat family.

"Call me around ten with the name of the bank you want the money sent to," Bari continued. "After you deal with your man, call me back with the name."

AFTER CALLING LUPO at the pool hall next morning, Cammy drove over the causeway to the city of Miami and randomly picked out a large bank on the main drag. He then called Bari who wired the fifty thousand dollars.

Lupo checked back by phone and Cammy gave him the bank's address. *If I ever get out of this fucking place* in one piece, I'll never come back again, ever, Cammy promised himself, as he walked out of the already blazing Miami sun, through the bank's huge bronze and glass revolving door and into a wall of frigid air.

No financial institution wants to hand over fifty thousand dollars in cash to anyone for any reason. Such a transaction violates every banking instinct. But mainly they don't want to do it because the money was traveling in the wrong direction: out the bank's door.

After trying and failing to get Cammy to take the fifty thousand in some other form - a cashier's check, or part in cash and the balance in a cashier's check - the bank vice-president shook his head at the doomsday impropriety of handing over that much raw currency.

After a dramatic show of reluctance, the vice-president nevertheless packed ten, five thousand-dollar bundles of hundred dollar bills into the soft vinyl zip-up document carrier that Cammy had provided.

Across the vast expanse of the bank's lobby behind an immense marble pillar, of which the classical Greeks would have been proud, sat Jackie Lupo, hidden by one of the bank's copies of the Wall Street Journal held up in front of his face.

Lupo folded the paper and placed it on a table next to his chair when Cammy walked up. Although he made an effort to be part of the scenery, Lupo looked like trouble with his low forehead and straight black hair gleaming with pomade. The mere sight of him would be enough to cause the bank guards to loose the flaps on their holsters.

Cammy sat the document carrier on the floor with a fluid motion, and Lupo handed him a folded piece of paper. It was a deposit slip that Lupo must have taken from one of the long tables in the center of the lobby. In the space that asked for the deposit amount, Lupo had scribbled a name.

No longer burdened with the document carrier, Cammy left the bank and flipped open his cell phone. He had read and re-read the name on the deposit slip. Unfuckingbelievable! His cell phone was dead, and wouldn't you know it, not a phone booth in sight. He thought about going back into the bank and using one of their phones, but decided against it. Not that it mattered. Cammy had done nothing illegal, but why give them something else to remember?

Cammy got back in the Mercedes and drove out toward the airport where his flight was due to take off in less than an hour. He barely had time to turn in the car and make the call to Roads Port.

The deposit slip with the name written on it was a time bomb, and he was grateful for the drive to the airport. It would give him time to figure out how to break the news to Joe Bari.

The map Cammy had gotten from the car rental place was sparse on details. He drove onto what looked like a frontage road on his way to connect with the Airport Expressway and started looking for an exit.

When he glanced in the rear view mirror, he could see an old beat-up muscle car bearing down on him fast, very fast, and he hugged the right shoulder to let that crazy S.O.B. go past. But the muscle car didn't want to pass. It hit the Mercedes rear bumper on the left side and spun it around. The Mercedes wound up going backwards down the right shoulder when Cammy hit the brakes hard and put the accelerator on the floor.

The tires spun on the grass, but the car didn't move. By the time he put it in reverse, there were grinning Haitians all around the car, wearing black nylon do-rags, yelling in voodoo French and armed with automatic weapons. The first thing that went through Cammy's mind as he got out of the car was *why the fuck is my piece always in transit when I get in a jackpot?*

Cammy tossed one of the banditos the keys and somebody fired. That was the last thing he heard until he opened his eyes in the emergency room and a doctor was telling him he was fine, that the bullet had just grazed his head. The concussion had been caused by his falling in the empty concrete drainage canal at the bottom of the shoulder.

Cammy was vain about his appearance and when he looked in the hospital mirror, his heart sank. His entire head was wrapped in what looked to him like a hundred yards of gauze.

"You're okay," said the ER doc. "The extra bandage is to protect your head in case you faint. After an injury like yours, people tend to faint for a day or two. Go to your doc at home and have him remove all that gauze in a week and replace it with a smaller bandage. In three weeks, you'll never know it happened.

"Thanks doc," said Cammy. *But what are you going to use for gauze the rest of the month?*

"Your rental getting stolen like that? It's a plague here in Miami," said the doctor. "They're supposed to tell you at the rental car place not to get on a residential street in a bad neighborhood or on a frontage road. We have hundreds of these every year."

"What is it down here, the Wild West?"

"Worse, Mr. Brown," replied the doctor. "Much worse."

THE ER DOC had suggested that he stay over night and get his legs back, but Cammy couldn't get out of south Florida soon enough. When he looked back on the carjacking, he thought he was going to die when he got out of the Mercedes to face those grinning idiots. He had been cool about it. No point in dropping to your knees and begging for mercy. They'd only laugh, then kill you.

"Will you call me a cab, nurse? I'm going to the airport." Miraculously, they didn't take his wallet with his credit cards, just his car. The thought of that perfectly engineered machine in the hands of those know-nothing, third world psychos, made him weak. He would have passed out had he not been lying down in the back seat of the cab.

He paid the cabby, who looked suspiciously like the clowns that took his beautiful car, and bought a ticket on the next commuter going north.

He found a phone booth, but his nerves got him and he had to dial Bari's number three times before he got it right. Busy! Sonofabitch, he grumbled as he redialed. He could see the last passenger head down the ramp. Bari's number was still maddeningly busy. If he can't keep the line open, fuck it, thought Cammy. I'll call when I get to Norfolk.

His flight to Norfolk was on a packed Jet Blue commuter with no seat assignments, and because of his futile attempts to reach Bari, he wound up with a detested middle seat in row twenty-six, bracketed by a couple of blimps that happened to be married to each other. They had taken a window and an aisle seat, probably hoping the plane wouldn't fill up so that their extra flab could spill over unimpeded into the empty middle seat.

Cammy sighed and somehow fought past the husband in the aisle seat and squeezed into what was left of the unoccupied middle seat. As he settled in, his head began to throb like a kettle drum. The jolly, perspiring, married twosome leaned toward each other and immediately began talking across him.

With a short stop in Charlotte, this flight will land in Norfolk in three hours, and then I will be released from this nightmare, he thought.

The name in his pocket would change everything - the investigation, the trial, everything, and he was anxious to dump it in Bari's lap the minute the plane landed.

"This is Cammy Brown. Put me through to Joe Bari. He's expecting my call."

"Cammy! What the hell happened? I've been tearing my hair out," screamed Bari.

"Your phone was busy, and the plane was about to take off. I'm in Norfolk now."

"Glad you're safe. Who's the . . . ?"

"You're not going to like this, Joe. The name Lupo gave me is your client's old man, David Feldman."

CHAPTER TEN

AFTER STIRRING UP CHAOS IN the endocrine systems of thousands of high school and junior high school students, spring had melted into summer on the Lower Peninsula, The dogwood trees had exploded like popcorn and hope had replaced despair everywhere, except in the offices of Bari and Louis.

"What the hell are you going to do, Joe?"

"I'm going to get his ass in here for a start and find out what the fuck this is all about."

"What can it be all about? Were Carey and old man Feldman business associates like Shilla and Carey? Did Carey screw him too?" asked Louis, throwing up his hands in surrender to a bizarre world.

"I can't even guess why he had Carey killed. But it's not so much *that* he had Carey killed, but *where* he had him killed. It's beyond me, Art."

"Can you imagine that shithead trying to cover his tracks by hiring an investigator, as if the S.O.B. didn't know who the guilty party was?" Louis, for whom loyalty meant everything, was personally offended by David Feldman's apparent betrayal of his son.

"This is a father whose son was indicted for a murder that he arranged. I'd bet a bundle that he hired the investigator before Carey was killed, not after," said

Bari, opening the door and peering down the hall for Helen and the coffee.

"His investigator sent his report, and the dates don't bear your supposition out," said Louis, pulling some pages from a file folder and tossing them on the desk.

"Fuck the dates. With his money, he could get the investigator to put down 1492."

"Call him."

Bari's call to David Feldman disguised its true purpose. They made a date for the day after tomorrow ostensibly to talk about help with Paul's mounting legal fees and the trusteeship of his assets should he be convicted.

"I'd like to be a fly on the wall when you talk to Paul's fucking, so-called father," said Louis, with a snort.

"Yeah, some father. I've got about a hundred very unpleasant questions to ask his sorry ass."

"I WAS TERRIFIED," said Cammy to Bari and Louis who were deeply engrossed. "I mean it was the end of the line. Here I was in a car with a racist mad dog, armed with a cannon, sitting right behind me, and I just finished telling him that I knew he was a paid killer. I will never do that again, you two, never." Cammy made a motion with his hands as he said "never" that was like an umpire calling a runner safe at the plate.

"Thanks, Cammy. I apologize, I really do. I knew it was too dangerous when I sent you down there," said Bari. "If it had been a different case . . . for someone other than Paul, I wouldn't have sent you in a million years. But I knew Paul was innocent . . . if only we could prove it. Now look at the fucking mess we've got on our hands."

Joe prepared for the Feldman interview by brooding for hours. David Feldman was a god to his son. Paul couldn't imagine a more loving father, as he never tired of telling Bari when they were housemates.

Bari had learned that like all gangly, bookish kids, Paul had difficulty making friends in grade school and later in high school, except with other lonely bookish kids. Girls were in a completely different category, like extraterrestrials. He could yearn until the stars went out, but he would never have one of his own. Of that, Paul had been certain.

In Paul's memory of those early years, his father seemed to know instinctively of his problems and social humiliations. He had patiently and lovingly explained to Paul that adolescence was no picnic for anyone.

They would go for long walks together, he told Bari, the father with his arm around his son's pitifully thin shoulders. The father had told his son comical tales of his own youth and stories about others that he knew had had it tough. He told true stories in which a boy was abused and laughed at only to win high honors and achieve greatness later on. He had made youth seem like a heroic quest, a journey fraught with stumbling blocks, but still an adventure wherein one acquired the knowledge and the skill to live a happy and fulfilling adult life.

Listening to Paul back then on Agate Street where they shared a house, Bari imagined how agonized Paul's dad must have been witnessing his son's suffering and struggle.

In the end, Mr. Feldman had told young Paul, the hardships, if faced and surmounted, would ennoble him and lead to wisdom. Even now, Paul firmly believed that he would have sunk had it not been for his father.

"JOE, MR. DAVID Feldman is here."

Helen might as well have said, "Abandon hope, ye who enter here," because Bari was beside himself with foreboding. He didn't even know what he wanted from this man, except to discover why in hell he had done such a thing. He had tried to imagine how he would have felt if his own father had committed such treachery and had refused to come forward. Because, if all the breaks went against Paul, and that could happen, he was looking at a death sentence. Then what?

"Come in Mr. Feldman, please have a seat." Bari found himself at a depth of somberness and gravity that he hadn't known existed. "I asked you here to tell you that I know about Jackie Lupo from Miami Beach. Now I want you to tell me what that was all about."

"My God, how did you find out? Does Paul know?"

"It wasn't through the usual methods, I can tell you that," said Bari. "And Paul doesn't know a thing, so your secret is safe, for the present."

After turning a dangerous gray and scaring the hell out of Bari, David Feldman placed some medication under his tongue and slumped into the sofa.

Mr. Feldman drew in several deep breaths to stabilize something - his heart, probably - and then he began to speak brokenly. "I had known for some time that my daughter-in-law was deceiving my son with that detective. As you said when last we spoke, I have resources." David Feldman rose from the sofa with great effort and began to pace like a defeated soldier.

"I went to Marian and begged her to stop. She laughed at me. She didn't even bother to deny it. At any rate, she continued seeing that S.O.B." Bari poured a drink of whiskey from his cabinet, and the broken old man downed it quickly.

"Next, I went to Carey. He denied it, at first . . . then I showed him pictures of his meeting Marian and embracing her outside a motel. The bastard dropped the act then, and told me that I couldn't use those pictures against him without hurting Paul." Mr. Feldman stopped his pacing and turned to face Bari who had taken a seat behind his desk.

Feldman held his hands out in a pleading gesture. "I offered him money, a great deal of money, but he turned me down. I think he was afraid the money might be marked or be otherwise traceable. In any event, they both refused me."

Bari came from behind his desk and went over to him. He gently put his hand on his back. "Why not sit for a moment, Mr. Feldman, and try to relax before going on?"

This was piss poor interviewing technique, Bari knew. Never, but never, interrupt the flow of a witness's story. But now this old man looked as though he might collapse if he didn't sit and relax for a few minutes. What good were facts if the witness had a stroke?

"I am all right. Thank you, Joseph," said Mr. Feldman who put his hands behind him and rested momentarily against Bari's desk. "That disgraceful thing they were doing was eating me alive. I couldn't sleep. I couldn't do my work. Rachel knew something was wrong, but I couldn't tell her. I'd die first." Bari was relieved to see that color was returning to Mr. Feldman's face.

"I knew that when Paul found out about them, as he was certain to do eventually, it would destroy him."

Even so, thought Bari, *that's a damn drastic way to handle a family problem.*

"I couldn't let that happen," said Feldman. "I thought that if I got rid of Carey, Marian would take it as a warning and behave herself. I know what you must be thinking, Joseph, but I would not permit a pair of unscrupulous fools to permanently damage my son and his mother, since she was bound to hear about it too."

"I'm simply listening, Mr. Feldman," Bari lied. "I am not passing judgment."

"I approached them, Carey and Marian, twice more with the same results. Finally, through an intermediary, I met with that assassin Lupo. I told him I wanted Carey dead. He said that unless I had any special requests, I could leave the details to him."

Bari thought of Cammy's description of Lupo and Lupo's family when he heard the words "special requests." He wondered where that crowd drew the line. Torture? Burning at the stake? Death by a thousand cuts?

"In my wildest nightmare I didn't think that lunatic would kill Carey in my son's home."

Bari interrupted to ask why he'd put anything past a paid assassin.

The distraught old man shrugged his shoulders. "I was given to understand that he was reliable." Feldman, who had resumed his pacing, stopped momentarily, smiling bitterly. "*Reliable*, an assassin, reliable. What a joke."

Reliable enough to get the job done, thought Bari.

"You know what happened next, Joseph. Paul became ill at the airport and returned home just in time to be suspected, and ultimately charged, with murder."

"Yes, that was hellish bad luck. Poor Paul" said Bari.

"I was horrified. The son I wanted to protect was

now accused of committing a murder that I, his trusted father, was responsible for. I didn't know what to do. I don't care about myself, you must believe that. I'm an old man near the end of his life. I'd gladly walk in front of a train for Paul."

"I have no doubt of it sir," said Bari.

"As if things could get much worse, my coming forward and admitting my role in Carey's death would have actually made things worse. By coming forward, I would abandon my helpless wife, whom I love with all my heart and I would cause my son to learn of his wife's infidelity and be branded a cuckold. It was Paul's deepest fear from early childhood that the world would someday make a fool of him."

"Have you ever heard the name Richard Kingman, Mr. Feldman?" asked Bari.

"Yes, I knew about him too. I was about to go to Kingman when Marian stopped seeing him. My source told me that she threw him over because he was indiscreet about their affair. In any case, it was no longer necessary to deal with Kingman."

Poor, foolish Kingman, Bari mused. *He would never know how close his pointless life had come to extinction.*

"Please tell me, sir. What would you have done if Marian had several lovers . . . at the same time? By my reckoning, there was a period when she was seeing both Kingman and Carey during the same time period. I mean, would you have had them all assassinated?"

"I've thought about that, Joseph." Trembling with exertion, Feldman sat down heavily on the sofa before Bari could steady him.

Thank god, his pacing was driving me up the wall.

"The best I can tell you," Feldman continued, "is that I wasn't faced with that situation, and so there's no point in considering it now. All I can say is that I tried everything I could think of to reach Marian and Carey before I acted."

Everything?

"I used all the influence I had to see to it that Paul was released on his real estate bond," said Feldman. "That judge in Richmond would never have released him if I hadn't stepped in."

Only now did Paul's release make any sense to Bari. No Virginia judge would ever release a defendant charged with capital murder without serious juice prodding him to do so.

Bari shuddered as a chill went through him. There couldn't be more than a handful of men in the entire state with that kind of money and influence. No telling how much Paul's release had cost David Feldman.

"Now, if Paul is convicted," said Feldman, "or it looks like conviction is imminent, I will of course come forward. I have tapes of my conversations with Lupo and photographs of the two of us in Miami."

This had been was a transforming experience for Bari. He had begun listening to Paul's father with severe condemnation, but he now felt only astonishment. How in the hell could this careful, successful man have screwed up so thoroughly this late in life?

Then it began to dawn on Bari that Mr. Feldman was probably no different from other wealthy, powerful men. If some fool, like Carey, raised the personal stakes high enough, any one of them would crush him.

"I don't want to add to your troubles, Mr. Feldman, but if Paul is convicted, your coming forward will change nothing. And, if you come forward toward the end of a losing trial, your testimony will probably not be allowed. Even if you come forward now, chances are it won't help."

"Why not, for god's sake?"

Oh shit. How am I ever going to get this across?
"Because you are the defendant's father, for one thing,"
replied Bari. "The court would view your testimony as a
Hail Mary to save your son, and therefore, unreliable.
And your testimony is all hearsay in any event. The
tapes won't come in, unless someone identifies the
voices on it, and who's going to do that? Certainly not
Lupo or anyone connected with him." Feldman sat
nodding his head in all the right places.

Although the old man wasn't a lawyer, it seemed to
Bari that he easily absorbed the complex evidentiary
rules recited to him. *I wouldn't be surprised if old man
Feldman had been through all this with another lawyer,*
he thought.

"This brings us to another problem, Sir. If by some
miracle, your testimony was admitted and you were
allowed to implicate Lupo, he'd come back here and
murder your entire family. That's a guarantee."

"I'll do anything you ask of me, Joseph."

"You are an influential man who makes things
happen, but I don't want you to involve yourself further
in this case. Your son's freedom - and maybe his life -
are on the line. Now I want your word that you will do
nothing more, absolutely nothing."

"You have it, of course. But what can you do for
Paul after all that I've told you?"

"Win."

CHAPTER ELEVEN

THERE WOULD HAVE BEEN NO point in telling that broken old man how desperate his son's case really was. The facts all pointed to Paul. And never mind that it would have been nearly impossible for Paul to have driven home from the airport in time to kill Carey, leave, and return after the cops arrived. It wasn't absolutely impossible, and that spelled real trouble. Plus, Harriet, that crafty bitch, had Miss Bernice Early as a witness.

Having coached his share of witnesses, Bari knew that once Harriet took the medical examiner and the pathologist to the woodshed, she could easily manipulate their testimony on the stand to fit the time constraints created by the time stamp on Paul's long-term parking receipt and Marian's 911 call. At the end of the medical testimony, Paul's guilt wouldn't even be a close call.

"Joe, remember I told you about Buzz's idea that the shooter probably entered the house as a FedEx or UPS delivery guy?" asked Cammy, checking through his report. "Well, I found a twelve year-old girl who lives down the street from the Feldmans. She'll testify that she saw a UPS man stop at the Feldman house on the morning of February fifteenth."

"That's big news, Cam! Why aren't you more excited about her?"

"I am, I am," answered Cammy. "It's just that she was home sick, and I don't know whether she'll stick with her story. You know how kids are today. They don't like being pinned down, but she seemed to take to me, so who knows. If she sticks, she'll be great."

"If she sticks, she'll be better than great."

"The cops didn't question her. Amazing, huh?" Cammy asked. "But hell, you know how they are. Once that lead detective, Ditsel, made Paul for the shooter, the only answers his cops were interested in then were the ones that fit his theory."

"Yeah, I know, Cam. They do that shit all the time. They want to close the case by making an arrest. They don't give a fuck whether the guy's guilty or not," said Bari.

"Yeah, and when Ditsel told them to question the neighbors, he meant come back with the right answers. Ditsel wouldn't have come right out and said it, but the cops all knew his message: 'Godammit, Feldman shot Carey, so don't tell me about some other fucking theory.'"

"Even if we can't bring Lupo in, who's to say he didn't dress up as a UPS man that morning?" asked Louis. It might help if we could find out about a professional hit that was done in disguise. On the internet, maybe?"

"I'll put Aaron on it. He's a whiz at that stuff," said Cammy. "Bernice Early said there was a UPS truck in the neighborhood on the morning of February fifteenth. She didn't see him stop at Feldman's, but she didn't see 'the big black car' leave either."

"The little girl is great, Cam, but we still have a problem. What do we do for a motive?" asked Bari, scraping an emotional bottom. "I mean, we're working backwards here. We know that it was a murder for hire. We know who hired the killer, and we know his motive. Finally, we know that we can't use any of it."

"Why the hell not?" asked Louis.

"Because the phony delivery man theory makes sense only if we bring Carey's problem with Shilla back into the case, and I don't think we can do that," Bari answered.

"The delivery man could have been a criminal that Carey put away," said Cammy.

"Maybe we don't need a motive." Bari and Cammy looked at Louis. "Criminal law is not my scene, I realize, but in my lack of experience, I think I probably see things as a juror might."

"We're all ears, Art," said Bari.

"Here's what I mean," said Louis, clicking off points with one hand in the palm of the other. "We put on an endless string of character witnesses in our case in chief. We humanize Paul. Hell, maybe we even put him on the stand." Bari wasn't sure where Louis was going, but he knew damn well they needed a motive.

"If we score with the jury," Louis continued, "they'll want to acquit, but they'll need a hook. The phony delivery man angle gives it to them," said Louis, tossing a pen on his desk top to punctuate his argument.

"Whoa," said Cammy. "We don't for sure have a delivery man yet. Give me a couple of days to ask some questions first."

"While you're at it," said Bari, "try to scare up a motive. The Commonwealth's case is all motive: jealous husband. If we don't offer a counter motive that's just as strong, we're dead."

STRESS BECAME THE unwelcome house guest at

the Bari residence. Joe responded to Ann's solicitude with coldness. She changed tactics and attempted merely to engage him in light conversation. Nothing. He answered her questions with a curt yes or no, then retreated to the library where he stayed until long after Ann went to bed, frustrated and angry.

He berated himself for the way he had treated her, and for a night or two things were better, but not glorious. They went out to eat, and when they came home they made love. Just when Ann believed she had reason to hope, her husband descended once again into his depression and solitude.

In her despair, Ann sought professional help. The psychiatrist she saw told her that he could do nothing unless her husband agreed to see him. Joe Bari, of course, scoffed and refused. Only after Ann threatened to go to the bar association did Bari agree to see the doctor. The bar had a program for burned out and depressed lawyers. Joe knew he couldn't be forced into that program, but he was alarmed that his colleagues would find out about his row with Ann. Wouldn't they have fun with that? The pricks.

Talking to a stranger about his emotional life violated every tenant of his stoic personal code; a code that dictated sucking it up and keeping his own counsel. He could ill afford to change such an integral part of himself with a murder trial looming, but he kept the appointment with the psychiatrist anyway. He would have lost Ann if he hadn't.

The psychiatrist prescribed some medication for anxiety and depression. As for Ann, he'd try to make it up to her after the trial. But worry was inescapable. Who the hell was going to make it up to Paul if the trial went south and he ended up on a gurney in the execution chamber or in prison for life?

EVERY SUMMER, JOE and Ann Bari's shrubbery and billiard-table lawn made the paper. An azalea hedge next to the house running its length, the inevitable dogwoods, a dozen championship rose bushes, wisteria over the entryway and a gnarled magnolia created a tableau of gracious, southern living. But it was their backyard, with its water hyacinth growing in the formal pool and its arbor with long-necked dipper gourds that clinched the prize for best yard year after year.

Inside, the Louises and Feldmans were being feted by the Baris. Cocktails were followed by endive salads and pan fried soft shelled crabs.

"These crabs are scrumptious," said Marian, who could stuff herself as often as she pleased without gaining so much as a milligram. Art's wife, Sally, who put on weight merely by reading recipes, moved the food around on her plate and feigned an appetite, which she had suppressed with a Dexamil.

Although Joe Bari's wife, Ann, was more in Marian's weight gain camp than in Sally's, she took no chances, terrified that she would follow her mother into a ballooning menopause.

"How's the beach cottage working out?" asked Sally of Paul and Marian.

"It's perfect," said Marian. "If things were different . . . if it weren't for the trial . . . I'd want to stay for autumn."

"Yes, the trial won't allow for any genuine pleasure," said Paul. "Otherwise, I think I'd love it."

Bari and Louis were reluctant to join in any discussion about the ongoing trial, and for that reason tonight's dinner party ground rules excluded talk about the trial. Impossible. The trial consumed everyone.

But Ann had no intention of letting her dinner party sink into the mire of trial talk. She got out the clippings from the *Daily Journal* showing their lawn in full color, and then, with oohs and aahs still hanging in the air, unfolded the Pictionary board as the table was cleared. Against long odds, it worked, and her guests got into the game and began to relax. Joe smiled and whispered "thank you" to his wife.

Bari fully appreciated that determined, well-bred, southern women, like Ann, with warm molasses drawls, were a force of nature. He also understood that very little of real importance ever got done in the South without them, from the protection of wetlands and wildlife refuges to the election of the governor.

It seemed to Bari that the Civil War - Christ! Would the South never be free of it? - had taught successive generations of southern women the foolhardiness of leaving all decisions to men. That lesson was one decent legacy in an ocean of bad ones left by what he called "that ruinous fucking war."

Bari was beginning to slowly give ground on Marian. She had warmed up to Paul and it appeared genuine. She was either a head case who realized when the jig was up, or she was a spoiled brat who was growing up. In any case, he thought, Marian was a gorgeous, desirable, enigma. And in a parallel universe, he'd love to make it with her just once. Well, at least once.

IT WASN'T OFTEN that Marian had trouble dropping off to sleep, but this night was different for some reason. Perhaps she ate too much rich food, or maybe it was the dinner table patter about the trial.

Paul was on his side breathing regularly, and Marian knew that he was in a deep sleep. She wanted to concentrate on happier times when she was in college. Maybe then she would slip into sleep.

Marian had graduated cum laude from a snooty Virginia women's college before meeting Paul. She had taken a series of classes from Wilberforce Hadley, an emeritus professor visiting from Cambridge University in England.

Professor Hadley perfectly fit Marian's picture of a college professor in appearance and mannerisms. Moreover, he had a deep knowledge of his field, and his class presentations were clear and frequently hilarious.

Hadley was returning to Cambridge at the end of the term, and he had handed back the students' graded term papers. Marian's paper wasn't graded. Instead, there was a note on the last page, "See me about this."

Marian and Professor Hadley had gone round and round over her notion that everything in life is ruled by self-interest. Hadley took the position that it would be a sorry state of affairs indeed if every consideration was ruled by nothing more than self-interest.

She made an appointment with the departmental secretary and two days later stood outside Hadley's open door as he was writing something in longhand.

She knocked softly. "Professor Hadley, it's Marian."

"Oh, of course, my dear," said Hadley with a warm smile, pushing his glasses high up on his hairless forehead. "Come in, come in," he said, pointing to the chair along side of his desk, which was a model of disorganization. "Please sit down. You're here about my note on your paper."

"Yes, Sir."

"I didn't ask you here to discuss your grade," said the Professor smiling sadly. "You will receive an A for the course. I sense something about you my dear that I can't quite put into words. Please permit me to ramble for a moment."

Marion loved Professor Hadley's clipped aristocratic manner of speaking. He could "ramble" away the afternoon as far as she was concerned.

"You are a beautiful young woman, Marian, and life will be pretty much as you want it to be. You are also exceedingly intelligent, which means you have an easy grasp of difficult material. But because you have an easy grasp you might overlook important aspects of a profoundly complicated world," said the professor. "I suppose I asked you here to give the hackneyed advice that the old invariably give to the young," he said, smiling again, "which is, live life to the fullest, and while you're at it, follow the Golden Rule," he chuckled. "It's in your interest."

Oh why do you have to go back to England and leave me? Marian would dearly miss this gentle old man, who understood her and loved her like a grandfather. Tears had welled up in Marian's eyes for the first time since she was a babe in arms. She left her chair and put her arms around her wizened old professor. "Thank you, sir. Thank you for everything."

Marian, now farther from sleep than ever, knew that if Professor Hadley were still alive and had heard the lurid tabloid account of the Carey murder, he would be brokenhearted about the fix in which she had gotten her husband and herself. And she understood completely for the first time that although brokenhearted, Hadley would not be surprised. It was what he was trying to tell her so many years ago - that she was beautiful, brilliant and ruthless.

ART LOUIS MOVED the court for its permission for the Feldmans to leave the state for the purpose of a four-day drive to Charleston and back. "This motion isn't going anywhere, Art. There's not a chance in hell of Jones's granting it. But Paul asked us to try, so give it a shot," said Bari.

Harriet went predictably ballistic, waving her hands and screeching that never had there been such flight risk as Paul Feldman and insisting that, at an absolute minimum, his passport be surrendered to the court at once. The Judge denied Louis's motion from the bench without explanation.

Thrusting copies at Louis, Harriet then gave the court formal notification in writing of the Commonwealth's intention to seek the death penalty. Her notice stated that the death penalty was appropriate in this case because the deceased victim was a policeman killed in the performance of his duty.

Bari groaned aloud. Everything about this case was wrong. Paul didn't kill Carey; Lupo did. Besides which, Carey was definitely not performing his duty.

Art Louis acknowledged receipt of the notification and moved for discovery of witnesses' names and statements not included in the Commonwealth's original packet of "discovery," which is the name given to the information that the prosecution is required by law to turn over to the defense.

Harriet responded that she was unaware of any witness statements that were not already in the defense's possession. The judge granted Louis's motion, saying that it would be treated as a continuing motion for discovery.

He told Harriet to find out for certain whether any outstanding witness statements existed and if they did to turn them over to the defense immediately. Steam was coming from her ears as she glared at Louis and said "Very well, Your Honor," in a clipped, but tightly respectful voice.

The cops had interviewed Bernice Early, and Aaron had fed her the names of the cuckolded husbands, thought Bari, watching Harriet's performance. *Harriet hasn't given us any names or statements, and now she'd denied having them to the judge. Jones will hang her by her tits for this.*

JOE BARI WAS thinking ahead to the trial. He had done criminal law for years and he knew all too well how it was *supposed* to work: Twelve strangers would look at the defendant as innocent until proven guilty, and in the meantime, suspend any judgment until after deliberations, during which they would decide if the Commonwealth had carried its burden of proof of the defendant's guilt beyond a reasonable doubt. If they decided that the Commonwealth had indeed carried its burden, they would vote to convict. If they agreed it had not, they would vote to acquit.

In fact, Bari grimly acknowledged, twelve strangers would look at Paul and say to themselves that if he's sitting here in court accused of murder, he probably did it. *What a goddamm farce.*

Paul's fate would lie in his and Art's hands. And they would turn themselves inside out to prove to this stonily predisposed southern jury that their client was innocent.

"WE DON'T HAVE shit to work with, Art. You

could get fucking character witnesses lined up from the courtroom to the sidewalk outside, and it wouldn't do a damn bit of good. If the trial was tomorrow, the jury would return with a guilty verdict in twenty minutes," said Bari, slapping the wall in disgust and exasperation.

"Christ don't take my head off, Joe. I'm not the enemy," said Art. "Maybe I can search through the rules of evidence and find some way for Paul's dad to testify."

"We can't use him. Paul would rather die than have his father involved," said Joe Bari with finality.

"I believe we have an ethical duty to tell him about his father and Lupo. Let Paul decide which way he wants us to go."

"I know him, Art. It would crush him to find out his dad had solicited murder for hire. About the ethics, find the rule. I don't think there is one that says I have to tell a client everything I know. If it bugs you, Art, you can withdraw . . . I'll understand, but at least go through the rules first."

"I'll hang in, Joe, but godammit we know who committed the fucking crime. WE KNOW!"

BARI HAD TO jump off the hamster wheel of worry about the case. He left his office for the men's room and doused his face and the back of his neck with cold water. He was about to commit himself to a dangerous course of action. Doubly dangerous with the Attorney General's cops watching his every move. If it became public, Paul would be convicted and he, Joe Bari, would be ruined and sharing a cell with Paul.

When Cammy came through his office door, Bari was in the middle of another lap around the room.

"I'm worried about this case, Cam. If you don't turn up something we can use, I'm afraid Paul's going down.

How are things?"

"I'll let you know in a few days," Cammy answered.

"What about those neighbor witnesses?"

"I've interviewed them all. Also, the 911 clocks check out. Somebody must have reset them. Aaron turned up eight murders by killers posing as delivery men. That's good. But they were all committed in 1964."

"Shit!"

"Look, I know you're worried. I'll do my best, Joe, you know that." Cammy paused for several moments. "But you didn't call me in here to give me a scare talk, did you?"

"No, I didn't, Cam. Jury selection begins next week. That's going to be a busy time for you and Aaron trying to get a line on our jury pool."

"After Miami, a piece of cake."

Joe walked back to his desk and sat down in his chair. He paused for several seconds and leaned forward. He ran his hands through his hair several times. "How long have we worked together now, Cam? Ten years, twelve?" he asked, leaning back and looking up at the seascape on the far wall behind Cammy. "How many times in all those years have we had a defendant that we knew for a fact was innocent? I'll tell you how many - zero, that's how many."

"Oh damn," said Cammy, as he fell into the overstuffed leather chair next to the sofa like a kite falling to earth when the breeze dies. He rested his head on the back of the chair so that he was looking straight up at the ceiling.

"Something told me when Helen called. I knew it, I knew it." Time stopped in the room. Cammy remained motionless in the chair. "It's the H-bomb, isn't it?"

"Yes," said Bari. "It's the H-bomb."

CAMMY WAS NO angel and he didn't come from angels. The only reason that he had gotten away with so much when he first started out as a PI was intuition and blind luck. He had no regrets. He performed a needed service that quite often made the difference between a much deserved jury award or destitution. And in criminal cases, it was the difference between freedom and years upon years in the penitentiary.

Now, a friend was asking him to do something neither of them had ever done, and had never dreamed they would ever think of doing. Sure, they had joked about it when some prosecutor was investigating the accusation of it in a far away state. The "H-bomb," he and Joe Bari called it, because the hydrogen bomb was unthinkable and it was built *not* to be used.

And yes, they had cut corners in the past. In fact, they'd cut a few in this case. But, if he and Joe used the H-bomb, even if no one ever discovered they had used it, they would be irreparably damaged.

In the future, they would never mention it. They would laugh together, they would get together for picnics and barbeques, they would be entertained in each other's homes. They would do all the usual, normal things that friends do.

Except, when they looked at each other, they would realize they had done something that they would not be able to forgive in each other or in themselves.

CHAPTER TWELVE

AS THE TRIAL DATE NEARED, preparations went into crisis mode. Character witnesses and experts were prepped. Bari made an appointment with Harry Ames, Paul's mentor and best friend at work. According to Paul, Ames had pushed him upward at every opportunity and had used his influence with higher ups to get their ear in Paul's behalf.

"Joe, Mister Ames is here."

Ames walked straight in, shook hands and took the seat in front of Bari's desk. He was next in line to the comptroller and was all business, as befits a top cost accountant.

Some people are notable for imposing physical characteristics, thought Bari. Others slouch or have speech defects. Some will try to get over with bullshit, but you know the line on them before they open their mouths. With Ames, it was the opposite. His inclination to get down to brass tacks immediately made all other approaches seem irrelevant. Before you knew it, you were dealing with Ames's razor sharp mind, and you had difficulty later saying exactly what he looked like. Had Ames known he had that affect on people, he would surely have cut loose with a rare wintry smile.

"When I asked Paul for a character witness from

work, Mr. Ames, he gave me your name instantly."

"I can tell you that Paul Feldman is a fine man, and that the charge against him is laughable."

"You are a man who comes right to the point, I can see that, but what I would like - for the purposes of the trial - is your appraisal of Paul, the human being. What, for example, brought him to your attention? Why are the two of you friends? That sort of thing." Bari had a yellow legal pad at the ready. The purpose of the pad was not so much to take notes as to give Ames the floor. Bari would look down at the pad and pretend to take copious notes while covertly observing Ames's gestures and his demeanor. "I have just met you, sir, and you strike me as utterly truthful and candid, which is valuable in all contexts. It will be of inestimable value in Paul's defense."

Ames sat back in his chair, put his elbows on the arm rests, made a steeple with his fingertips, and crossed his legs. "Most of the people who work for a large successful enterprise at the executive or management level are competent and smart. Generally, those people are also dedicated to the status quo. After all, they have families and children in college or private schools, and they tend to live beyond their means."

I know the type well, Bari thought.

"Paul, on the other hand, is an innovator," said Ames. "Not in any flashy sense and not simply for the sake of innovation. He knows the direction a company must take to be profitable in five years or in ten. That's no small gift in the modern world where circumstances reverse overnight.."

"I agree," said Bari, thinking, *if I had Paul's talents, I'd own the Peninsula outright.*

"Unfortunately, there are those who are jealous of

Paul, and there are those who steal his ideas and take the credit themselves.   This issue came to a head at the company picnic last August."

The company picnic was an annual event at one of Richmond's city parks on the banks of the James River. Actually, there were two annual company picnics - one for the wage earners and supervisors held in July and one for company officers and upper management in August.

"At any rate, a small group of us in management were talking business and one of this bunch began reminding us of an idea of his.   It was an idea that I knew originated with Paul, and I called him on it.   There was an argument and I could see that I was a minority of one," said Ames pursing his lips in distaste.   "I could hardly believe my ears.   They all knew I was right, yet they sided with that idiot.   I suspect the reasons for it were equal parts envy and anti-Semitism."

In enlightened Richmond? Perish the thought, Bari smiled to himself. *They might nail you Paul, but they'll have to come through Ames here first.*

"Paul's position with the company is unaffected by such monkeyshines," Ames continued.   "Top management knows his worth and his future is secure."

Bari lifted his head and looked at Ames.   The jury's going to love this guy. He's a straight talker and a man of few words.   "I appreciate your filling me in on the company politics.   I suppose those guys at work are gloating over Paul's misfortune, but we won't get into any of that on the stand.   I'll ask you how long you've known Paul and what you think of him.   If you testify in court just as you spoke here today, Paul will be grateful." *And so will I.*

BARI'S DOMAIN WAS criminal law.   He did lots

of civil law work too, but all the criminal cases that came into his law firm automatically went to him.

In Paul's case, there would be more expert witnesses than in the ordinary criminal case, and experts were Louis's forte. True to his word, Louis would present three experts from Roads Port University. One, a pathologist, would testify to the time of death. Another was a traffic engineer who would testify to the condition of the road, the amount of traffic, and the number and duration of traffic signals between the airport and Feldman's home. A lucky break: when asked if Paul could have driven home in the amount of time at issue, the traffic engineer would emphatically say no, not in his opinion.

The third was a criminologist who would testify about the behavior of husbands who murder rivals. Louis had learned that, for complex reasons, some husbands kill wives, some kill wives and their lovers, and some kill only the lovers.

According to that expert, "it would confound every piece of research in the U.S. and Europe for Paul Feldman to have acted in conformity with the Commonwealth's theory of the case - he isn't the type."

The big problem with the criminologist was that the judge's every inclination would be against letting him testify. Judges don't like anything that smacks of social science. Nor do they like studies that speculate how someone will act in a particular circumstance. Too mushy, and proves little.

"I have to interview the cops, and Harriet has ignored request after written request. She says it's up to me to arrange interviews. When I call the cop house, I leave messages but I get no replies."

"Fuck her, Art. Note a hearing and make a motion

for a continuance. Tell Jones that Harriet is stonewalling on the cop interviews. Show him copies of the memos you sent her and her smart-ass answers."

HARRIET WAS UNPREPARED for Louis's argument, just as he had guessed. She came to court probably expecting Louis to plead with Judge Jones for a continuance based on some lame defense excuse about not being able to fully prepare by trial date.

"Good morning, Your Honor. Art Louis for the defense in *Commonwealth v. Feldman*. The defense moves for a thirty-day continuance. We haven't been able to interview any police witnesses. We have asked the Commonwealth to arrange interviews and have been refused . . ."

"Your Honor, I'm perfectly willing to help," Harriet cut in with a barely concealed, condescending smirk. "But it's really up to defense counsel to arrange interviews with the police."

Louis looked at her blankly, and reached in his briefcase and pulled out a sheaf of duplicate memos that he hastily shoved in front of Harriet for a glance before handing them to the clerk who handed them up to Judge Jones.

"In addition to the memos asking for help, I have called the station a dozen times, leaving messages for all the detectives and police officers involved in investigating this case. To date, I have received no reply," said Louis. Judge Jones's demeanor darkened and Harriet began to fidget.

"The victim in this case was a police detective, Your Honor. I don't expect cooperation from other police without help from the Commonwealth or compulsion from this court."

The Commonwealth, as represented by Harriet Atkins, was about to make a grievous error.

"That's what his client gets for killing a cop," she sniffed. "Maybe next time he'll think twice."

The judge leaned forward on folded elbows and looked straight at Harriet, waiting to speak until he was certain he had her full attention.

Louis looked over at Harriet. The crazy bitch has stepped in it now.

"Ms. Atkins, I want you to take a seat at counsels' table and draft an order that states clearly that you, by name, are to set up interviews with all the police witnesses at the Commonwealth Attorney's office in Richmond. These interviews are all to be completed within two weeks from today." The judge looked over at Louis. "That all right with you, Mr. Louis? Good." He turned back to Harriet. "If you fail in this, I will cite you with criminal contempt and make a written complaint to the bar association. Sit down. Write the order now."

The court waited silently while Harriet wrote furiously. When she was finished, she handed the order to Louis for his signature. Louis signed the order and handed it to the clerk who gave it to the judge. The judge signed the order and had copies made for both lawyers.

"Mr. Louis, today is Monday. Call my clerk next Monday with a progress report. Adjourned."

Bari helped Louis pack up his briefcase while fighting the smile playing on his lips.

THROUGHOUT RECORDED HISTORY, it has been open season on poachers who make sport with married women at their homes in the marital bed. There are laws against killing them today, but sympathies are still with the husband, and those sympathies are especially strong in other women.

Joe Bari knew about those sympathies and he planned to lean on them hard. He knew juries too, and what he knew frightened him. Get male and female jurors with a wide divergence of ages, some black some white, maybe an Asian or two, some very religious jurors, some not religious at all, and you couldn't begin to account for all the treacherous crosscurrents and bizarre alliances in the jury room during deliberations.

He was all too aware that jury selection is like the serve in tennis - it's the game's most important shot, yet so few had mastered it.

Once, in his early years, he had picked an aging Birkenstock-wearing hippie female because he thought she was certain to favor his black defendant on trial for possession for a few pathetic rocks of cocaine. To his horror, he discovered after trial that she had led a one-woman crusade for a guilty verdict.

During that same early time so many eons ago, he had exhausted all his challenges in a case in which his gay client was on trial for killing his lover with an axe. He had cringed when the prosecutor seated a sour redneck who turned out to be the one defense hold-out in a hung jury.

Bari's ability to pick a favorable jury had improved immensely since those years. But most lawyers had trouble trusting their own judgment. Hence, that modern phenomenon, the jury consultant.

"I think we should hire one, Joe."

"They cost a fortune, Art, and they're wrong half the time."

"I hear the Commonwealth will have one."

"I don't blame the Commonwealth," said Bari with a

mirthless laugh. "That Atkins bitch doesn't know shit about people who aren't fascists like her own miserable fucking self."

Civil litigators like Louis rely almost entirely on experts at trial. All kinds of experts: doctors, other lawyers, statisticians, actuaries, engineers of every stripe: civil, structural, aeronautical, electrical, acoustical, name it.

Louis had shaken his head in dismay. This was jury selection, an entire appalling area of their upcoming trial for which there was no expert.

And another thing. Louis had thought that he was Bari's best friend. Okay, so he wasn't. So fucking what? But here was Bari defending an even closer friend in a murder trial without the services of a jury consultant. Insane, thought Louis. "How are you going to feel if we lose this damn case and the appellate lawyer cites us both for 'ineffective assistance of counsel' as a ground for appeal?"

"Let not thy heart be troubled, Art. No Virginia appellate court is going to set aside a guilty verdict because of a defense lawyer's misconduct that is short of punching out a prosecution witness on the stand or passing out in the middle of trial with a blood-alcohol level of at least point four."

Louis continued to mutter darkly about a jury consultant. And Bari continued to question a jury consultant's usefulness and their enormous expense. Louis countered that in a case this costly already, what's another hundred thousand?

But Bari had other reasons for not hiring a jury consultant - the dreaded H-bomb. Cammy would attempt to tamper with jurors who were financially strapped. A jury consultant might rely on criteria other than financial need. What red flags might it raise if Bari had to overrule the consultant so as to keep those jurors Cammy had chosen as candidates for bribery?

Lawyers don't go around hiring hundred thousand dollar experts only to overrule them. If word of it got back to the AG's office, his investigators would be all over those jurors. Once that happened, Bari knew that he was looking at disbarment and prison.

CHAPTER THIRTEEN

THE CLOUDS PARTED, AND THE sun flooded the west side of Joe Bari's office with light. Ten minutes later, a hard rain was falling on the balcony outside his sliding glass doors six floors above the busy, irritated city traffic. The changeable late summer weather exactly matched his moods.

"We'll have some touchy questions for them about the death penalty. Jones won't seat a juror who's opposed to the death penalty in a murder case. Virginia law forbids it. What the law doesn't speak to is the juror who hasn't made up his mind."

"Harriet will, of course, challenge such a juror," said Louis, bristling at the thought of Harriet Atkins saying anything on any topic.

"I think we should take turns," said Bari. "You voir dire four jurors and I'll do four. Something like that. Oh, and we have to remember to inoculate the jury against our objections - 'You will hear objections from both sides in this trial, ladies and gentlemen. When we think a rule of evidence has been violated, we object.'"

"Right, I got it," said Louis. "And however you want to play the voir dire is okay by me."

Bari, who came across as a little edgy, envied Louis his simpatico with ordinary people.

After Louis left his office, Bari thought about the pact he had with Cammy. It was an odd state of affairs. He and Louis were closer in many ways than he and Cammy. Would Art go to the mat for me? Certainly. Give me the shirt off his back? In a heartbeat. But there were limits to closeness. If Louis knew what he and Cammy were cooking up, he'd call 911 without hesitation and report a felony in progress.

HARRIET INTRODUCED HER second chair, a tallish young woman in tortoise shell glasses and a dark business suit. Her blonde hair was pulled back in a tight bun, and she didn't smile - at anything. "Your Honor, I'd like to introduce Assistant Commonwealth Attorney, Priscilla Mimms, to the court. Ms. Mimms will be second chair for the Commonwealth."

Mimms has done everything humanly possible to present herself as a prosecutor and not as a woman, thought Bari. But all she's done, really, is make everyone wonder what she's like when the glasses are off and the hair comes down.

Judge Jones started off jury selection with some general questions of his own about whether anyone in the large group of prospective jurors was related to the defendant, the prosecutors or anyone employed by any police department? Whether anyone on the panel had any religious or personal objection to the death penalty?

Whether he could decide a case in which the death penalty was a possibility?   And finally, the killer question: whether any prospective juror, or juror's family, had ever been the victim of a violent crime?   In some cases, Bari had seen half a jury panel raise their hands "yes" to that question - today it was more than half.

"Mrs. Hegel, it says on your juror questionnaire that you've worked at the shipyard for some time now." In fact, the questionnaire said that Earline Hegel had worked at Newport News Shipbuilding & Drydock Company for exactly twenty-eight years. Mrs. Hegel appreciated that Bari was treating her age with delicacy and she smiled her thanks.

Bari carefully took her through the meaning of reasonable doubt. You can scare up a reasonable doubt about the days of the week. If jurors really took it seriously, they'd never convict anybody of anything.

As he had done with Mrs. Hegel, Bari took up a single topic with each of the succeeding jurors. Louis, the same.   Mrs. Hegel was examined on reasonable doubt. The next prospective juror was examined (taught, actually) about burden of proof and about which side was responsible for carrying that burden. The juror after that was asked/taught about the presumption of innocence.

Each question was designed to engage the prospective juror being questioned and also to instruct the others about the defense's theory of the case. The heart of the defense's theory was physical impossibility: Paul couldn't have made it back from the airport in time to kill Carey. The rest was window dressing.

"Mr. Wythe, the case against Paul Feldman is circumstantial. That means that the Commonwealth will present no eye witnesses in this case. Neither will they present any physical evidence tying Paul to the shooting death of Detective Carey, the victim. Will you be comfortable deciding a case based solely on circumstantial evidence?"

"Yes sir, if there's enough there."

The touchy questions came toward the end of selection. "The Commonwealth will characterize its case against Paul Feldman as 'marital jealousy' or as adultery. Will you accept those descriptions from the beginning, or will you listen to all the evidence before deciding for yourself what kind of case it is?" Harriet was poised to object all through that question. In the end, she decided to let it go. Judge Jones would probably overrule her objection and the jury would resent an objection to a question asked directly to one of them.

Bari always included a nice fat pitch among the hard questions just to ease the tension. "You will take an oath to listen to all the evidence and determine the facts in this case. You will also promise to discuss the case with other jurors in an effort to reach a unanimous verdict. Is there any reason why you couldn't take this oath?"

"No sir. I have an open mind. I could take that oath."

"Has there been anything you've read or anything you've heard that has swayed you one way or another?"

"No sir. I heard about it on TV, but they didn't say much."

When the Commonwealth questioned the jury panel, it zeroed in on the death penalty. The last thing Harriet wanted was a stealth juror concealing an anti-death penalty bias, because that juror would vote to acquit rather than risk a death sentence, regardless how strong the evidence of guilt.

"If the defendant is convicted and sentenced to

death, he will be injected with compounds that will stop
his heart and render him dead. Will the possibility of
lethal injection prevent you from finding the defendant
guilty if the facts so dictate?" And, "Have you ever
taken a position or expressed an opinion on the death
penalty?"

THE DAYS HAD grown longer, and everyone's
mood lifted. The clerks and bag boys and girls in
Cammy's neighborhood grocery store were less sullen.
Cammy, who was young enough to feel the sap rising,
was too busy with jury selection to act on it.

As jurors were passed by both sides and seated, Bari
gave copies of the juror questionnaires to Cammy, who
was in court watching the selection process,
optimistically called voir dire, which meant truth telling.

There was one juror who appeared to be ideal for
Cammy's purposes. Mr. Duane L. Castle was thirty-
four, white, a high school dropout, and a father of three
little girls with Kim, his stay-at-home wife of ten years.

A little digging around had revealed that Mr. and
Mrs. Castle had some equity in a three bedroom home
with past-due mortgage payments and threats of
foreclosure. Like Mrs. Hegel, Castle worked at the
shipyard, until three months ago when he had been laid
off. Now, he couldn't find work. His unemployment
compensation, which was barely keeping his family
afloat, would run out in three more months. Then what?

Judge Jones closed up shop at four and Mr. Castle
took the city bus to Marty's, his neighborhood bar, a
stale, dingy cave, with an old pockmarked shuffleboard,
where he was hailed by the bartender and the regulars.

Castle had two straight shots of Cabin Still with
small draft beer chasers before heading for home two

blocks away.

When he left Marty's the following day, Castle was met by an elderly, well-dressed black gentleman with a neat beard and a cottony head of hair.

"Excuse me, Mister Castle, I wonder if I could speak with you for a moment," said the old man walking along, aided by a handsomely carved black cane, trying to keep up with Castle.

Castle stopped and faced the stooped old man.

"How do you know my name?"

"I'm a journalist assigned to the Feldman murder trial, sir," he replied, with the courtliness of a long lost era.

"What can I do for you?" asked Castle, his eyes narrowing.

"My publication is interested in an account of the trial from a juror's point of view. We will pay handsomely for an article about the jury's deliberations."

"Oh yeah? How much?" asked Castle, resuming his walk.

"Well I suppose that depends," the old man said, stroking his beard with his free hand.

"Hey, are you the cops? Is this legal?"

"Heh, heh, no I'm not the police, and as far as I know you can say anything you want to after the trial. But I'll tell you what, why don't you think about it overnight and we'll talk some more tomorrow."

Castle looked deeply skeptical. "Can you give me a ballpark figure?"

"Can you keep it strictly to yourself?"

"Yeah, I won't tell a damn soul."

"Twenty thousand dollars."

"You're putting me on," said Castle.

"No. I said 'twenty thousand dollars,' young man,

and I meant twenty thousand dollars."

"Holy shit!"

THE FOLLOWING DAY after adjournment, Duane Castle stopped at his neighborhood bar and had the two shots his meager juror compensation scarcely covered. He left the bar, looked around and saw no one. Disappointed, he jammed his hands in his pockets, muttered darkly to himself and started for home.

"Mr. Castle. Mr. Castle!" cried the old man as Castle reached the end of the first of the two blocks to his home.

Castle turned to see the old man at the other end of the block, attempting to trot and waving to him with his cane. He held up his hand for the old man to stop, and he stepped off the distance between them in seconds.

"Okay, I've decided I want to hear more about your offer," said Castle, congratulating himself for being cautious and businesslike.

"Let me catch my breath. You young people are so lucky," said the old man, taking deep breaths through his nose.

"I'm sorry," said Castle, not quite putting a sympathetic hand on the old man's shoulder, but the old man saw the gesture.

"Thank you, son." Recovering, but still short of breath, the old man said: "The title of the article my publisher wants you to write is 'Why I Voted to Acquit Paul Feldman.'"

The old man's offer sunk in very slowly. "Yeah, but what if I vote guilty?"

"Well, my publisher doesn't believe that would make an interesting story. He has authorized me to offer you twenty thousand dollars now for the acquittal story and five thousand more after the trial is over, if there is a hung jury."

"What's that? I think I know, but just to be sure."

"There's a hung jury if the jurors can't all agree on a verdict," said the old man, fully recovered now, but leaning heavily on his cane.

"Then what happens?"

"Well, the judge dismisses the case and the prosecution retries it just like a brand new case."

"Yeah, I thought it was something like that, but I didn't know what happened afterwards," said Castle.

"But here's the good part. If there is an outright acquittal, then the offer is twenty thousand now and thirty thousand after trial," said the old man, and Castle swallowed hard.

"There is one more wrinkle," continued the old man. "If you are picked to be an alternate juror, you will not deliberate. In that case, you simply keep the twenty thousand dollars that I'm offering right now and then we're quits."

The old man could hear the gears whirring inside Castle's head: This old black guy could make all my problems go away if he's on the level about the money. My house payments are behind, my credit cards are maxed, the girls need braces, and I'm about to go bankrupt.

"There is only one small problem, Mister Castle." He put a grandfatherly arm around Castle's shoulder. "If you decide that you are interested, and we pay you, you can't spend the money in a way that will draw attention."

Until that moment - the moment when the old man said "in a way that will draw attention" - the full import of his proposition had eluded Castle. Now he reluctantly faced the fact that he was actually being bribed.

"Make up only one back payment on your house, not several, if you get my drift," said the old man. "Then when you go back to work, you can blend in the money we pay you with your paycheck a little at the time."

"How do I know that you'll come through with the rest after the trial is finished?"

"I can't give you a written guarantee, so here's the way it will happen," he said softly, as if to a frightened child. "Sometime within forty-five days after the trial, I'll approach you again. It might be here, it might be somewhere else, but you may be sure that I'll find you and give you the balance in cash. Do we have an agreement?"

"Let me see if I follow you," Castle replied. "You're going to pay me twenty thousand now and another thirty thousand after the jury says that Mr. Feldman is not guilty?"

"Yes, if you are among the twelve jurors doing the deciding."

"I don't know. If I get caught, it's prison. I've got a family; I can't go to prison."

"Nobody except you and me will ever know." The old man could guess Castle's calculations. If Castle never saw another dime, the twenty thousand dollar bird in hand was itself a much-needed answer to his prayers. The thirty thousand dollar bonus, if paid, would be all velvet.

"Okay, you have a deal."

"The money is wrapped in a watertight package beneath the front stairs of your home," said the old man. "To be extra careful, Mister Castle, I wouldn't even tell Mrs. Castle about this agreement. It's best left between us."

"Yes sir, I understand," said Castle solemnly.

BARI HAD EXPLAINED the jury setup to scores of defendants he'd represented over the years. The jury of twelve was in actuality a jury of fourteen, twelve regulars and two alternates. No one knew who the alternates would be until right before deliberations began. At that time, the names of all the jurors were placed in a hat and two slips of paper were blindly drawn by the judge's clerk holding the hat above her head. Those two names were the alternates.

The reason behind this method was that in a long trial, one or two jurors might become ill or unable to go on. In that case, the alternates would fill in, having heard all the evidence.

Bari's Defendants always asked, "Why the secrecy?" And he always gave the same answer: "Because if the alternates knew they were alternates in advance, they wouldn't pay attention to the evidence or surely not as much attention as the regular jurors. No, better to have all fourteen jurors paying strict attention to the evidence believing they might have to deliberate over it."

An additional juror would therefore have to be bought to be on the safe side. If Castle were chosen as an alternate, he would not deliberate and he would have no vote. But, if two jurors were successfully approached to sell their vote, the odds were against both being blindly chosen to be alternates.

The second juror Cammy chose was a woman in her early sixties with rheumatoid arthritis in the knuckles of both hands, which she rubbed together whenever she believed that no one was looking. Betsy Stevens was a widow with two grown children and seven grandchildren. One set of grandchildren lived in Boston and the other set in Portland, Oregon. That much came out in voir dire.

Cammy made a few long-distance phone calls, talked to a couple of neighbors and discovered that Mrs. Stevens saw her grandchildren during the holidays. She saw the little ones in Boston at Thanksgiving, and the others in Portland at Christmas time. She would visit them more often if she had the money. Mrs. Stevens lived on a small pension and a piddling disability income from Social Security. She saved all year to make the Thanksgiving and Christmas visits.

Her children, both divorced, were up against it themselves and couldn't help her with traveling expenses. Perfect. Cammy had also discovered that her late husband had been a gambler and a thief. He'd heard of the guy years ago.

A middle age black woman approached Mrs. Stevens at the Post Office with the same pitch that was used on Mr. Castle: "Why I voted to acquit Paul Feldman."

Mrs. Stevens was not nearly as dense as Mr. Castle in these matters, and she apparently knew a paying proposition when she heard it, because she jumped at this one. To Cammy's mind, the one bright spot in this sorry business was that with fifty G's, Mrs. Stevens could visit her grandchildren whenever she damn well pleased.

Bari, meanwhile, was in the grip of anxiety, bordering on panic. He had been picturing himself being transported to the Virginia State Penitentiary in chains when his office phone rang.

"Joe Bari here."

It was Cammy. "We're in!"

CAMMY STOOD IN his bathroom and carefully removed the makeup that had taken hours to apply. His makeup and acting artistry went some distance to balance the queasiness he felt. He had helped undermine the system that paid his bills, and he had corrupted Duane Castle.

In time, disgust would dissolve the pride he took in his performance, and he would be left with only disgust. But today was different, and he was going to enjoy it, dammit.

BARI, ON THE other hand had nothing but the icy comfort of knowing that the worst he could do at trial was a hung jury - that is, unless both his crooked jurors were chosen as alternates. He no sooner banished that horrible thought than others took its place.

Bari weighed sequestration. If the jurors were sequestered, they'd be put up in a hotel with guards around. There would be no further chance for Cammy to communicate with them. He and Louis certainly wouldn't push for sequestration, but Harriet and her young deputy might, in order to deprive the defense of an issue on appeal, namely, that the jury had been tainted by all the ongoing media hype.

No, on second thought, the Commonwealth wouldn't dare move for sequestration and earn the jury's collective hatred for interfering in their lives merely because it couldn't trust them to ignore the publicity.

Judge Jones, Bari knew, was another matter. Jones didn't approach his job as a popularity contest. If he thought the jury would be influenced by the media in any meaningful way, he'd order sequestration on his own. Let the jury hate him if it wanted. He wouldn't give a damn.

CHAPTER FOURTEEN

EVEN THOUGH HE HAD SWORN not to let the prosecutors get to him, Bari had worked up a loathing for both Harriet and Mimms. There had been so much bloody combat between the prosecution and the defense even before the fourteen unsequestered jurors were seated and trial began.

Harriet's opening statement condemned Paul Feldman for murdering a police detective who, in the line of duty, had been seduced by Marian Feldman.

So that's her angle, thought Bari. She's insisting Carey was shot in the line of duty even though he was banging Marian when he was shot. Why? Because Carey went to the Feldman home with the best intentions, only to be waylaid by Marian. Brother, what crap!

With her adultery theme, Bari had mistakenly believed that Harriet had given up the death penalty for sure. Her claim all the while was that Carey was making it with Marian, and that certainly wasn't during the course of his duties. How could she argue for death penalty in her closing argument? Now he knew.

And after cowardly shooting the much decorated Detective Carey in the back of his head with his own weapon, she argued, the defendant left the house only to appear after the police arrived, pretending that he had just returned from the airport.

"With the cruel killing of Arnold Carey, the City of Richmond lost a star . . ." said Harriet with a choking voice, looking heavenward. She then strode determinedly over to the defense table, planting herself before Paul and, with a look of theatrical contempt, continued: ". . . to a cold, calculating killer."

Bari and Louis turned slightly toward each other and Bari mouthed "bullshit."

Bari sat back as Louis opened for the defense. He wanted Louis to be the jury's first impression of the defense. But Bari had planned to close.

Louis methodically pointed out that there was no physical evidence connecting his client with Detective Carey's death. No mystery there, since it had been impossible for his client to have driven home from the airport in time to shoot the detective.

Moreover, there was no evidence that the detective was having a liaison with Mrs. Feldman. That fairy tale had been dreamed up, Louis asserted, to serve as a motive for the killing.

Predictably, Harriet objected. Judge Jones sustained the objection, telling Louis to save it for closing argument.

Harriet's objection and the judge's warning alerted the jury. If the prosecutor fails to prove that the detective was diddling Mrs. Feldman, then the defendant had no motive to kill him.

Louis finished by asserting his client's innocence and asking only that the jury listen carefully to all the evidence, promising that having done so they would reach the conclusion that Paul Feldman was innocent of the charge against him.

Bari had made notes throughout Harriet's opening statement. Stripped of its emotional appeal to the jury, her opening spun out an ancient tale. Husband returns home unexpectedly and kills wife's lover. It was mythic and powerful and Bari could feel the underarms of his shirt go damp. Even a juror sympathetic to the defendant would think that it was unfortunate, but true.

Louis's opening urged the jury to put a different construction on the known facts of the case. Detective Carey was killed while investigating an attempted burglary. The Commonwealth's assertion that Carey and Mrs. Feldman were lovers was slander, not a provable fact.

In any event, Paul Feldman could not have gotten home in time to murder Detective Carey, and the timed exit receipt from airport parking and his wife's timed 911 call proved it.

Court was adjourned after opening statements. Bari and Louis gathered their folders and legal pads, packed them into briefcases, and walked back to the office a block away.

A tear-away memo from Harriet greeted them when they walked through the front door into the reception area. "This came fifteen minutes ago," said Helen, handing the memo to Bari, who quickly read it. "Oh shit, she's added Richard Kingman to her witness list." He handed the memo to Louis. "According to this, Kingman will testify to his involvement with Marian and say that she broke up with him when she started seeing Carey."

"Kingman's relationship with Marian is irrelevant and anything she told him is hearsay," said Louis grabbing the offending document. "Besides that, Kingman's testimony is a thousand times more prejudicial than probative. Jones will never let it come in, especially at this late date, with no prior notice."

More prejudicial than probative . . . Bari wondered how many times in a career a lawyer would put that phrase in a brief or say it in open court? It was the ultimate balancing test all evidence had to pass. Did the evidence inflame more than it proved? Would the risk of prejudice outweigh its evidentiary value to prove the point at issue?

In this case, Harriet wanted to introduce Kingman's testimony that he had an affair with Marian in order to prove that Paul killed Carey. It would poison the jury and prove nothing.

"I agree," said Bari, "but I don't blame her for trying. Who knows, the judge might let it in. I wonder how she found out about Kingman. The prick probably walked right in her door and offered his services. I'll put Cammy on him again."

Bari went to his office and lay on the couch. It was either reflux or ulcer, he couldn't determine which. More worrisome was the pain in his left chest that was either indigestion or the foretaste of a heart attack.

"HELLO, MARIAN? THIS is Joe Bari. Can you come to the office right away? There is something important I want to discuss with you."

Marian was in Bari's office within thirty minutes of his hanging up the phone. This is a good omen, he thought. She takes the case seriously enough now to hurry when I ask her to.

Bari sat her in the chair facing his desk where he could see her only from the waist up. Half of Marian was distraction enough. "I want to ask you about Richard Kingman. He's on the Commonwealth's witness list. I don't think the judge will let him testify, but I want to be ready just in case."

Marian didn't blink. "He's a delusional egotist. Before I knew what he was, I had a few drinks with him at a bar in Richmond."

"What is Kingman's testimony likely to be about?"

"The prosecution will call him to trash me, I suppose. Apparently, he told his lawyer that he and I were lovers. This lawyer also works for Rocket Science, Paul's company."

She's not lying, not really. Marian's no fool. She knows that I know that she and Kingman were lovers, thought Bari.

"Anyway, that S.O.B.'s name is Dave Harrison, and he made a pass at me at last year's company picnic."

"What can you tell me about Kingman's background?"

"Not much," she replied. "Richard would like to be a playboy, but he doesn't have the money. He gets by on a modest trust fund, I think. That's the talk anyway. He's closer to a gigolo for horsey, older broads. Richard trains horses and gives lessons. In the summer, it's tennis too. He's a frivolous, forty-year old child."

In other words, thought Bari, if Jones lets him testify, he can hurt us bad.

Bari appreciated that so much of what a jury was permitted to hear was strictly up to the trial judge. This was chief among a hundred reasons why trial lawyers were well advised not to piss off the judge.

Because there was so much judicial discretion, experienced judges could make a case come out any way they damn well pleased and juries were none the wiser. Occasionally, there was a lawyer from out of town who would bring a fight with the judge out into the open and let the jury figure out who was the asshole. But this was a dangerous tactic, too dangerous to try in a murder trial, because juries always kowtow to the man in the black robes.

ON HER WAY back to the beach cottage, Marian thought about Kingman. He was a good lover for a while, but my God, what a bore, especially when he drank, and he drank often.

Then, as Marian had begun to pull away from him more and more, he became impotent. He was of no use to her with a limp dick, and she told him so. She regretted it now.

One would think that pride would prevent his retelling such a sorry tale to another man, but no. Kingman had told his lawyer, that despicable Dave Harrison, of all people. And that lecherous jerk had approached her himself at last year's company picnic. Marian hated the goddamn picnics in the first place. "Flea markets for gossip," she called them.

She and Paul were on opposing softball teams. Marian remembered clearly that she was leaning against a tree waiting for her turn at bat when Dave Harrison walked up. Harrison was head of the company's in-house legal department, which had just lost its third dispute in a row to the I.R.S.

"Hello Marian. You're looking as sexy as ever."

She gave him a dioxin smile as she thought, *when the ship is sinking, anybody can be captain. Ahoy, dingbat.* "Oh hello, Mr. Harrison. I don't feel very sexy."

Regardless, Marian knew she looked sexy even when she was trying least. Her black hair gleamed in the sun like a rich vein of coal, and her faded jeans and white

T-shirt accentuated her mouth-watering figure.

"Call me Dave. We in legal are democratic," he said, chuckling self-deprecatingly and lying through his teeth.

Harrison wore an expensive Egyptian cotton shirt, doeskin gabardine slacks and hand-stitched Italian loafers, all new. He had obviously spent a lot of money for the occasion just to appear casual; however, the styling gel in his hair ultimately scuttled the effort.

"By the way, Marian, I keep a small outside practice, and one of my clients tells me he knows you."

"Really, what's his name?"

"Richard Kingman. Rich tells me that the two of you are very close."

"We were," said Marian, working her jaw muscles.

"Well, Richard has a big mouth," Harrison added. "This certainly isn't something that should reach Paul's ears. Perhaps we could discuss it sometime soon, and I could advise you. I don't think that Richard . . ."

"I've got a better idea, Dave, let's tell Paul about it right now. Oh Paul! PAUL!"

"Marian, you're crazy," said Harrison trying to keep his voice down. "I'm walking away from here this minute."

"Wait awhile, prick. You ever approach me again and I'll burn you. Understood?"

Dave Harrison, protector of the strong, was chastened. His self-assurance collapsed, and he looked stricken as he stumbled away, nearly falling.

"HEY MARIAN," called a teammate, "YOU'RE UP!"

"HELLO RICH," SAID Cammy, taking a seat next to Kingman at Stoney's bar laminated with Civil War memorabilia and Mathew Brady photographs.

"Well hello. I haven't seen you for awhile. What's your name again?" Kingman, resplendent in a windowpane tweed sport coat with leather patches at the elbows, was already gassed.

"Cammy. Cammy Brown," said Cammy extending his hand to shake Kingman's. "Still drinking Black Label Scotch?" He ordered two more from the bartender and gave Kingman a light punch of camaraderie on his upper arm, "We still haven't gotten together for tennis."

"I'm in the middle of something. Maybe in a couple weeks."

"Okay, I'll call you," said Cammy. "My usual partner was transferred to L.A. by his company. Say, did you get things squared away with that gal you told me about— Marian, I think her name was?"

"Fuck getting squared away, as you put it. I'm going to get even with the bitch."

Cammy took a drink and adjusted his tie. "How's that, Richard?"

"I'm going to testify against her in court. That'll fix her fucking ass," said Richard, checking out his preening image in the mirrored back bar.

"What's she on trial for?"

"Marian? Nothing. But her simpleton husband's on trial for murdering a cop. The prosecutor's going to say he shot the cop because the cop was fucking his wife. Marian's going to deny it. I'm going to testify that I had an affair with the bitch and that she stopped seeing me when she started up with the cop." Kingman's eyes tightened with malicious satisfaction as he appeared to imagine himself slamming Marian in open court.

"Wow! I've been following the case in the paper and on TV. A guy like you must have lots of classy friends. You think it's a good idea to . . ."

"To what?" asked Kingman.

"Oh, I was just thinking that you might get back at her, all right, but you'd probably have a hard time getting laid in Richmond after that," said Cammy, who read Kingman like a billboard.

Cammy actually pitied him. His investigation revealed that Kingman was a social animal and a superb athlete. But his doting upbringing and good looks had stunted his growth as a man. He loved beautiful women and beautiful horses. He also loved cocktail parties, benefit balls, football games in Charlottesville and fox hunting in Winchester.

And here he was mixed up in a messy murder trial. That alone could put a serious, perhaps fatal, crimp in his social life. And now he was going to cop to an affair with the married femme fatale in the case.

Kingman should have known, thought Cammy, that if word of his courtroom treachery ever reached the women in his set, they'd shun him, and that would be the end of his social life in Richmond. And, when the feminine tom-toms had sent out the news, Kingman would be finished in Washington, Charleston, and Savannah as well.

After a couple more rounds, at Cammy's expense, Kingman breathed a drunken sigh of relief at his close call. "You know, Cranny, It just goes to show you what can happen when a guy gets obsessed with a broad."

It's Cammy, you lush. "Yeah, I know. I've been there."

"If I hadn't run into you, I might have made a bad, bad mistake," said Kingman. "I'll have to think of something to tell that goddamm prosecutor when she calls. She'll want to know why I changed my mind."

PAUL AND MARIAN were in the outer office. Bari was about to round up Louis and leave the office for court when Cammy walked in. "Kingman's cool. Don't worry about him."

Bari waited while his gut did a somersault. "Why not?"

"He won't testify. I pointed out to the dumb shit that if he dropped a dime on Marian Feldman, he'd never get laid in Richmond again."

"Art is strictly out of the loop on this. He'd come apart if he knew you rolled Kingman now that he's on the witness list."

"I'm with you. Art is out on all the sticky stuff."

Bari grabbed his trial case, which resembled a beat up black suitcase from some pawn shop. "You're going to get fucking rich off this case, Cammy."

Cammy snorted: "Swell. Maybe I'll make enough to pay for my nervous breakdown."

CHAPTER FIFTEEN

WHEN THE FOUR OF THEM walked in, Bari noticed that the courtroom was rapidly filling up with media people, courtroom regulars, relatives and young lawyers there to observe and learn. He nodded to those in the spectator benches that he recognized, and hoped they couldn't tell that his stomach was doing acrobatics.

"Listen up," said Judge Jones. "Both sides have two lawyers. The lawyer who objects during a witness's direct testimony will also cross examine that witness. One lawyer per witness, got that? Anything before I call for the jury?"

Bari nudged Louis, who rose to his feet at once. "Yes, Your Honor. May we speak to you in chambers?"

"Is that really necessary, Mr. Louis? I don't want the jury waiting in the jury room any longer than . . ."

"It's important, Judge."

Both sides plus the court reporter followed Judge Jones to his chambers and gathered around his desk. The court reporter set up quickly and was ready to go.

"All right, we're on the record. What is it, Mr. Louis?"

"Your Honor, the Commonwealth informed us late yesterday afternoon that it was adding a Mr. Richard Kingman to its witness list. Trial is underway. The defense moves that this witness be barred from testifying."

Bari had urged Louis to strenuously argue the motion to exclude Kingman's testimony. If Louis hadn't, Harriet might have suspected defense trickery when Kingman refused to testify.

"Ms. Atkins?"

Harriet, with a roll of the eyes and an audible sigh, affected exceeding weariness at what through her eyes must have been a transparent defense effort to keep honest, straight-forward testimony from the jury. Surely, her body language said, Your Honor will see through this unethical defense sophistry. "Your Honor, this witness came forward the day before yesterday. The Commonwealth had no idea he existed before that. There is nothing in the case law or the court rules that would bar this witness from testifying."

"Rebuttal, Mr. Louis?"

"Yes, Your Honor. In addition to springing a new witness on us, his testimony is both irrelevant and hearsay. According to Ms. Atkins's memorandum, the witness will testify that he had an affair with Marian Feldman."

"So what?" asked the judge, and Bari felt a tingle of anxiety.

Louis pushed on: "Even if true, which it isn't, that testimony is irrelevant. It is inflammatory and probative of nothing. The witness will also testify that Ms. Feldman told him that she was jilting him for Detective Carey. That testimony is classic hearsay. It couldn't be more unreliable."

"Is that true, Ms. Atkins?"

"Your Honor, the witness's testimony will directly contradict Marian Feldman's testimony, in which she will deny an affair with Detective Carey. The heart of the Commonwealth's case is that the defendant caught his wife and Detective Carey together and that's why he shot him."

"Ms. Atkins, would you mind telling me how your witness knows that Ms. Feldman was having an affair with Detective Carey?" asked Jones.

"Ms. Feldman told him so when she dump . . . pardon, when she called off her illicit relationship with Mr. Kingman."

"I see. Then you're telling me that unless I admit that garbage, the Commonwealth can show no motive, which under Virginia law you don't have to prove anyway?"

"Yes, Your Honor. But I would hardly characterize the witness's testimony as garbage."

"The defense motion is granted. The testimony is excluded."

Outside the judge's chambers, Bari exhaled a low whistle of relief. Now, after the judge had barred his testimony, Harriet wouldn't call Kingman and so would never suspect a thing. These machinations were doubly difficult because Louis wasn't privy to any of them.

Harriet was a stop-at-nothing type herself, and Bari knew that it was critical they do nothing to stir up her prosecutorial suspicions, lest she begin to put every facet of the trial under a jeweler's glass, including the jury.

That increased degree of scrutiny could lead her to interview jurors separately after trial, which could in turn lead to the discovery of tampering, of which Louis was still blissfully ignorant. Bari was confident that had he known, Louis would have gone straight to the judge and exposed the whole thing.

Bari stole a glance at his friend and client standing next to him in chambers. He and Louis had driven home to Paul the importance of not reacting in court, especially in front of the jury. It mattered in chambers too. If the judge hadn't yet formed an opinion of the case, Paul's demeanor could affect the judge's evidentiary rulings.

Their worry was misplaced. If Paul was reacting, it was viscerally. His face betrayed nothing except dignified sorrow. Once witnesses were called, every man in the courtroom, including the judge, would have to wonder how it felt to be on trial for your life and hear slimy accusations about your wife and the murder victim. *Man, I don't know if I could sit there without punching somebody's lights out*, thought Bari.

"If there is nothing further," said the judge reseating himself and smoothing his robe, "the bailiff may bring in the jury." Everyone rose when the jury filed in, and resumed their seats as the jurors took theirs. The jurors smiled politely and whispered pardons to their fellow jurors as they squeezed past each other to find their seats. Once they were seated, the smiles were replaced by grim game faces.

HARRIET ROSE QUICKLY, causing her tits to bounce. *That move was for the benefit of the male jurors,* Bari observed. *Harriet, you tacky bitch.*

"The Commonwealth calls Detective Lieutenant Ditsel to the stand," she announced.

Ditsel walked smartly to the stand and was sworn in. Veterans like Ditsel were a nightmare for criminal defense lawyers, because they appeared in court so often that it held no fear for them. Their smoothly flawless testimony showed it. Trying to nail a vet like Ditsel with an inconsistent statement was like trying to nail jello.

Ditsel was especially nightmarish in that he was as pleasant and inoffensive as a priest at a baptism. Bari would have to guard against taking it easy on him by reminding himself that Ditsel wanted to send Paul to the execution chamber.

"Will you give your full name and spell your last name for the court," said Harriet with exaggerated deference, which she conveyed with a musical voice and clasped hands.

Her smiling glances invited the jury to join her adulation of Ditsel. The jury responded with an impassiveness stoney enough to chill any trial lawyer's heart.

"Samuel Ditsel, D-I-T-S-E-L," said Ditsel, leaning slightly into the witness microphone, which screeched with feedback. The judge's clerk moved quickly to adjust the tuning controls on the console in her area behind the witness stand. She mouthed a silent "sorry" to Harriet and the jury when she was done.

Harriet, bowing to the hapless clerk, made a show of being big about it before continuing. "I'd like for you to tell the jury about your experience as a member of the Richmond Police Department."

"Yes ma'am. I joined the Richmond PD fifteen years ago. I worked as a patrolman for four years. I was promoted to detective in the vice division, where I worked for three years. Then I was moved to the fraud division and promoted to detective sergeant. I investigated frauds for four years until I joined the homicide division. After two years in homicide, I was promoted to detective lieutenant, which is my current rank."

Bari had Cammy digging everywhere for dirt on Ditsel. Nothing. His marriage was in trouble, but that wasn't exactly dirt in the twenty-first century. Half the marriages in the country were tanking.

"Did you receive any awards during that time?"

"I was awarded citations for valor twice when I was in the vice division."

Bari rolled his eyes. Oh great! Valor, no less.

"Thank you detective. Were you the detective in charge of investigating the murder of Detective Carey?"

"Yes ma'am, I was."

"Will you please describe your investigation for the jury?"

On cue, Ditsel repositioned the mike and sat back comfortably. "On February fifteen at 10:50 a.m., a call came in from the 911 operator reporting a shooting at 807 Broadmoor in the Madison Park area. That address was the home of Mr. and Mrs. Paul Feldman."

"Who called in the shooting to 911, Detective?"

"The caller identified herself as Marian Feldman."

Bari and Louis knew this question was coming and that it was hearsay, because it was an out-of-court statement offered to prove the truth of its assertion, namely, that a female caller identified herself to the 911 operator as Marian Feldman. It was actually double hearsay, because Ditsel was repeating the statement of someone else who heard the caller say that she was Marian Feldman. Nevertheless, neither Bari nor Louis objected at this stage; there would be other more important and damaging hearsay testimony offered later to which they would object, and they didn't want to give the jury the impression early on that they wanted to keep anything from them.

"What time was Marian Feldman's call to 911?"

"A few minutes before eleven. Ten-fifty a.m., I think it was."

Harriet repeated, "ten-fifty," and looked over at the jury, arched an eyebrow, and slyly smiled. Bari knew that she was trying her damnedest to make the jury think that Ditsel's testimony about the time of the 911 call helped the Commonwealth's case, but it did no such thing.

"Please continue."

"When I arrived at the scene, police officers had secured the crime scene with yellow tape. I walked into the upstairs bedroom and observed Detective Carey's body on the floor near a window."

"Where was Mrs. Feldman when you arrived?"

Ditsel picked Marian out of the court spectators with a slight lift of his head. "She was sitting in the living room in the company of a uniformed officer."

Bari was becoming increasingly frustrated. While Ditsel's weaselness made him look crafty and crooked, his courtroom performance totally offset his appearance.

"Would a diagram be helpful to you in describing the crime scene to the jury?"

"Yes ma'am, it would."

Lawyers have to set up all this choreography with the judge's clerk ahead of time. With the clerk's help, Harriet moved an easel and adjusted its placement. She then put up a three-foot-square Styrofoam display board on which was a diagram of the bedroom, moving the easel a few inches here, a few inches there until she was satisfied that the judge, the jury and Ditsel could see it.

"Is this diagram an accurate representation of the Feldman bedroom, detective?"

"Yes, it is."

"Your Honor, may the witness leave the witness stand to point out features on the diagram as he testifies?"

"Go ahead, detective."

Ditsel moved the mike aside by its stem to avoid the screeching and stepped down.

"Detective Ditsel, would you take that pointer and point out the door you walked through and the locution of Detective Carey's body."

"I came through this door, which is near the top of the stairs, here," said Ditsel, using the pointer, standing to the side, careful that all could see.   Ditsel's professionalism was on full review in front of the diagram. He had testified like this a hundred times and was entirely at ease, pointing and explaining.

Bari grimaced. *Wait till I get you on cross, you rodent sonofabitch.*

"Carey's body was here, where you see the red X." said Ditsel circling the red X with the tip of his pointer. "His body was facing toward the window at the right side of the bed as you face it."

"What was the body's position?"

"The body was face down - the left hand was at the side and the right hand was up at head level."

"Was there anything unusual about the body?"

"A wound to the back of his head was exposed, but there appeared to be very little loss of blood for that kind of wound."

"Anything else?"

"The suit he had on was smooth and not disheveled as expected. And his necktie was in a four-in-hand knot, and not the Windsor knot he always wore."

"Thank you. You may return to the witness stand, Detective." Ditsel carefully placed the pointer sideways on the lip of the easel and returned to the witness stand without ceremony and resumed his seat. The clerk quietly moved diagram and easel out of the way.

Unfortunately, for the defense, Ditsel gave the impression that he was a truthful detective who meant everything he said. It was true that on the witness stand Ditsel was an advocate for the Commonwealth's case, but he was a cop, and the jury would understand that no cop wants to see his arrest end up in an acquittal.

According to Ditsel's profile, which Cammy had given to Bari, Ditsel always trusted his own detective's judgment first, which was good. But Ditsel's supreme self-confidence had sometimes caused him to prematurely halt an investigation when he had mistakenly believed he had the bad guy, and that was not good. Bari was poised to argue that's exactly what happened to Paul.

"Detective Ditsel, I will hand you eight photographs and I will ask if you can identify them," said Harriet showing the photos to Bari and Louis, who made a production of going over them as if for the first time. When they were finished, she walked them over to Detective Ditsel who fanned them like playing cards.

"Yes, these are pictures that I took of the body and the bedroom. Three of the pictures are close-ups of the body, and the remaining five are of the bedroom and there is one of the bath included in that group of five."

"Your Honor, I would like permission to publish these pictures to the jury at this time." The judge nodded and Harriet gave the stack of pictures to the juror on the far left in the lower of two rows and the jurors began looking at them. She folded her arms and waited as the jurors passed them around.

Bari and Louis looked at each other in disbelief. A greenhorn right out of law school would know better than to give the jury a stack of pictures to look through in the middle of an examination.

"Please resume your examination of the witness, Ms. Atkins."

"I had hoped to resume after the jury had a chance to look at the pictures, Your Honor. I believe that Detective Ditsel's testimony will be clearer if the jury has an opportunity to look quickly through the pictures."

"The jury will have ample time to view the photographs in the jury room during deliberations, Ms. Atkins. Resume your examination, if you have additional questions."

Harriet looked at the jury, helplessly waving her arms in desperation. The jury was too interested in the pictures to have picked up on Harriet's predicament, and they leisurely continued to go over them.

The judge had spoken. Now Harriet's dilemma was whether to resume her examination of Ditsel while the jury was looking at pictures and paying no attention, or to collect the pictures right in the middle of their inspection of them.

Harriet could finally take no more. She went over to the jury box and politely but firmly retrieved the pictures, getting into a minor tugging match with one juror who hadn't seen quite as much as he wanted.

Bari figured that maybe Harriet took a calculated risk that the judge would let her slide, on the theory that prosecutors often get breaks from judges that defense attorneys never get.

"Was Detective Carey armed?"

"Yes, he had a shoulder holster with a Beretta 9mm semiautomatic pistol."

"Did you locate the gun with which he was murdered?"

"Yes ma'am. It was the same gun Detective Carey was wearing."

The spectators began murmuring and shifting in their seats. Judge Jones had to bang his gavel twice to quiet them: "Bailiff, prepare to clear the courtroom if there is another disruption."

"That's hearsay, Your Honor," said Bari, standing to make the objection.

"I'll allow it," said Judge Jones, still glaring at the spectators.

If the jury came away with the idea that Carey was shot with his own gun, Bari knew he would never get an acquittal, because the only logical way that could have happened is if Carey had his clothes off.

Harriet walked to the prosecution table and returned with a glassine bag containing a dark object. Noting that the bag had been marked for identification by the clerk, she asked Ditsel to identify the evidence tag with his name on it to demonstrate that he, the ballistics tech, and no one else, had had possession of the bag and the object inside.

"Please break the seal and remove the object it contains, Detective. Is that the gun Detective Carey was wearing?"

"Yes, it is."

"What kind of gun is it?"

"It is a 9mm semiautomatic handgun manufactured by Beretta U.S.A."

Ditsel put the gun back in the bag and handed it to Harriet, and she returned it to the prosecution table after offering it to the court as evidence.

Bari smiled. When a weapon is an exhibit, it isn't removed to the jury room automatically with the other exhibits. If the jury wants to examine the weapon, they call for the bailiff who retrieves it and remains in the jury room while the weapon is being examined. It wouldn't do for an angry juror to maim another juror with evidence from a murder trial. When Bari was first in practice, one juror stabbed another during deliberations when the bailiff accidentally left a knife among the exhibits in the jury room. The prosecution had moved the court for a mistrial, but the judge denied their motion and the defendant walked.

"After looking at the body, what if anything did you conclude at this point?"

Bari leapt to his feet. "Objection. Argumentative."

"Overruled. The witness may answer."

"I concluded that the body had been naked at the moment of death, and redressed afterwards," said Ditsel, brushing an imaginary speck of lint from his sleeve.

The collective intake of air by the spectators was audible, and the judge raised his head and glowered. "One more sound and you're gone," he told them.

Harriet had the jury's attention now. They leaned forward so as not to miss one delectable, prurient word.

She had Bari's attention too. Ditsel's testimony on this one issue could sink their case if Bari couldn't knock it down.

"What else did you notice, Detective?"

"In examining the body for bloodstains, I located a bloodstain on the lower heel of his left sock, but nothing on his left shoe."

"What, if anything, did that indicate to you, Detective Ditsel?"

"That his sock had been on when he was killed, but his shoe had been off."

"Did you find any other bloodstains? On Detective Carey's suit, for example?"

"There were some blood smears on his shirt, but nothing on his coat. And let me add that there should have been blood spatter on the back of his coat with that kind of head wound."

"Did you find blood anywhere else in the room?"

"No, which indicates a cleanup by someone."

"Objection. That answer is unresponsive," said Bari.

"Overruled."

Harriet then asked: "When did the defendant, Paul Feldman, become a suspect?"

"Almost immediately.

"And why was that?"

"The shooting took place in the defendant's bedroom. The victim was shot in the back of the head. The victim was redressed after having been nude, indicating sexual activity and a cover-up. Also, the defendant returned unexpectedly from the airport in time to have committed the murder."

This was the part in the movie where the defendant stands up and says, "How dare you say that about my wife!" But when Bari checked him in his peripheral vision, Paul was sitting motionless.

Bari knew it was worse than useless to object to this litany of suspicion. The jury wouldn't like it and Jones would let it in anyway.

"Anything else?"

"Well, that gave me opportunity and motive. When the ballistics report came back stating that Detective Carey was killed with his own gun, I also had means."

Well done, Ditsel, you prick, thought Bari, who made a note on his yellow legal pad.

"How did you know that the defendant returned from the airport in time to kill Detective Carey?"

"The time of death was between 10:00 a.m. and 11:00 a.m., and the defendant had a timed receipt from the airport's long-term parking."

After Ditsel identified the receipt, Harriet entered it into evidence.

"What was the time printed on the receipt, Detective Ditsel?"

"9:55 a.m., Monday, February 15th this year."

"No further questions. Thank you, Detective.

Having canonized Carey in her opening statement, Harriet didn't dare ask Ditsel about Detective Carey's predilection for married women or the traces of human feces on his penis. She could have, and the testimony would have been admissible, Bari thought. She was probably afraid that if she elicited the seamy details of Carey's reputation from Ditsel, the defense might plunge in with questions of its own.

It was wasted energy. Prior to trial, Bari and Louis had decided against painting Carey as a womanizer. That could only help Harriet prove premeditation.

"Cross examination?"

"Thank you, Your Honor," said Bari coming from behind the defense table.

Bari placed himself directly in front of Ditsel. In that position, the jury was on his immediate right. Okay, Detective, now it's my turn.

"Who else did you investigate in this case?"

"I looked at people Carey arrested and helped to convict. All but three of them are still incarcerated, and those three are out of state."

"Surely, Detective Carey had other enemies. Why did you stop investigating others and settle on Paul Feldman?"

"When he stopped cooperating with us, I knew we had our . . ."

"OBJECTION!" Bari and Louis shouted in unison. "Your Honor, may we approach?"

Judge Jones motioned to Bari to come forward. Louis, on Bari's right and Harriet, with her prim second chair, Priscilla Mimms, lined up before the bench as Bari pressed his objection.

"Your Honor, the exercise of the Fifth Amendment right to silence is not evidence and Detective Ditsel knows it," whispered Bari, vibrating with indignation. "I move that the answer be stricken and the witness be admonished before the jury in the strongest terms."

"Mr. Bari opened the door, Your Honor," Harriet hissed. "He can't be heard to complain now. The witness was merely answering his question."

"Stand back," said the judge. "The objection is sustained. The witness's answer will be stricken in its entirety, and the jury will disregard it." The judge leaned over and after covering the mike, whispered: "You pull that again, Ditsel, and I'll lock you up. Understood?"

Ditsel's professionalism was slipping. He had a little thug smirk on his face, like a mean kid caught pulling the wings off of flies.

The judge had more than neutralized the effect of Ditsel's answer, but Bari still hadn't recovered. He could feel the extra heartbeats warning him to calm down.

The courtroom door suddenly opened and Aaron, Cammy's associate walked quickly down the center aisle to the defense table where he conferred with Louis in whispers. Louis signaled Bari who turned to the judge, "Your Honor, may I take a moment?"

"Make it quick, Mr. Bari."

The three of them huddled and Bari walked over to face the bench. "Your Honor, the defense requests a meeting in chambers to discuss an urgent matter."

"Is this necessary, Mr. Bari? Can't it wait until the end of the day?"

"I believe that it is essential that it be heard immediately, Your Honor."

"ALL RIGHT, BARI, make it good," said the judge who was right on the edge of being pissed off.

After they were gathered in Jones's chambers, Bari began: "Your Honor, it has just this minute come to the defense's attention that the Commonwealth has been withholding *Brady* material."

Before Jones could reply to Bari, Harriet yelled, "WHAT IN THE HELL IS HE TALKING ABOUT?!"

"Keep your voice down, Ms. Atkins. Yes, Mr. Bari, what are you talking about?" the judge asked.

"This, Your Honor," said Bari handing the judge a copy of a police investigative report listing the married women that Carey had been screwing around with. It was the same report that Aaron had stuffed in Harriet's in box three weeks ago, without a word to Louis.

Bari had decided to spring the trap in the middle of Ditsel's testimony. Now, let Harriet try to explain why she had failed to turn this exculpatory information over to the defense.

"Do you know anything about this, Ms. Atkins?"

"As a matter of fact, I do. First, there is no *Brady* material in this report. Second, I was never able to run down the detective who made the report. If Your Honor will notice, there's no name on the report."

"Mr. Bari?"

"Your Honor, if Detective Carey was having serial or simultaneous affairs with married women, then he had a lot of jealous enemies. The Commonwealth had a duty to give us the report. The information is exculpatory and it guts their case.   Moreover, the Commonwealth's opening statement made Carey out to be a saint. That was an intentional lie."

"Your Honor, may I be heard?"   asked Harriet who had turned a deathly white.

"In a minute, Ms. Atkins," answered the judge. Turning toward Bari, he paused stroking his chin and looking directly at Bari first, then Louis. "I don't agree that the material in this so-called report is exculpatory. However, I do believe that in the spirit of accommodation, which lawyers no longer see fit to exercise, you should have given the report to the defense, Ms. Atkins."   The judge stood, pushed his chair aside and turned his back on the assembled lawyers and looked out the window in silence.

After minutes, he turned back with a sigh, addressing no one in particular: "I find the sudden appearance of this document in the middle of Detective Ditsel's testimony on cross suspicious, to say the least.   If anything like this happens again, somebody will explain it to the Bar's disciplinary committee.   Am I coming through loud and clear?"

"Your Honor, the defense has also learned that the prosecution plans to call Bernice Early as a witness. We never received any notice of this witness . . ."

"Your investigator interviewed Miss Early and videotaped it.   How much notice do you need?"

Judge Jones said nothing, which told Bari exactly where he stood.   Never before had he so badly overplayed his hand.   He had wanted to rattle Harriet Atkins and get a favorable ruling from the judge.   He got the opposite, and now Harriet had the upper hand.

Leaving the judge's chambers, Bari stole a look at Harriet and Priscilla Mimms.   They had their noses sanctimoniously elevated. Well, why not? He had fucked up and everybody knew it.

"DETECTIVE DITSEL, YOUR investigative notes reveal that you first thought the victim's death was a professional assassination. A 'hit,' you called it. Correct?"

"Notes, what notes?"

Bari walked to the defense table and retrieved a sheaf of papers. "These notes, Detective."

Ditsel looked helplessly at Harriet, who came to her feet and objected, without a clue what the grounds for her objection might be.

"Overruled. The witness can authenticate the notes if they are his, but only if they are his. Detective?"

"These are my notes, but that's all they are. Notes."

"Your Honor," said Harriet, recovering from her befuddlement. "The detective's notes are just raw impressions, not part of his official report, and I think that counsel should be made to tell this court how he came into possession of these confidential papers."

Bari felt his heart stutter and his blood pressure go through the floor. Deep steady breaths. Now relax.

"Ask your question again, Mr. Bari."

Reprieve!

"Thank you, Your Honor. Detective, according to your notes, you believed that the deceased was assassinated by a professional hit man, a paid assassin. Didn't you?"

"At first, yes, but I changed my mind in a hurry"

"Thank you, Detective." For a few panic-stricken moments, Bari thought the judge might actually throw the notes out as stolen property. But these were copies and fair game.

"You didn't record your change of mind in your notes, did you?" asked Bari.

"No, but . . ."

"Thank you Detective.   You have absolutely no physical evidence linking Mr. Feldman with the murder of Detective Carey, isn't that right, Detective?"

"That's right, but there's more to a case . . ."

Bari cut him off: "In fact, the only connection that Mr. Feldman has to this case is that the crime took place in his house, correct?"

"No, that isn't correct.   He's also married to Marian Feldman, who, by her own admission, was with Detective Carey when he was murdered."

Gloat, asshole, thought Bari. You think you got over on me, but you just told the jury exactly how fucking thin the Commonwealth's case really is.

"You said on direct examination that there appeared to be very little loss of blood, given the wound. Wasn't that your testimony?"

"Yes sir, it was," answered Ditsel, once again on his best courtroom behavior. This infuriated Bari who knew only too well how badly a jury wants to believe a police witness. Unless Ditsel screwed up again, the jury would overlook his previous lapses.

"Was there an exit wound?"

"No."

"Where a bullet penetrates the skull, but does not exit, there is typically very little loss of blood, isn't there sir?"

"It depends on the wound," answered Ditsel. "Some wounds bleed more than others."

Bari grabbed the stack of photographs from the prosecution table and thumbed through them withdrawing one.

"You have identified this picture as one that you yourself took, correct?"

"Yes sir."

"This picture shows the body face down, with the wound in the center of the head, doesn't it?"

"More or less in the center, but yes, that's right."

"In that position, the wound is not bleeding, is it Detective?"

"No, it isn't, but . . ." Ditsel trailed off.

Bari returned the pictures and paused for a drink of water, signaling to the jury that he was changing topics.

"Will you explain livor mortis to the jury, Detective?"

"You mean lividity?"

"Yes, livor mortis and postmortem lividity are the same. Please go ahead."

"Objection, the witness is not a pathologist, Your Honor," said Harriet in a sing-song voice, mocking Bari's earlier objection on the same grounds.

"This is basic police work, Your Honor."

"Overruled. "The witness may answer."

"Lividity," Ditsel answered, "is when the blood settles to the lowest point of the body; the part nearest the surface where it lies. You know, because of gravity."

"So if the body is lying face down, livor - sorry - lividity will cause the blood to settle on the front of the body rather than on the back. Isn't that right?"

"Yeah, that's right."

"Did you examine Detective Carey's body for lividity, Detective Ditsel?"

"It was much too soon."

"Isn't it true, Detective, that lividity can make an appearance on a body in an hour?"

"Not usually."

"*Not usually*," repeated Bari, giving the jury time to digest Ditsel's answer. "When lividity is present, you can also tell if a body has been moved, correct?"

"Yes, but before you can determine whether a body has been moved, lividity has to be fixed."

"But since you failed to check for lividity in the first place, we don't know if lividity was fixed, do we detective?"

"Objection. Argumentative."

"Sustained. Save it for closing, Mr. Bari."

I'll save that and a lot more, Judge.

Another pause and another change of topics.

"I'd like to ask you some questions about the victim's clothes. I believe that you said the victim's clothes were 'unexpectedly smooth, not disheveled,' correct?"

"Yes sir, that's correct."

"And that led you to conclude that the victim had been redressed after having been naked. Right?"

"That's right."

Bari went to the defense table and retrieved a stack of photographs from a closed folder, out of the sight of prying prosecutorial eyes.

"I request that these photographs be marked for identification," said Bari, handing the pictures to the clerk who attached tags. He then handed duplicates to Harriet who handled them as if they smelled of raw sewage.

"I'd like for you to look through these police photographs and describe the condition of the clothes worn by the deceased."

"Objection. Those photographs have not been authenticated. Detective Ditsel can't say that the photographs portray the subject with reasonable accuracy," said Harriet, with triumph in her voice.

"I'm very sorry, Your Honor. I neglected to have the detective identify the pictures. You recognize these photographs as your own, don't you Detective?"

"Yes. My initials are on the back in the lower left hand corner." Ditsel's face darkened and he slid down in the witness chair.

The police photographs Bari was showing Ditsel were "borrowed" from Ditsel's own file and copied at a cost of five thousand dollars by one of Cammy's inside cop informants. The half-dozen Bari was using to impeach Detective Ditsel were culled from a stack of over seventy-five photographs Ditsel had taken since joining the homicide division.

"Very well. Are the victims' clothes in these photographs 'disheveled,' Detective?"

"Well, I'd say they were disheveled."

"You are not in any case prepared to say that the victims in these photographs were naked at the time of their death and redressed afterward. Correct?"

"I never said they were at the time, and I don't say it now," said Ditsel, fidgeting and looking cornered.

You're shook now, aren't you weasel?

"Your Honor, I move these photographs into evidence as exhibits."

"I object. Those photographs are irrelevant to any issues in this case." Harriet was so enraged at having her star witness's testimony questioned that she could barely spit out the words.

"Your Honor," said Bari, "the witness made a claim about the victim in this case based in part on the condition of his clothes. The defense challenges that claim and is prepared to leave the final judgment to the jury when they compare the photographs of Detective Carey's clothes with the clothes of other victims."

Harriet slammed a copy of the court rules on the prosecution table causing Mimms to jump. She'd been sucked in by Bari and made to look foolish in front of the jury.

"Overruled. The photographs are accepted into evidence."

"I have another photograph for you to identify, Detective. Do you recognize the subject in this photograph?"

"Yes, that's Detective Arnold Carey, the murdered victim in this case." In this picture, Carey's body had been turned over and was face up.

"Did you take this picture, Detective Ditsel?"

"Yes. I took it at the scene after turning the body over."

Bari took the picture over to the prosecution table. Harriet snatched the photograph from Bari's hand. A puzzled look came over her as she looked at the photograph. She started to hand back the photograph, stopped, and took another look before placing it on the table and sliding it toward Bari.

Once Bari and Louis read Ditsel's police report, they knew what his testimony would be. They knew the knot in Carey's tie would be an issue, and they dispatched Cammy to find a picture of Carey wearing a different knot.

Cammy had given this assignment to the assiduous Aaron, who began wading through news photos, departmental pictures, Carey's high school graduation picture, until he finally struck pay dirt. A class picture from the junior college where Carey received an Associate of Arts degree in forensic science. The picture clearly showed Carey in the middle of his classmates, smiling and wearing a four-in-hand knot in his red and blue striped rep tie. Aaron had copied the picture and had blown up the section with Carey into a handsome eight by ten glossy for court.

"Now you testified that that the victim's tie had a four-in-hand knot, which led you to conclude that he had been redressed. Correct?"

"Yes, that, his clothes, the blood on the heel of his sock, and the negligible amount of blood from the wound."

"Look closely at Detective Carey's tie in this photograph, detective. What kind of knot is in his tie?"

"That picture is twenty years old . . ."

"Move to strike, Your Honor, the witness's answer is unresponsive."

"The jury will disregard the witness's answer. Answer the question, Detective Ditsel."

"It's a four-in-hand knot," mumbled Ditsel.

"Please speak up, Detective. I don't believe the jury could hear you."

"It's a four-in hand knot," said Ditsel directly into the mike.

"Thank you, Detective."

Bari admitted the picture into evidence, walked over to the defense table and glanced at a legal pad filled with notes. As he turned back to the witness, he looked briefly at the jury, making as much eye contact as he could. Harriet stood. Bari thought she was about to make an objection. Then she reconsidered with a look of utter disgust and sat back down.

"What kind of shoes was Detective Carey wearing at the time of his death, Detective Ditsel?"

"He was wearing tassel loafers."

"Were they new loafers, Detective?"

"No, they were not."

"Is it possible that when Detective Carcy was shot and fell forward his shoes momentarily slipped off his heels and then settled back when he hit the floor?"

"I'm sorry. I don't know what you mean."

"May I demonstrate, Your Honor?"

"If it isn't time-consuming, go ahead."

"I'm wearing tassel loafers, Detective. Now watch." Here, Bari stood on his tiptoes and reached upward, and as he did, his loafers slid off his heels. Next, he stood away from the defense table and leaned forward, his back to Detective Ditsel. As Bari caught himself with his hands on the edge of the defense table, his loafers slid off his heels.

"So, when Detective Carey was shot, it's possible that he fell forward and his shoes momentarily slipped off his heels?"

"I suppose it's possible, but I doubt it," said Ditsel, with obvious resentment, shifting uneasily in the witness chair.

"May I ask if you carry a weapon, Detective?"

"Objection; whether or not the detective is armed is irrelevant," said Harriet.

"I'll tie it in, Your Honor."

"Be very sure that you do, Mr. Bari. I'll reserve my ruling for the time being."

"What kind of weapon is it, Detective?"

"It's a nine millimeter Beretta semiautomatic handgun."

"May I see it?"

Harriet slammed her trial manual shut. "Objection! Your Honor, the defense is wasting the court's time with this meaningless display."

"It's all right, Detective, but make sure it can't be fired," said the judge who looked fully prepared to destroy Bari in front of the jury if he didn't make a relevant point in the end.

Ditsel appeared dubious, but he reached inside his suit and pulled out his gun. He removed the magazine and the round in the chamber, but did not hand it over to Bari.

Bari went to the prosecution table and brought back Carey's gun, which Harriet earlier offered into evidence.

"Now Detective, this gun that belonged to Detective Carey is identical to your own, is it not?"

"Yes, they are both nine millimeter Berettas."

"This is a very popular gun among Richmond PD detectives, isn't it?"

"A lot of guys carry them, yes."

"It's also popular with criminals, isn't it?"

"I have removed this model from perpetrators, yes."

"In fact, sales records show that the nine millimeter Beretta is by far the most popular handgun sold in Virginia, isn't it?"

"Objection. Sales records are hearsay."

"You may answer if you know, Detective," said the judge.

Bari knew that Ditsel was in a quandary. He didn't want to give the answer Bari wanted, but he also didn't want to show ignorance of information that detectives should know. Pride won out.

"I believe it outsells other handguns, yes."

"You testified that Detective Carey was killed with his own gun, didn't you?"

"Yes."

"You don't really know if he was in fact killed with his own gun, do you?"

"I know what the ballistics report said, which is that he was killed with his own gun."

"Fair enough. Paul and Marian Feldman were tested to discover whether either had recently fired a gun. Were they not?"

"Yes."

"What were the results of those tests?"

"Both tests were negative."

"Which means?"

"That neither one had recently fired a gun, but you can get that same result . . ."

"I have a question about fingerprints, Detective. The only fingerprints found on this gun belonged to the deceased, Arnold Carey, isn't that right?"

"Yeah, that's right."

Bari's questions came rapidly now, no pauses. "Returning to your testimony that, based on his timed parking receipt, Mr. Feldman had time to return home from the airport and shoot Detective Carey. Mrs. Feldman called 911 at 10:50 on the morning of February 15. Correct?"

"That's what the 911 records say, correct."

"Then you agree that the shooting occurred before 10:50 a.m., right?"

"That's right."

"10:45?"

"I don't know."

"10:40?"

"I said 'I don't know.'"

"Very well, Detective. But assuming that the shooting took place at 10:40 a.m., Mr. Feldman, according to his timed parking receipt, had just forty-five minutes to drive home, park his car somewhere, walk to his house, climb the stairs, grab the gun and fire. Correct?"

"The distance can be driven in that time."

"By Mario Andretti?"

"Objection, counsel is mocking the witness."

"Sustained. ENOUGH, Mr. Bari!" barked the judge.

"My apologies to the witness," said Bari without looking at the judge. "On a different point, Detective, when did all that redressing of the deceased take place?"

"It could have happened before the 911 call."

"I see. How long would it have taken?"

"I'm not a hundred percent sure - five minutes, ten."

"And all the cleaning up you say happened?"

"Minutes, if you were in a hurry."

"Which brings us to the question of who did the redressing and cleanup?"

"It was either Mrs. Feldman or Mr. Feldman."

"Your report theorizes that it was Mrs. Feldman, doesn't it?"

"Yes, but it could have been Mr. Feldman too."

"And if Mr. Feldman redressed Detective Carey and cleaned up the bedroom, it would have been after he shot him. Correct, Detective?"

"Yes, that's correct."

"So, on the theory that Mr. Feldman redressed Detective Carey after shooting him, the chain of events would likely have been as follows: Mr. Feldman shoots Detective Carey at 10:40; Mrs. Feldman calls 911 at 10:50; With the police on the way, Mr. Feldman, for reasons known only to the Almighty, takes the time to redress Detective Carey and clean the room. And finally, after redressing and cleaning up, Mr. Feldman leaves seconds before the police arrive at 11:15 a.m. Do you agree with that timeline, Detective Ditsel?"

"Actually I arrived at 11:15 a.m. The uniformed officers arrived at 11:05 a.m." When Bari stole a look at

Harriet, she looked like she was having an attack of peritonitis.

"You don't really believe that ridiculous timeline, do you Detective?"

"Yes, I do."

"One last question, Detective.   Was any blood discovered on the defendant or his wife?"

Blood rushed to Ditsel's face and neck.   "They weren't checked for blood stains."

"When you Richmond detectives think somebody's guilty, you don't let troublesome facts get in the way. Do you Detective Ditsel?"

"OBJECTION!"

"Thank you Detective Ditsel. No further questions," Bari said, shaking his head and smiling.

Judge Jones called a fifteen minute recess and the defense and prosecution stood as the judge left and the jurors filed out.

Paul left the courtroom for the break, his hand on Marian's elbow. Bari was torn. He loved the picture of marital devotion that Paul and Marian presented to the jury. On the other hand, Bari could only shake his head at his friend's naïveté. Paul was on trial for his life because of Marian's shenanigans. *Jesus, Paul,* thought Bari, *wake the fuck up!*

Bari and Louis headed for the men's room. There was a line, of course. They took the stairs down a floor to one that was empty.

"What do you think?" asked Louis.

Bari knew that if, in a criminal trial, one side can actually score points during cross examination instead of merely pecking and finding tiny faults with the witness's testimony, there's a multiplier effect on the number of points scored.

"The guy's credible, Art, but I think we're ahead, and we've got a lot to argue about in closing. If Atkins continues to insist that Carey was there for a tryst, the jury will laugh at her, and there goes her fucking motive."

Louis was subdued, and Bari knew why. It was because of the "report" he had made a stink about in chambers. Bari was afraid that Louis would quit when court was adjourned at the end of the day. An unsigned police report? Exculpatory evidence? An allegation of misconduct? He knew the whole production was as much of a surprise to Louis as it was to Harriet Atkins. Louis would have some pointed questions, and Bari was at a loss to think of any answers.

THEIR NEXT HEADACHE was up after recess, and Louis would do the cross. It was the medical examiner who went over Carey's body at the scene, and who would establish the cause as well as the time of death.

The ME would be a dangerous witness, because juries perceive medical examiners as having no axe to grind and usually take their testimony at face value. That perception of impartiality is reinforced by the flat, techno-medical flavor of a medical examiner's testimony. In actuality, the job of medical examiner is a political appointment in hundreds of jurisdictions across the country just as it is in Richmond, Virginia.

But if ever a medical examiner's testimony, regardless how accurate, begins casting doubt on the Commonwealth's case in high profile trials, his - and frequently, her - job is on the line. So while the ME would knock himself out to appear unbiased, he would be anything but.

Louis loved experts. He was well acquainted with his own strengths and he knew that he would be a perfect foil for this witness. Let him be dry and scientific; Louis would be engaging and human.

CHAPTER SIXTEEN

"THE COMMONWEALTH CALLS DOCTOR Eldred Mason to the stand."

Mason was a thin defensive man with a mincing walk and effeminate mannerisms. His grey gabardine suit was shiny and cheap and the collar of his shirt was a size too large, as if he hated anything tight around his neck.

Everything about this quiet, little pathologist told Louis that he would react aggressively to any attempt to trick or humiliate him on the stand. This was a man who could not have risen to his present position without having steel in his spine and a powerful sponsor. Colleagues would have run him off otherwise. He would also have to know his stuff.

"Doctor Mason, would you please identify yourself for the jury."

"Yes, I am the chief medical examiner for the city of Richmond."

Harriet took him through his extensive medical training, publication of monographs on forensic pathology and his experience in the field.

"Will you please tell the jury what happened on the day in question?"

"Of course. I received a call at around eleven a.m. on February fifteenth and drove to a home at 805 Broadmoor, where I arrived at eleven twenty-five. Detective Sammy Ditsel showed me where the body was located."

Harriet once again pulled her easel and diagram into position. "Is this a fair representation of the room where the body was located?"

"Yes. The body was located at the red X."

Harriet motioned to the doctor to join her at the easel. He shook her signal off. Harriet had a frozen smile on her face, but her eyes were death rays aimed directly at the ME.

"What was the cause of death, Doctor Mason?"

"Massive trauma to the brain caused by a nine millimeter lead projectile fired from a distance of over ten feet. Death was instantaneous."

"Were you able to determine the time of death, Doctor?"

"Within certain parameters, yes."

Harriet winced, but she soldiered on. "Please describe for the jury the methods you used to arrive at the time of death."

"I first took the deceased body's temperature. A body begins losing heat at the time of death and will continue to lose heat until it reaches the ambient, or surrounding, temperature. I noted very slight signs of rigor mortis and lividity, both of which indicated that the time of death must have been no later than eleven a.m. I also talked with the homicide detective."

Mason's testimony matched Ditsel's on important points. That the actual time of death was sometime prior to Marian's call to 911. Also, that there was very little blood. Louis knew that, if allowed to stand, Mason's testimony would be enough to convict Paul. Harriet proudly turned Mason over to him.

Louis rose from the defense table with his suit jacket open. When he was squarely in front of Mason, he noticed his open jacket like a man might notice that his fly was unzipped. Embarrassed, he fumbled nervously to button it. Shameless theater, but it helped Louis introduce himself to the jury as one of them, a decent Joe, an everyman. If it worked, the jury would pull for him to do well.

"Time of death is simply an estimate, isn't it Doctor?"

"That's correct, Mr. Louis. Time of death analysis isn't an exact science." Louis knew that Mason had been through cross examinations like this so many times that it was like a Gregorian chant: *You can't be precise, can you doctor?*

No, but I can be very close.

"Let me see if I understand you, Doctor Mason. You based your estimate on four factors; body temperature, degree of rigor mortis, lividity, and Detective Ditsel's theory of the case. Isn't that right?"

"Yes. You have to use every indicator at hand."

"But you didn't use the time of the 911 call, did you?"

"Given all the other indicators, I concluded that death occurred near the time of Mrs. Feldman's 911 call, as it happened. In other words, the time of the call was irrelevant to my analysis."

"You say *now* that the time of death was closer to eleven than ten?"

"Yes."

"But on your report, you said the time of death was closer to ten, correct?"

"Yes. I have since reevaluated the facts."

"You estimated the time of death as closer to 10:00 a.m., when the big issue was whether the decedent had been redressed after death. Isn't that right?"

"Well, yes but . . ."

"But that was before you knew that Mr. Feldman had a timed receipt showing he left the Richmond airport at 9:55 a.m., wasn't it?"

"What are you suggesting?"

Quick as a bunny Harriet was out of her chair. "Objection. It's improper for an attorney to answer questions put to him by the witness." Her objection was a little too loud. What the hell is she complaining about? thought Louis. Mason is her witness.

"Overruled. If the witness wants clarification, Mr. Louis can give it."

"I am suggesting that you have tailored your estimate of the time of death to fit the Commonwealth's so-called case. Isn't that right, Dr. Mason?"

Mason half rose from the witness chair. "THAT'S AN INSULT, and it is *not* right."

"Very well, let's return to rigor mortis. It takes hours for rigor to set in, doesn't it?"

"Ordinarily yes, but full rigor can set in minutes after death."

"Also with lividity. It takes hours for lividity to appear, doesn't it?"

"As a rule, yes, but not always."

"Shall we go through them one at a time? In your report, you state that the victim's body had heat loss."

"There was some heat loss, although very little. There was a gas fireplace in the bedroom that I factored in when I calculated the heat loss in the victim's body."

"But there was appreciable heat loss, wasn't there Doctor?"

"No, but that could have been because the room was very warm and there wasn't sufficient time after death for the body to have registered significant heat loss."

"Had the body been nude, as the prosecution alleges, the heat loss would have been greater, isn't that right?"

"In theory, yes, but there are a number of factors that affect heat loss."

"Such as?"

"Obesity, position of the body, drafts, and so forth."

"Come now, Doctor Mason," said Louis. "The victim wasn't obese or curled up, so there should have been significant heat loss corresponding to your first, ten a.m. estimate of time of death. Correct?"

"Well, I've reevaluated my first estimate. Since I now believe that the time of death was closer to 11:00 a.m. than to 10:00 a.m., it makes perfect sense that there was negligible heat loss."

"In light of your reevaluation, the body's temperature told you nothing about time of death. It didn't figure in, isn't that correct?"

"That's right. 'It didn't figure in,' as you put it," said Mason with a sneer.

"The victim's lividity didn't indicate that his body had been moved, did it?"

"No, it did not, but there was a reason . . ."

"Thank you, sir. Doctor Mason, let's cut through the underbrush here. Your estimate of the time of death was mainly influenced by Detective Ditsel who told you his theory of the case at the crime scene and later, after he found out that Mr. Feldman had proof that he was at the airport at 9:55 a.m.?"

"It was certainly a factor, yes."

"Furthermore, you dismissed the time of the call to 911 because it conflicted with the detective's theory?"

"I discounted the time of that call as misleading, given the detective's compelling analysis of the case."

"What would you think about the time of death if the detective's theory was all wrong?"

"But I don't believe the detective's analysis is wrong. On the contrary, I believe it is right on."

Louis paced close to the witness chair and when he came even with Mason, he stopped. Louis was now facing the jury and Mason would have been looking at his left ear.

"You performed the autopsy, right?"

"Yes, I did."

"In your autopsy report, you stated that the victim showed signs of recent sexual activity, correct?"

"As I testified, there were spermatozoa in the victim's urethra."

"Do you stand by your testimony that the sexual activity was recent?"

"I stand by all my testimony."

"Sperm can be found in a male's urethra up to three days after sex, isn't that so, doctor?"

"Yes."

"So by recent sexual activity, you mean within the last three days. Isn't that right?"

"Yes."

"I suppose that for some of us three days is recent, but with regards to this case, calling three days 'recent' is misleading, isn't it, Doctor?" Louis was still facing the jury and three of them stifled laughs. *YES!*

Both Harriet and her deputy jumped out of their chairs. "Objection, Your Honor," said Harriet. Louis was making a fool of her witness, and her wrath was apparent to everyone in the courtroom. "That question is improper and irrelevant."

"The question permits the witness to explain his testimony, Your Honor," said Louis.

"I'll overrule the objection, Mr. Louis, but enough of the wry comments. I'll stop you myself next time."

Louis knew that Harriet would think hard about having Mason explain his lividity testimony. Lividity can prove that a body was moved only after several hours when it has become fixed in the body. Once lividity is fixed, no amount of turning the body over can cause the blood to flow back to the other side.

After dealing with hundreds of experts, Louis knew that, sure as hell, if Harriet questioned him on redirect, Mason would go technical on her and she'd lose the jury for sure.

"One final thing, Doctor. Did you find any finger prints in the body?"

"No."

"Wouldn't dressing or moving a body leave fingerprints, Doctor?"

Louis knew there were no usable prints found on Carey's body because Mason's report plainly said there weren't. Cammy had interviewed the ambulance drivers who took the body to the morgue. The drivers apparently weren't told to be careful, and their prints were everywhere they came in contact with flesh. The morgue attendant who undressed the body had made the same mistake. These errors were then compounded when the body had been refrigerated. The low temperature had the effect of slowly eradicating the fingerprints, and by autopsy time, there was nothing usable.

"Handling the body should leave prints on the exposed portions of the body that came in contact with fingertips," Mason said.

"Your report doesn't indicate that you concur with Detective Ditsel's theory of the body's having been moved."

"My report is mute on that point. That doesn't mean I disagree; it simply means that there was insufficient bodily evidence to reach that conclusion."

"So to sum up, Doctor, your time of death was really guess work based on Detective Ditsel's analysis with which you don't entirely agree. Isn't that correct, Doctor Mason?"

"Objection, Your Honor," said Harriet, who must have been on the edge of a stroke. "Counsel is testifying again."

"I don't think so," said Jones. "Objection overruled."

"As you established from the beginning, Mr. Louis, time of death is an estimate," said Mason. "I am comfortable standing by my estimate, which was that the time of death occurred about eleven a.m. on February 15."

Now it was Louis's turn to get pissy. "I'm beginning to think you could be comfortable in a sandstorm, Doctor Mason."

Harriet came out of her chair like a bronco, knocking it over with a loud crash. "OBJECTION!"

"All right, Mr. Louis, that's enough. Do you have anymore questions for this witness?" asked the judge, whom, Louis was certain, wasn't nearly as put out as Harriet would have liked.

"No, Your Honor. I'm finished with the witness."

Still, Louis was unhappy with Mason's cross. You can show that an expert is wrong, that his assumptions are flawed, that he's totally out to lunch, but if you can't demolish him, and if the S.O.B. won't back away from his testimony, the jury is left hanging. His only hope was that the jury would dislike Mason as much as he did.

MS. RHONDA JAMES, the ballistics technician, established the chain of custody by testifying that the automatic that Harriet handed her was the same gun that Detective Ditsel had booked into evidence on February 15, which she had marked with a file. To complete the chain, the technician further testified that she had given the same gun to Harriet that morning before trial.

She described the process of firing into a water tank and retrieving the expended round for testing. Priscilla Mimms, Harriet's expressionless second chair, showed the technician two enlargements: one of a badly deformed round taken from the victim's head, and the one that she retrieved from the tank. "Ms. James, what can you tell the jury about the bullets in these two photographs?" asked Mimms, handing the two photos up to the technician.

"Those are photographs I made of the two projectiles," the technician answered.

"What else?"

"If you will notice how the lands and grooves on both projectiles match each other . . . There is a *reasonable probability* that both projectiles were fired from the same gun."

"Had the victim's gun been recently fired?"

"Good police procedure requires that a gun be cleaned after firing. The victim's gun had not been cleaned. There was powder residue all over the barrel and firing mechanism."

Bari elected to take the ballistics expert. He knew about guns from past cases and from his hitch in the service. He had fired so well on the firing range that his company commander tried to talk him into sniper training.

Even so, Bari believed that they might have to live with the fact that Carey was killed with his own gun. But he didn't dare concede that point. It was by far the strongest evidence that Paul had pulled the trigger.

Detective Ditsel's testimony was that in his opinion Carey was banging Marian when Paul came into the bedroom. Paul saw the action and shot Carey with his own gun, which was hanging somewhere nearby.

The jurors might want to acquit, but they were bound to go over and over the ballistics evidence during deliberations. They were certain to ask themselves, and each other, how the hell else could it have happened? Bari knew he had to give the jurors a way out— some believable alternative theory.

Bari knew exactly how it happened, of course. Paul's old man hired that psycho Jackie Lupo to kill Carey. Paul's parents were sitting next to Marian on the bench directly behind the defense table, and Bari turned to catch David Feldman's tortured eye for a brief moment. Then, as the dark cloud of resignation rolled in, the ballistics technician unexpectedly said those magical words "reasonable probability."

"Cross examination?"

Bari rose and began his first question as he moved his chair back and walked around the defense table, "The test bullet you fired into the water tank and the bullet taken from the deceased's skull were both round nose lead projectiles. Isn't that right?"

"Actually, the test bullet was a round nose bullet. I'm not a hundred percent sure about the bullet retrieved from the victim's head. That bullet could have been a round nose or a hollow point."

Good ballistics practice would have been to fire several test rounds taken from Detective Carey's Beretta, and Bari was positive this witness had done just that. But since the second chair hadn't asked and the witness hadn't volunteered the information, Bari would be nuts to nail it down.

"And your doubt is because of the condition of the bullet retrieved from the victim; right?"

"Yes, that's right. There wasn't a lot of surface left for comparison."

After saying a silent prayer of thanks for this witness, Bari set up a diagram of his own. He exchanged his diagram for Harriet's crime scene diagram, and moved the easel to the spot Harriet had used, so that judge, jury and witness could easily see it.

"Now, all nine millimeter Beretta semiautomatic handguns have six lands and six grooves and a left twist, correct?" asked Bari, pointing to the large perspective drawing of a cross section of a gun barrel. The drawing clearly showed left-twisting grooves and the raised metal spaces between them, called lands.

"Yes, all semiautomatic Beretta handguns of that caliber have the same rifling, the same number of lands and grooves with a left twist," the technician answered.

"Ordinarily, you can determine if a particular bullet was fired from the handgun in question even though all other handguns of the same manufacture and caliber have the same rifling. Correct?"

"Yes. The bullet is marked by the weapon's distinctive rifling. There are always microscopic differences in the barrel due to the sharpness of the blade cutting the grooves during manufacture. After cutting each barrel, the blades are a tiny bit less sharp than they were on the previous barrel. These microscopic differences are transferred to the bullet when the gun is fired."

Bari quietly asked the clerk for the photograph Mimms had used during her direct examination of the witness and placed it in front of his diagram still on the easel.

"And yet, you are not sure beyond doubt that the test bullet and the bullet retrieved from the victim were fired from the same gun?"

"If you'll notice, that tiny black dot at the base of the deformed bullet does not appear on the bullet fired into the test tank."

"Would you please step down and point to that tiny black dot?"

The ballistics expert bent over prettily with her knees locked and her ample butt facing the jury. "It's ri...ght there," she said closing one eye and pointing with her index finger. Bari looked over at Harriet, who had taken on the stoical impassivity of an Easter Island statue. Mimms was her usual hard-to-read self. *Mimms is a screamer, I'd bet my life on it,* thought Bari. *If you made it with her in a motel, somebody would hear her and call the cops.*

"But yet you are still not one hundred percent sure?"

"No, because the tiny black dot could be a photographic artifact, or it could have been put there by a skull chip, or even during its retrieval from the skull," said the technician. "As you can see, there is very little left of the bullet to compare."

"Including the lands and grooves?"

"Well, *I* can see them, but I do this all the time."

Bari's eyebrows shot up dramatically for the jury, but he said nothing. Instead, he had another question. "Ms. James, when a bullet is deformed, you can often identify the weapon that fired it by markings on the shell casing. Isn't that correct?"

Bari had kept Louis in the dark about Cammy's involvement in the missing shell casing. Nevertheless, Louis, as well as Bari, had seen a shell casing listed on the evidence sheet, but there was no mention of it in the ballistics report.

The technician couldn't now testify to tests she hadn't done, nor would Judge Jones allow her to speculate about what the probable results would have been.

"Yes, that's right, but no one turned in a shell casing to me."

"The police report clearly inventoried a shell casing. Are you telling this court that you received no such item?"

Mimms stood, all business. She removed her glasses and held them at the ready. "Objection. That question has been asked and answered."

"Sustained."

What a chicken shit objection, thought Bari. It took more time to make the damn objection than it would for the tech to answer it.

"Did you inquire what happened to the missing shell casing?"

Ms. James looked over at Mimms and gave a tiny, helpless shrug of the shoulders, "Yes, I did. More than once."

"And what answer did you receive, Ms. James?"

"No one seemed to know where it was."

"That's too bad. A shell casing can rule out a particular gun as the weapon that was used. Isn't that right?"

"Yes sir, a shell casing is an excellent way to identify a weapon or rule it out."

"Thank you, ma'am. You have been most helpful. No further questions."

Bari figured, gleefully, that it was probably just beginning to dawn on Harriet and Mimms that Carey's gun was both the proof and the problem. If Carey was killed with his own gun, then the defendant was the most likely killer. On the other hand, the use of Carey's gun drained the case of premeditation. The defendant returns home to confirm his suspicions, happens on the gun and, in a jealous rage, shoots Carey. That's not premeditation and it's not a cop-killing, legally. It's murder two, tops.

Also, the Commonwealth had the lingering problem about what to do about the nausea that caused Paul to cancel his flight. Her cop witnesses believed Paul's nausea was on the level.

And now that it had come to light in chambers that Harriet knew that Carey was making it with other married women, Judge Jones would never permit her to seek the death penalty based on Paul's having killed a cop in the line duty. What duty? Bagging yet another married broad?

The jury might accept that Marian screwed around on her unsuspecting husband. Husband leaves on a legitimate business trip, gets sick, returns home and discovers his wife and Carey making the beast with two backs. Bada boom! The hand of God, working through the defendant, smites the offender with his own weapon. Beautiful. Christ, Bari thought, if only the jury would see it like that, they'd acquit Paul and feel good about doing it.

"Redirect?"

"Your Honor, may I have a moment?" asked Priscilla Mimms.

"Make it brief, Counsel."

The prim young woman and Harriet had a furious whispered conversation at the Commonwealth's table. Their dialogue ended abruptly.

"Thank you, Your Honor," said Miss Mimms. "Where did you get the cartridge you fired into the water tank?"

"From the same gun. I removed the magazine, took a cartridge from it, and chambered it. Then I fired into the water tank."

"Has it been your experience in your ballistics work that cartridges with different bullets are found in the same clip?"

"I'm sorry, I'm not sure I understand the question."

Bari bounced up. "Objection, Your Honor. The question exceeds the bounds of cross examination." *Goddamm it. Somebody always pulls this on redirect*, he thought. Redirect examination, as a rule, is for the purpose of clarification and not for a brand new examination with questions that should have been asked the first time around. Bari felt a stab of pain in his left arm. After a second or two, it passed, and he vowed to cut way back after this trial. If only God would let him bring this one home a winner.

"Overruled, I'll allow it."

Thanks a lot.

"Would you expect to find a round nose bullet and a hollow point bullet in the same handgun?"

"Okay, I see. No, I wouldn't expect to see that. Every handgun that I've examined, and I've examined hundreds, were loaded with the same bullets - all round nose or all hollow point."

"Would you please sum up your analysis of the ballistics comparison for the jury?"

"Yes, ma'am. Despite the tiny abnormality on the bullet retrieved from the victim's skull, I believe that bullet was fired by the victim's gun. Even though the bullet was deformed by the wound it made, there are other good points of comparison with the test bullet."

"Thank you . . . Your Honor, I'd like to pass this witness subject to recall."

"Very well, Counsel."

Bari suddenly felt weak all over. The emotional roller coaster was too much. He had the ballistics tech right where he had wanted her, until Harriet's snippy second chair asked the tech to sum up. Now they were almost back where they started with the goddamned gun.

BARI WAS DELIGHTED that Harriet's next witness was Detective William "Billy" Mitchell, one of the detectives that had questioned Paul and Marian. Cammy had discovered that Mitchell had an infuriating reputation among his fellow detectives for honesty in court. Several times in his career, the bad guy had walked because Detective Mitchell would not shade the truth.

Harriet took Mitchell through the preliminaries, then quickly got to the meat of her direct examination. "What time did the defendant tell you he left for the airport, Detective?"

"He couldn't remember at first, and he asked for some time to figure it out. After a minute or so, he said he left at eight a.m."

"Did the defendant give you the impression that he was playing for time?"

"I don't think so. He was heaving into a trash can every few minutes."

Harriet would probably have shot Mitchell in the back of his head at that moment, if she could have gotten away with it. Bari didn't smile. He was careful not to anger the trial gods by glorying in Harriet's distress at being crossed up by her own witness. It had happened to him in the past and would happen again, though not, he pleaded, in this case.

Mitchell went on to testify to the times Paul had given him, and say that he had gotten a timed parking receipt from him also. Harriet asked Mitchell to identify the receipt and had it admitted into evidence.

"At what time did the defendant arrive home from the airport?"

"He didn't know for sure. He said his block was cordoned off when he got there. He said he parked his car up the street and walked to his home."

"Then he could have arrived at any time?"

"Mr. Feldman said that the EMT people were just placing the victim's body in the ambulance as he walked up."

"Were you at the scene, Detective?" Harriet sighed.

"Yes ma'am, I was."

"Did you see the defendant?"

"Yes ma'am. He identified himself to me when he walked up."

"Your witness."

Bari decided to show Detective Mitchell the respect and care that so helpful a witness deserved. He wouldn't try to trick him and he wouldn't try to make him eat his words.

"Was the defendant pale, Detective?"

"Yes sir, and his shirt was soaked with sweat."

Harriet rose to make an objection, thought better of it, and sat down peevishly.

"Was the defendant a suspect at this time, Detective Mitchell?"

"He was to me, yes sir."

"And that was only because he was the husband, isn't that right?"

"He was the husband, and he was near the crime scene."

"Did you test the defendant and his wife for gun powder residue?"

"Yes sir, I did. We used the FAAS technique for detection of gunshot residues."

"What does FAAS stand for Detective Mitchell?"

"It stands for Flameless Atomic Absorption Spectrometry."

"What were the results?"

"Negative for Mr. Feldman and inconclusive for Mrs. Feldman."

"Inconclusive?"

"Yes. Her test showed slightly elevated amounts of barium and lead on her right palm. Elevated amounts of barium and lead could indicate firing a weapon, but they are usually found on the back of the hand and the front of the hand near the thumb of the shooter. Also, the lipstick she uses contains barium and lead in trace amounts."

"Which means?"

"We have no evidence that either Mr. or Mrs. Feldman fired a gun on February fifteenth."

"Thank you, Detective. No further questions."

"Redirect, Ms. Atkins?"

Harriet swished over to face Detective Mitchell. "Thank you, Your Honor. Detective Mitchell, if someone wore gloves when firing a handgun, that person's hands would test negative for gunshot residue, correct?"

"Objection," said Bari. "There are no gloves in evidence."

"Overruled. The witness may answer."

"Correct. Yes ma'am."

"If that person washed his hands after firing a handgun, his hands would test negative, correct?"

"Yes ma'am."

"If that person was wearing a coat, gunshot residue would be found on the sleeve and front of the coat of the coat. Isn't that correct?"

"It might be, depending on the size of the gas cloud blow-back."

"Did you test the defendant's clothing for gunshot residue, Detective?"

"No ma'am."

"So he could have fired . . ."

"Objection. Detective Mitchell has testified that there is no evidence that Mr. Feldman fired any gun."

"Overruled. I'll allow it."

"To repeat, Detective, the defendant could have fired a handgun on February fifteen last and still have tested negative for gunshot residue. Isn't that right?"

"Yes ma'am, that's right."

"No further questions."

CHAPTER SEVENTEEN

"WHAT DO YOU think, Art?" asked Bari on the way back from court.

As soon as the September humidity and late afternoon sun hit Louis, he began to perspire. By the time they had walked two blocks, he was dripping. "I think we're behind. If the trial ended now, Paul would probably be convicted, because, as you said, it's really up to us to prove he didn't do it. Forget the Constitution and reasonable doubt. A cop is dead and the jury will want to nail somebody."

"I think you're right, Art. And the jury hasn't heard from Bernice Early."

"THE COMMONWEALTH CALLS Miss Bernice Early to the stand," announced Priscilla Mimms, looking at a legal pad she held in one hand.

A model of elderly dignity, Miss Early made her way slowly through the gate and, refusing assistance, stepped up to the witness chair. Let others her age wear pant suits; Miss Early wore a soft linen skirt with bag to match and a flowery silk blouse.

Mimms swore her in and went through the preliminaries. Bari was astonished. Mimms was apparently trying to be polite, but she was making classic errors. She was too loud, even though Miss Early displayed no difficulty hearing, and she was condescending. Mimms must have also believed that all elderly people were senile, because she spoke to Miss Early as if she were seven years old.

"Can you remember back to February fifteenth of this year, Miss Early?"

"Young woman, if I couldn't remember February fifteenth, you wouldn't have called on me to testify," answered Bernice Early, drawing herself up and fixing Mimms with a reproving stare. "And keep your voice down. My hearing is unimpaired by age or anything else."

"Very well, Miss Early. I apologize." But it wasn't an apology. Mimms seemed determined to humor the witness. Bari was baffled. Certainly, she must have known she was insulting Miss Early. Then it hit him. *Mimms doesn't have a drawl. She isn't from the South!*

"Miss Early, will you tell the court where you live in relation to the defendant, Mr. Feldman?"

"Directly across the street."

Mimms continued her examination, establishing that Bernice Early had lived in her home for thirty years; that Paul and Marian had moved in across the street seven years ago; and that Miss Early considered them friends.

"On the morning of February fifteenth, did you have occasion to look across the street at the Feldman home, Miss Early?"

Miss Early testified that she was watching TV at ten thirty when she looked across at Paul's and Marian's house. There was a light blue sedan parked in the driveway, and just as she got up to get coffee a large black car pulled up. She became distracted in the kitchen wiping down the counter tops. By the time she returned to the TV room, ten or fifteen minutes later, the big black car was gone.

"What color is the defendant's car?"

"Paul's car is black and much smaller than the car I saw."

"Your Honor, the witness's answer is non-responsive. I move that everything after 'black' be stricken."

Judge Jones leaned over to the witness: "Bernice, I'm afraid I'll have to ask that you confine your answers to the questions Ms. Mimms asks." The Judge apparently knew Miss Early. In any case, he had no trouble at all showing the proper deference to the witness.

"I'm sorry, Harley. I was just trying to save time. I know Paul's lawyer is going to ask me about the car's size."

"Go on, Ms. Mimms, said the judge, smiling slightly."

Priscilla Mimms shook her head in disbelief at this delicate, complicated reel. It would have taken her a lifetime in the South to understand it. Bari, grinning, looked over at Louis.

"I believe you said there was also a light blue car parked in the driveway?"

"Yes, I did say that."

"Did that light blue car leave?"

"No."

"Do you wear glasses, Miss Early?"

"Only to read."

"When was the last time you had your eyes checked?"

"Last week when I renewed my driver's license."

"Pass this witness, Your Honor."

Bari knew Miss Early would be popular with the jury. She was irascible and no one could lay a glove on her and she knew it.

"Good morning, Miss Early, ma'am."

"Good morning, young man."

"Early is an old Virginia name, isn't it Miss Early?"

"Yes it is. My great-great-grandfather was General Jubal Early."

"Oh my, yours is an illustrious name indeed!"

"Yes. General Early fought with high distinction. He was Robert E. Lee's right hand man."

Before getting into his cross, Bari paused theatrically to honor the late warrior.

"Ma'am, you testified that a big black car pulled into Mr. Feldman's driveway at ten thirty on the morning of February fifteenth. Is that right?"

"That's right. Just as my news program ended."

"You also testified that you got up and went to the kitchen to get a cup of coffee at that time."

"Yes, that's right."

"And that when you returned ten or fifteen minutes later, the big black car was gone?"

"It was gone, but I didn't see it leave."

At first, Bari had been floored that Mimms hadn't nailed Miss Early. She had told the cops that Paul's car was maroon. He suddenly realized with a thud that Mimms was waiting for redirect. Bari hadn't believed his luck when Mimms ended her direct on such a downer. But she had tucked the car color issue in her pocket to use on redirect and end on a high note. It would be a discrepancy in Miss Early's testimony that the Jury would not forget.

Bari had to inoculate her testimony much as he hated to. He knew that if he made an issue of the color of Paul's car, it would be damaging, but not nearly as damaging if were brought in by Mimms. "Miss Early, you were questioned by the police on February sixteenth, weren't you?"

"Yes I was."

"At that time, you told the detective that Paul's car was maroon, didn't you ma'am?"

"I did."

"But Paul's car is black, isn't it?"

"Yes, it is."

"Can you account for that discrepancy?"

"I believe I can. There is a maroon awning right there by the garage. That awning was reflected in the car's finish, making me think the car was maroon. I had a friend park her black car in the driveway where I've seen Paul's car, and . . ."

"Objection. The witness is introducing very unscientific and unreliable testimony into evidence."

"Sustained. Next question, Mr. Bari."

Miss Early's explanation of the color discrepancy was plausible! Bari could see that she was a woman who hated to be wrong about anything.

After she had talked to Cammy, she must have begun searching around for an explanation for having believed Paul's car was maroon. She noticed the maroon awning by the driveway, and then called a friend with a black car to test her reflection theory. Right on, Miss Early!

"Miss Early, I believe you testified that Mr. Feldman's car was much smaller than the big black car that drove into his driveway at ten thirty in the morning of February fifteenth?"

"Yes, the car that drove up was a ponderous thing. It must have been a good twenty feet long."

"And Mr. Feldman's car?"

"Paul's car is much smaller. It's Japanese, I think."

Bingo! Got what I needed.

"Miss Early, did you happen to see any other vehicle stop at the Feldmans' on the morning of February 15?"

"No, I didn't. After I finished my coffee, I went grocery shopping."

"Thank you Miss Early. It's been a pleasure. No further questions."

Mimms rose with a quizzical look on her face. "Miss Early, the strange blue car parked in front of the defendant's house surely made you curious?"

"No. People have visitors all the time."

"Well ma'am, when the big black car drove up, that certainly piqued your interest?"

"Objection. The prosecutor is leading the witness."

"Sustained."

"I'll rephrase, Your Honor. When the big black car drove up, were you curious about who it was?"

"Young woman, you want the people in this room to think that I'm a nosy old woman. I'm not. When that car drove up, I thought that Paul was probably having a business meeting. I didn't see who was in the car, because I got up to go into the kitchen. Furthermore, I didn't care who was in the car."

"I'm sorry if I offended you, Miss Early, but the fact is you do notice quite a bit from your window in the TV room. Don't you?"

"Objection, leading. The prosecutor is attempting to impeach her own witness."

"Sustained. Cut out the leading questions, Ms. Mimms."

Smug, after having gotten what she wanted, Mimms said, "I have no further questions for this witness, Your Honor."

THE COMMONWEALTH RESTED its case against Paul Feldman without the flourish it wanted. But Bari knew that it had done serious damage. Despite the jury's normal inclination to side with the husband, the sympathies were really all with the Commonwealth. The victim was a decorated cop and nobody likes a cop killer.

During jury selection, it had became clear that the jury believed there was a "thin blue line" that stood between law-abiding citizens and anarchy. Everybody believed it. Bari believed it. The jury would want to convict, and the Commonwealth had given them more than enough ammunition.

If they survived alternate selection, Bari could count on the two ringers on the jury to at least hang it and give the defense a mistrial. Yeah, and the Commonwealth would re-file the case the same day. Then what? Paul would have to face another trial with God knows what results. Bari wasn't sure how, but he knew that they had to win it all the first time. This time.

CHAPTER EIGHTEEN

PUTTING TOGETHER BILLING SHEETS IS at once a royal pain in the ass and a gratifying pleasure. As he went through the sheaf of receipts and the items on his check register, Cammy saw that expenses in the Feldman case would exceed any case he'd worked on. The fun part would be figuring the cost of his services.

There was an unopened bill from Causeway Investigations sitting on his desk. Cammy played the game of trying to guess what he would have billed a brother PI for the same services he had received, as he slid the letter opener in the envelope.

Inside, there was a cover letter from Clyde Harrow that said: "Dear Cammy, I've got to bill you something, so how about you buy dinner next time you're out my way? If I can be of further help, let me know. Regards, Clyde Harrow." There were three more pages stapled together with a Post-it note at the top that said, "This is Lupo's criminal history."

Lupo's rap sheet was surprisingly thin. He had pulled time for extortion and mail fraud. There were two assaults (dismissed) and a felon-in-possession of a firearm. His most recent arrest, which Harrow had helpfully highlighted, was on a warrant for nonpayment of a traffic fine. That arrest was on February 14. He was released from custody at noon the following day. "Omigod!" Cammy shouted. He drove the three blocks to the law offices, bounced up over the curb, and parked half-assed in the parking lot. He then sat, stood and paced in Bari's outer office for a half hour reading and rereading Lupo's rap sheet.

When Bari and Louis finally got back to the firm after court, Cammy was a wreck. "Joe, we have to talk right away" said Cammy, as he followed Bari to his office.

"Sure Cam." Bari put down his trial case and poured them both a drink. "Damn, you sure are jittery. What's up?"

"I got a bill today from that PI I worked with in Miami. He included Lupo's rap sheet. Lupo couldn't have killed Carey. He was in custody in Miami on February fifteenth until noon on a fucking traffic warrant."

Bari hung up his suit coat slowly. "You sure about that, Cammy?"

"Here it is; it's highlighted."

Bari took the rap sheet from Cammy and tried to penetrate its meaning as though it were an unfamiliar code. But there was no hidden meaning to be mined from the blunt recitation of facts: "Lupo, Jackie, DOB: 08/06/72, aka James Lunt, aka Jack Limo, $256.00 warrant nonpayment of fine: reckless driving 06/20/03. Custody: 5:00 p.m. 2/14/04, released: 12:00 noon 02/15/04."

"What the fuck does it mean? Did Lupo send an associate? What?"

"Let's work backward, Joe," Cammy answered. "You got Lupo's name from Manny Shilla. I flew to Miami and paid Lupo fifty large for the name of the man that hired him. That man turned out to be Paul's old man, who came to your office and copped to hiring Lupo. That should have closed the circle. Except it didn't. We now know that Lupo couldn't have shot Carey, even though he was hired to do it. Ergo, somebody else did the work and Lupo got the credit. The question is, did the real shooter know anything about Lupo?"

Bari was much too far along in the trial to have a mystery dropped in his lap. The prosecution had rested, and he and Louis would begin their case in chief tomorrow morning. He gulped down his drink and poured another. "Jesus Christ!" he said, hitting his desk hard with the palm of his hand.

"Think about this," said Cammy, picking up the pace. "Somebody - not Lupo - shoots Carey. Lupo, who was hired to do it, reads about it in the paper or sees it on TV. What does he do? Does he refund the money old man Feldman paid him? Fuck no. He puts that money in the dark hole and forgets about it. Then here I come and give that asshole another windfall. But, credit where credit is due, I approached him, and all I asked him for was the name of the man that hired him. That greasy cocksucker must be laughing his ass off this very minute. That's a funny, ha-ha, story, but we still don't know who killed Carey. I tell you, Joe. I smell a big fat Lebanese rat."

"Oh, come on, Cam. You think Shilla had it done and blamed it on Lupo. Makes no sense."

"Well, think about it," said Cammy, knitting his brow in concentration. "Shilla gets wind of the deal that Lupo has with Paul's old man. But he decides to do it himself, knowing that if it comes unraveled, it'll be Lupo who goes down. It's too perfect. Only Lupo gets himself arrested and is in custody at the time Carey's brain explodes. Who does that leave? Manny Shilla, that's who," said Cammy.

Bari was seated at his desk making despairing faces and running his fingers through his hair. It also leaves Paul, he thought. "I can't fucking believe I was taken in like that . . . by Shilla himself! Why?"

"Of course, that theory opens up another can of worms," said Cammy.

"Please, Cammy, no more."

"Sorry, Joe, but why, if Shilla wanted Carey dead, would he want to beat Lupo to the punch? Why not just sit back and let Lupo do his dirty work for him? It doesn't cost him a dime, and his hands are clean. Now that's perfect."

"Who the hell knows? I can't think straight right now," said Bari.

"On the other hand, maybe Shilla has him killed because he wanted the satisfaction of taking out somebody who fucked him," said Cammy.

"Manny Shilla? Not in a million years," said Bari. "I talked to him. That Shilla is a practical sonofabitch. Money comes first, always. Do you think he would have lasted this long if he were ruled by petty emotions?"

Cammy took the seat in front of the desk. "We're talking about a Lebanese syndicate guy, right? And you call revenge 'petty'? Not with those fuckers. They invented revenge. All right, suppose I change the facts. Shilla has Carey iced before he learns about Lupo. He waits until Paul goes out of town and then he strikes," said Cammy with a chopping motion.

Bari and Cammy had brainstormed before, but never under this kind of pressure. Regardless, what they finally came up with today would determine whether Bari brought Shilla into the case. Bari knew that if he brought Shilla in, everyone connected with the defense was in mortal danger.

"Why would Shilla lay himself wide open for trouble? Hell, everyone in that world knew that Carey fucked Shilla," Bari suggested.

"I don't think Shilla cared," said Cammy. "He might have thought that since Carey was on his payroll, that made Carey fair game. The cops have Paul, because Paul makes the most sense as a perp, but if they thought it was Shilla, they'd go after him."

"Yeah, Cammy, I see your point," said Bari too exhausted to argue further.

"Shilla won you over, Joe."

"I suppose. But fuck Shilla. Now I'm thinking about calling Stubby Minetti as a witness."

"When I served Stubby with your subpoena back before you met with Shilla, he acted like it was his death warrant. Even without Shilla, Stubby would just as soon take a seat in the electric chair as the witness chair, but now he's scared out of his gourd."

"I can imagine, Cammy, but goddamm it Stubby has personal knowledge of Carey relieving Shilla of that forty Gs," said Bari. "And Shilla, that *scrifosa,* has no one to blame but himself in this fucking deal. He had Carey zeroed out, and then he tried to throw us off with that phony Lupo story,"

Cammy was lying on Bari's sofa "resting his eyes." His fingers were laced on his chest and his knees were hooked over the armrest. "I don't know if I told you, but Stubby and I go way back. I lived with Stubby one summer. I was six years old, and my daddy was doing ninety days for pandering. Daddy asked Stubby if I could work for him till he got out. Stubby was good to me, and I had a lot of fun that summer."

"If you felt a loyalty to Stubby, why didn't you let Aaron serve the warrant?" asked Bari.

"Wouldn't dream of it. Stubby would know Aaron worked for me, and he wouldn't like it," replied Cammy not moving. "You know as well as I do that if a bookie like Stub testifies that he knows something about the Carey business, the cops will be all over him."

"And you know that a case like this always has its casualties. I'm sorry about Stubby, Cam, but we've got to have him."

"The thing is," said Cammy, "even if he doesn't testify, it'll be the same thing with the cops. Either way, Stub loses his livelihood. He's also got to tell Shilla."

"WE HAVE TO face facts, Joe," said Louis. "We're barely staying even with the Commonwealth. And the jury . . . the goddamn jury looks like fourteen tombstones sitting there."

"But if we dwell on those facts, Art, we'll lose," said Bari. "They don't have a case, in my view. In fact, now that it's half time, we should hit Jones with a written motion for dismissal."

Half time comes at the end of the prosecution's case. A half-time motion to dismiss for lack of sufficient evidence is standard in every criminal trial in every courtroom throughout the United States and its territories, but they are usually perfunctory voice motions. "Your Honor, the defense moves for dismissal because the prosecution has failed to present evidence sufficient for a conviction."

Bari knew that defense lawyers flirt with malpractice if they fail to bring a half-time motion, despite the fact that well over ninety percent of them are denied by the trial judge. Still, trial judges are paranoid when it comes to the court of appeals and the horror of being reversed. Bari's hope was that he could make Jones look over his shoulder and grant a persuasive written motion to dismiss.

"Okay, I'll get right on it," said Louis, gathering himself and trying hard to ignore the hyenas of defeat laughing and howling in his ear.

"COME ON IN, Paul," said Bari motioning to the sofa. "How are you and Marian bearing up?"

"I'm doing fine, Joe. Marian, not so good. She knows she has to testify, and she's worried about it. She can't stand the head prosecutor, and she's afraid she'll blow up at her on the stand."

"I think maybe I should talk to her again. Just remember one thing, Paul, as long as Marian limits her answers to 'yes' or 'no' with little or no elaboration, the prosecutor can't lay a glove on her."

"How do you think it's going, Joe?"

"I'm encouraged by how it's going," he lied. "The Commonwealth's case is a house of cards. They jumped too soon and indicted you, and now they're scratching to get past reasonable doubt."

"You seem a little tense."

"That's normal, Paul. As long as this case lasts, I'm tense. *If you knew what I knew about this fucking case,* thought Bari, *you'd understand why I'm tense, old friend.* "But don't worry - that's what Art and I are for, and like I said, it's normal."

"Do you think I'll have to testify?"

"My golden rule is that defendants never testify, but in truth, I never know until I begin putting on my case," said Bari. "It's a matter of feel. If I think the jury wants to hear from the defendant, then yes, I'll have the defendant testify. You have to be prepared and ready in any case."

Bari knew from hard experience that you could know somebody for years and see them operate in every conceivable situation, and still be surprised at their performance on the witness stand. Paul might be as cool as Thelonious Monk on the stand, but you never knew for sure. You go over a defendant's testimony again and again; then they take the stand and start arguing with the prosecutor. Damn.

"Now, we've gone over your testimony. On direct, listen carefully and answer truthfully, but don't elaborate. On cross, keep your answers brief without seeming curt, and again, don't elaborate - she'll nail you if you do. Would it help you to go over it again?" asked Bari.

"No, I've got it. I do think that Marian might benefit from another session; I think that it will shore up her confidence."

Even though an acquittal might turn on the credibility of her testimony, the thought of an alley cat like Marian having a crisis of confidence perversely warmed Bari. "Of course, Paul. Ask her to come by tomorrow after court, and Art and I will go over her testimony."

"HELLO, BARI HERE."

"Mr. Bari, my name is Sidney Foxe, and I represent Emmanuel Shilla, whom I believe you've met."

"Yes, I have met your client, Mr. Foxe. How can I help you?" asked Bari.

"Mr. Shilla met with you on my advice. I thought if you met him, you wouldn't involve him in your trial strategy without a good faith basis to do so."

"You're entirely correct. However, your client gave me a name and implied that he was the guilty party. After a huge outlay of money to investigate that man, it turned out that he was in custody in Miami at the time the victim was killed. I believe that my client and I were ill-used. Expectations were raised, and both time and money were wasted."

"Mr. Bari, I don't believe that Mr. Shilla had any idea that man was in custody at the time, but please allow me to look into the matter further and get back to you."

"Sure. Nice talking with you."

Shilla's lawyer seemed like a decent sort over the phone, and Bari suspected that Shilla was using him too. Stubby Minetti must have told Shilla about his subpoena, and Shilla had sent his lawyer to put the train back on the track. In Bari's view, Shilla had the balls of an elephant.

CHAPTER NINETEEN

"COME IN, MARIAN, and have a seat." Marian was her same gorgeous self, but without the cocky edge this time. "Paul tells me that you'd feel more at ease if you went over your testimony one more time."

"To tell the truth, I'm more worried about style than substance. What I mean is, I want the jury to like me. I don't want them to take one look and say 'I'll never believe this bitch.'"

"I've been thinking about it a lot," said Bari. "Where does that leave them if they don't believe you - logically, I mean? Does disbelieving you make Paul guilty in their minds? I'm going to ask Art to come in, Marian. He knows nothing about our prior conversation, so let's play it just as you say it happened. Okay? And while we're at it, I'll think I'll ask Helen to step in too. She's sharp and I trust her judgment."

What was the rule? Male jurors like beautiful female witnesses and women don't. No, women dislike *sexy* female witnesses. Marian, therefore, had to appear guileless and unself-conscious. Moreover, she had to walk and sit in a way that played down her beauty. It was important to speak evenly; don't be breathy and don't dazzle, and please, don't bat those striking blue eyes.

Bari knew that Louis was even more susceptible to Marian's charms than he was but, in a triumph of character, Louis appeared to keep his mind strictly on her testimony and presentation.

"You were having an affair with Detective Carey, weren't you, Mrs. Feldman?" asked Louis, taking Harriet's role.

"I certainly was not having an affair with Detective Carey, Ms. Atkins."

"You would have this jury believe that he was in your bedroom on police business while your husband was away on business?"

"That is what happened."

"You told the investigative officer that you and Detective Carey were standing side by side looking out the bedroom window when he was murdered?"

"Yes. Actually, we were trying to open the window."

"Isn't it true that you and Carey were in bed together when he was shot?"

"Objection," said Bari. "Your Honor, that question has been asked and answered. Sustained. Harriet will return to it as often as she can get away with it, Marian, so stay loose. What do you think so far, Helen?"

"I like her testimony," said Helen. "She wants to tell the truth - that's what comes through. She has the right amount of outrage at questions about intimacy between her and Carey. If you continue to give straight answers, with a touch of indignation, Mrs. Feldman, you'll be fine. If you get angry, or if you dissolve into tears, I think you'll lose them."

"I agree," said Louis. "Keep your head, and let Atkins's questions wash over you like surf on stone. She'll be the one the jury ends up hating."

They went through Marian's full direct and cross until everyone was satisfied, including Marian. At the end, they all shared a drink of single malt Scotch, courtesy of Louis.

"Thanks for coming in, Marian. I will be handling your direct testimony and you're good to go," said Louis.

After Marian had gone, the three of them did a private post mortem. "I wish she wasn't such a knockout," said Louis. "The jury will think that Carey was a fool if he didn't make a move on her."

"I can tell that she's a hothead when she's under attack," said Helen. "That's your biggest worry. If the prosecutor gets under her skin . . ."

JUDGE JONES DENIED their beautifully reasoned half time motion to dismiss for insufficiency of the Commonwealth's evidence. "Yeah, I know you're disappointed, Joe," said Louis. "So am I, but at least we made a good record."

Big fucking deal. Bari shuffled through papers to avoid responding. He knew better than Louis that the Virginia court of appeals wouldn't overturn a criminal verdict against a white guy in a million years. The record be damned.

The defense led off with Harry Ames, with Louis doing the questioning. As Louis was taking Ames through his history with Paul, Bari was all admiration. Never had he seen a more credible witness. Ames's praise of Paul was neither too little nor too much, and Harriet's cross did nothing to reduce his stature as a character witness.

We picked up a few points with Ames, thought Bari. Too bad the system doesn't allow paid witnesses. I'd have Ames testify in all my trials.

Bari called the roly-poly cashier from long term parking at the airport. She identified the timed receipt she had given to Paul as he left.

"Oh, yes sir, I recognize him. He's sitting right over there," she said pointing to Paul. "He looks a lot better today. He looked terrible on that day he paid me for parking. He gave me the money and then opened the door and threw up right on the black top."

"No further questions."

Mimms came crisply to the point. "You were arrested for possession of cocaine two years ago, weren't you?"

"Objection, irrelevant, and the Commonwealth knows it's irrelevant," said Bari. "Whether or not the witness was arrested for possession does not bear on her competency or truthfulness."

"Sustained. Cut it out," said Judge Jones.

But the damage was done. The average juror assumed that anyone who fooled around with cocaine would do anything, including lie under oath. Harriet's young protégée had learned her lessons well. She'd be ready to step into Harriet's poisonous stilettos in no time.

LOUIS CALLED THE twelve year old neighbor who lived diagonally across the street from Paul and Marian. She had been home sick with a cold. From her bed upstairs, she could easily see the front of the Feldman home and the driveway.

"A UPS delivery man parked his truck in Paul and Marian's driveway and went in. I saw him leave five minutes later."

"How do you know it was February fifteenth?" asked Louis.

"Because it was Monday and I was, like, sick."

"Your Honor, I have her class attendance record here. It's on school stationery, and it has been notarized. This document has been marked by the clerk for identification, and the defense offers it as evidence."

"Ms. Atkins?" asked Jones.

Harriet inspected the school record with an attitude of exaggerated skepticism, before giving a grudging: "No objection."

"Did you happen to see any car parked in the driveway?"

"There was a blue car there."

"Any other car beside that one?"

"No, but I was asleep off and on."

"Nothing further."

Harriet rushed over like a playmate. The little girl scrunched down in the witness chair.

"You wear glasses, don't you?" asked Harriet in her most cloying voice.

"Yes."

"You didn't have them on while you were lying in bed, did you?"

"I don't know. I could still see."

"I'm only suggesting that you might be mistaken about the UPS man and the day he stopped on your street."

"No ma'am."

"Now you were absent from school on February fifteenth *and* February sixteenth, weren't you?"

"Yes."

"Then you can't be sure whether you saw the delivery man on the fifteenth or the sixteenth, can you?"

"Yes, because on Tuesday, February sixteenth, my mom took me into the clinic early in the morning, and we didn't get back home until, like, late in the afternoon."

Harriet ended her cross of the little girl with as much grace as she could summon under the circumstances.

Neither Bari nor Louis could guess how much weight the jury would give to the testimony of a twelve year old girl who wore glasses and was sick at the time. The important thing was that Harriet hadn't made a dent in her.

Louis called a UPS supervisor as a witness. The supervisor testified that there was no scheduled UPS delivery to the Feldman address. He also testified that UPS had received calls reporting a truck in the neighborhood on the fifteenth.

This was a fortuitous confluence of skillful questioning, hard work, and a lucky break that defense lawyers dream about. Cammy had placed the fictional UPS deliveryman in the little girl's mind so firmly that the picture of him parking his truck at the Feldmans and making a delivery on the morning of the fifteenth was unshakable.

Cammy had also discovered that on the morning of the fifteenth, a real live UPS man who had something going with a housekeeper a block over was in the neighborhood. Seems he had dropped by for a morning play date in the guest bedroom. These happy circumstances teed up the tale of an assassin disguised as a UPS delivery man for Bari's closing argument.

Next, the defense put on its traffic engineer from Roads Port University. He testified that given the amount traffic the morning of the fifteenth and the number of traffic lights between the airport and Paul's home, it would have been virtually impossible for him to have driven home from the airport in time to park and murder Carey.

"You said 'virtually impossible.' You don't mean absolutely impossible, correct?"

"I mean that there might be some ideal race car driver in an ideal race car together with ideal conditions - little or no traffic and green lights all the way - that would allow for the possibility that the distance from the airport to 800 Brentwood could be driven in thirty-five or forty minutes."

"How long would it take a sick man to drive the same distance?"

"If he stopped along the way, well over an hour, maybe two hours."

Bari and Louis followed up the traffic expert with their forensic pathologist, also from Roads Port University.

"Doctor, are you saying that it's impossible to nail down the time of death?"

"What I'm saying about the time of death generally is that it's always an estimate, except in cases where there is some disinterested party present with a watch, as there is at an execution. In this case, there is a dispute whether the victim died before or after ten o'clock, and I'm saying that there is at least a two hour range in which he died, and that it's impossible to be more exact than that."

"Was the victim's body moved after death?"

"There is no way for a forensic pathologist to know whether the body in this case was moved. After lividity is fixed, which takes several hours, then perhaps if the body is repositioned so that the lividity is upside of the body or the top of the body, then yes. That wasn't the case here. There were signs of lividity in the body, but they were right where you'd expect to find them in a body lying face down, namely, on the belly, thighs and chest."

Harriet tried to make hay out of the fact that the defense's forensic expert hadn't actually examined the body and wasn't therefore entitled to express an expert opinion. "No I didn't examine the body. I didn't need to. I read Doctor Mason's report, a careful reading of which will demonstrate that he and I agree, or at least we don't disagree."

BARI CLEARED THE firm's conference room of other lawyers and had sandwiches delivered by a lunchroom up the street. Bari, Louis and the Feldmans huddled around the end of the long conference table that was used mainly for depositions and settlement conferences.

"I'll put Marian on right after lunch," said Art. "It'll go fine, Marian, if you don't let Harriet get to you. Actually, I'm not worried about you at all."

"Will I take the stand?" Paul asked.

"I don't think it'll be necessary, Paul," said Bari. "You'll testify only if there's something to gain, otherwise no."

"Gain? How?"

"Let's say that S.O.B. Atkins muddies the waters somehow," Bari replied. "Then it might be important to put you on to clarify. I can't think of a specific example right at the moment, but . . ."

"You mean if we're losing, don't you Joe? Then you'll put me on."

"If we're losing, Paul, then certainly you'll take the stand. You might also take the stand if Atkins and her young torpedo begin screwing up. If they cross-examine the defendant and don't do any damage, then we win for sure. None of that is clear as we sit here. You understand, Paul, I know you do," Bari said.

"I'm going to pass on the sandwich," said Marian. "I'm a little jittery."

BOTH THE DEFENSE team and the Commonwealth made their way into the courtroom through the judge's chambers to avoid the crush of spectators and media.

"The defense calls Marian Feldman to the stand."

With her head high and shoulders back, Marian walked quickly to the stand and was sworn in. She couldn't have looked lovelier or less likely to have committed adultery with Detective Carey. When she took her seat, her suit skirt remained over her knees, which she held to one side, her legs crossed at the ankles. Bari was proud of her, so far, for her willingness and skill in looking the part of the much-maligned, but unquestionably irreproachable, wife of the accused.

Louis smoothly guided her through the preliminaries, which included her education and her extensive service with noble and sympathetic charitable organizations. Once again, Bari admired how monstrously clever of Marian to have carefully built so unassailable a resume that had until now insulated her from gossip.

"Mrs. Feldman, please tell this court in your own words what happened the morning of February fifteenth."

"Twice during the previous week, I heard noises outside our home. At first I thought that it was a tree branch in the wind scratching on the side beneath the bedroom window. I woke my husband and he heard it too."

"Objection. The witness can't testify as to what the defendant heard," Harriet said.

"Sustained."

"Continue, Mrs. Feldman," said Louis.

"Then on the night of the fourteenth, I heard it again. This time, it sounded more deliberate, like a person trying to get in. I woke Paul again, and it stopped."

"What happened next?" asked Louis.

"The next morning, Paul left on a business trip, and I was afraid of someone breaking in while I was at home alone. I called Detective Carey and asked him to investigate, if he had the time."

"Why did you call Detective Carey?"

"I had met Detective Carey at a book fair the Junior League was sponsoring. He was talking to another League member, Liz Harris, and she introduced us, and he gave me his card."

"Please go on."

"Detective Carey came by, and I showed him where the noises had come from: below a window in the bedroom. As we were trying to get the window open, there was a deafening noise, and Detective Carey fell to the floor on his face."

"Then what happened?"

"I had no idea what had happened until I saw the wound in the back of his head. I shook his arm and screamed out his name, but he didn't move, and I knew he was dead. When I stopped trembling, I called 911."

"Did you see who shot Detective Carey?"

"No. At that moment, the Detective and I were trying to open the bedroom window - it was painted shut - and our backs were turned to the door where the shot came from."

"Your witness." Louis walked to defense table, winked at Bari and took his seat.

Bari had decided that of the two of them, Louis would do far better with Marian on the stand. Louis's knowledge of Marian was limited, and she would be much more comfortable with him because of it. Bari congratulated himself. He was right. Marian was perfect so far.

Harriet rose from the Commonwealth's table and walked over toward the jury and then turned to face Marian; her jaw was set sideways, and her whole upper body was puffed up with incredulity and contempt.

"Those mythical noises you heard the week prior to February fifteenth were simply to provide you with a reason to invite Detective Carey over, were they not?"

"No, they were not."

"You knew the defendant was supposed to go out of town, so you planned to bed Detective Carey well in advance, didn't you?" Harriet's tone dripped malice.

"No," answered Marian, looking straight into Harriet's eyes. A hint of color showed high on Marian's cheeks. Louis, alarmed, looked over at Bari.

"Then why didn't you simply call the police to investigate the so-called noises outside your bedroom window?"

"Because, with Paul leaving, I wanted the disturbance investigated right away."

"And you knew Detective Carey wouldn't disappoint, correct?"

"I knew nothing, but I thought I'd call anyway."

"In fact, you had other plans for Detective Carey and yourself, didn't you?"

"I don't know what you're getting at, Ms. Atkins."

"That you planned to have sex with Detective Carey right in the same bed you share with your husband?"

"No. Absolutely not."

"You were, in fact, having sex with Detective Carey when he was shot, weren't you?"

"No."

"And you redressed Detective Carey and cleaned up the blood and yourself before you dialed 911?"

"Your question is offensive and wrong," answered Marian, who hadn't changed position in the witness chair nor taken her eyes off Harriet.

"Are you here to tell this jury, Mrs. Feldman, that you've never been unfaithful to your husband?"

"Objection. Irrelevant. Your Honor, the Commonwealth has no basis for asking such an insulting question."

"Approach."

Both teams approached the bench. Bari was steamed. That bitch Atkins would stop at nothing to nail Marian.

The judge bent forward to whisper, "Is what defense counsel said true, Ms. Atkins?"

"First of all, Your Honor, this question goes to motive," Harriet replied. "The defendant might not have known anything about his wife and the victim in this case, but he might have had good reason to suspect that his wife would misuse his time away from home, you know, for assignations with others. As for a basis, I do have a good faith basis, and I will prove it before this trial is over."

Bari's heart sank, and he could feel Louis shift nervously beside him. Harriet's promise to prove a good faith basis could only mean that her question about fidelity was a trap. She was going to parade as many of Marian's past lovers as she could find to testify in rebuttal if Marian's answer under oath was negative.

The defense's case had suddenly sprung a dangerous leak, and they'd have to get Cammy on it right away.

"All right, everyone get back . . . the objection is overruled. The witness may answer."

"No, I have never been unfaithful to my husband."

Louis inclined his head away from Paul and whispered to Bari: "Settle down Joe, we'll find a way to keep whoever she has off the stand."

Bari was silent for a moment. Then, he whispered back: "That's the problem. We don't know who the fuck she has."

Harriet walked up and back in front of Marian, the index finger of her right hand against her cheek, her right elbow cradled in her left hand. Suddenly she stopped and faced the witness chair, hands on hips. "Tell me, Mrs. Feldman, what did Detective Carey conclude about the disturbance outside your bedroom window before your husband blew his brains out?"

"Objection, Your Honor!" Louis roared, his fists on the defense table as he stood trembling with fury. "The question assumes facts that are embarrassingly not in evidence. The prosecu*trix* is trying to harass Mrs. Feldman."

"Dial it back, Ms. Atkins," said Jones.

Harriet's attempts to goad and rattle Marian availed nothing. Bari knew the rigatoni would hit the fan on rebuttal, but for the moment he gloried in Marian's conduct under cross. Harriet's final questions elicited answers that crowned Marian's performance with laurel.

"You testified that you didn't see who murdered Detective Carey. Isn't that right?"

"As I said, my back was turned."

"Was it that your back was turned or that your legs were up?"

Louis and Bari jumped from their chairs, but before either could yell, Marian stood. Looking down at

Harriet, she answered in a loud, clear voice. "Ms. Atkins, you are a filthy woman."

The spectators loved it! There was clapping here and there and laughter and other sounds of approval before Judge Jones shut it down. Bari stole a look at the jurors. They were scowling at Harriet, and a few were whispering to their neighbors. Louis caught it too, and fought back a smile; might as well enjoy the fun while it lasted.

Some of Bari's anxiety eased. If Harriet had been successful on cross in showing that Marian was a slut instead of a respectable young society matron, the jurors would turn on Marian and Paul. The punch line would then be inescapable: The defendant, suspecting his duplicitous wife was fucking around on him, returns from the airport and kills her lover. Q.E.D.

Harriet would realize, of course, that under that theory premeditation was easy, but premeditation to do what? The defendant obviously didn't plan to shoot the victim in advance. He used the victim's gun, which he could not have known would be handily hanging from his holster when he arrived.

So what? Harriet had already offered Bari and Louis murder two in exchange for a plea. She no doubt thought that Paul Feldman would go away for a minimum of fifteen years, and the case would still go in her win column.

But with a rebuttal witness in the wings, one who would directly contradict Marian Feldman's claim of marital fidelity, capital murder was in play again.

Nevertheless, Bari knew that he still had his two bent jurors to fall back on. But a successful rebuttal witness would make it impossible to get an acquittal. The two ringers could argue for a not guilty verdict until they went hoarse, and the remaining ten would ignore them.

CHAPTER TWENTY

CAMMY COMBED RICHMOND FRANTICALLY looking for Richard Kingman. He sailed in and out of all the hotel bars and the college hangouts. He finally found Kingman half drunk in another uptown bar, one that catered to politicians and their constant companions, the press.

This joint didn't figure to be in Kingman's bailiwick. There were too many hard asses and too few jazzy women. Cammy thought that maybe the jerk was hiding from one of his horsey mommas.

"Hey Rich, didn't think I'd see you in this joint. Can I buy you a drink?" Cammy signaled the bartender to bring two of what Kingman was drinking.

"Oh hi. I needed a change of pace. What are you doing here?"

Cammy chuckled. "I come here sometimes to catch up on the political dirt. It's fun to see how the sausage is made, so to speak."

"But man, the broads that come in here . . ." Kingman held his nose.

"Not Miss America."

"Phew!" Kingman exclaimed, making a face.

Cammy paid for the drinks from a money clip, with the crossed tennis rackets motif, and pulled a barstool under him.

"Rich, a little bird told me that you're going to testify in the Feldman trial after all."

"Yeah, the fucking prosecutor is going to make me."

"How's she going to do that, Richard?"

"Says she's going to prosecute me for an old assault unless I testify I fucked Marian Feldman."

"Was that a felony assault, Rich?"

"I'm afraid so."

"When was it?"

"Oh shit, I don't know . . . two years ago, I think."

"Hang on a minute, Richard. I've got to make a phone call."

The public phone was back by the restrooms. Cammy could see Kingman bobbing and weaving at the bar while he called Bari. Booze was beginning to take a toll on Kingman's features. The flesh on his face was losing its tone and it hung heavily from his cheek bones. His eyes were bloodshot and hooded. Even his fingers were swollen and his college ring looked like it would have to be hack sawed off.

The simple fuck probably feels bad about getting kicked out of UVa, thought Cammy. But he's got to know that only dorks wear their college rings.

"Well?"

"Tough luck. There is no statute of limitations on felonies in this state," said Cammy.

"Shit, I didn't even think about any statute of limitations."

"One thing I'm curious about, Richard," said Cammy. "Was Marian Feldman making it with anyone other than you and the cop?"

"I wouldn't put it past the bitch, but I don't think so."

"By the way, Rich, if you change your mind about showing up in court, the prosecutor will lock you up as a material witness. So mum's the word."

"How do you know so much? Hey, who the hell are you?"

"I'm your friend, Richard," said Cammy putting his arm around Kingman's shoulders.

As an inducement to blow off his court appearance, Cammy planned to mail Kingman an irresistible all-expenses-paid week for two for race week at Laguna Seca, California. Included were air fare, a four star hotel, and invitations to all the best parties. Race week fell just when Harriet would need him in court.

That prize would be wrapped in some phony contest that Kingman would have forgotten he had entered. "To you, Richard Kingman, for winning dumbbell of the month award . . ." He wouldn't care that he didn't remember it or what the hell it was for when he saw "Laguna Seca", "all-expenses paid," and "parties."

"YOUR HONOR, THE defense calls Anthony Minetti to the stand."

Stubby rose to enter the Bermuda rectangle, that space on the judge's side of the rail that separated the spectators from the court. As he came through the swinging gate, Harriet jumped to her feet. "Your Honor, may we see you in chambers?"

"There will be a ten minute recess," said the judge. The bailiff led the jury from the courtroom. The judge nodded and Bari, Louis, Harriet, Mimms and the court reporter waited briefly while the judge descended from the bench and headed for his chambers. He motioned wordlessly for everyone to sit in front of his desk, and he took the high-back leather desk chair behind it.

Leaning forward to give Judge Jones a good look at her tits, Harriet said, "The defense is putting that Minetti witness on when they know he's only going to take the Fifth Amendment to all their questions."

"Your Honor, the witness is a small-time bookmaker," said Bari, "and he's afraid of prosecution when his bookmaking necessarily comes to light under oath. We request that the court grant the witness use immunity so that he can give very important testimony."

"The Commonwealth objects, Your Honor," said Harriet urgently, "Minetti's testimony is irrelevant, and should not in any circumstance be a shield for his illegal activities."

"This is a capital murder trial, Your Honor," said Bari.

"All right, Mr. Bari, I'll grant your witness very narrow use immunity. I'll rule on the relevancy issue when it comes up."

"I'd like a few minutes alone with the witness to explain the situation to him, Your Honor."

"Hurry it up, Mr. Bari."

Bari and Louis ushered a befuddled Stubby Minetti out to the hall. "Mr. Minetti, Judge Jones has granted you something called 'use immunity.' That means that you won't be able to take the Fifth, but it also means that you can't be prosecuted now or in the future for anything you say on the stand ever, unless the prosecution can show that they developed information about your bookmaking from some other source," said Bari. "They'll never be able to make that showing."

"What happens if I still refuse to testify?" Bari could hear the tumblers in Stubby's nimble mind falling into place. Stubby was a man who dealt with hustlers and thieves every day, and now here were two lawyers trying to doubletalk him. Not a chance.

"The court will hold you in contempt and either fine you substantially or put you in jail until you agree to testify. Maybe you should talk to your own lawyer first before you do anything," said Louis, taking an elbow shot from his partner.

"Yeah, that's what I want to do," said Stubby, relieved.

Bari, Louis and Stubby filed back into court and Bari approached the bench. "Your Honor, the witness would like to speak with an attorney before testifying."

"I don't blame the witness," said the judge. He looked at the clock approaching four o'clock and put the court in recess until one-thirty the following afternoon.

BARI AND LOUIS walked back to their offices in a shower that ended in minutes. The moving clouds parted and the sun shone hot enough to force them underneath building overhangs and business awnings. "I wish you wouldn't have suggested that Minetti talk to a lawyer, Art," said Bari. "We might never get his testimony now."

"Come on, Joe. The man's got exposure. We can't advise him; we represent Paul. It's a clear conflict of interest. I'm surprised the judge or Harriet didn't insist on it."

"The judge wants to get this trial over with, and I bet Harriet didn't think of it," said Bari. "It's no wonder. Her whole bent is to nail some poor bastard, not protect him."

Louis had had more contact with Harriet than Bari, for which Bari was thankful. But he could see that the very idea of any witness consulting a lawyer before testifying would be anathema to her. In a universe of her own design, everyone would put their trust in the perfect justice of the Commonwealth and in Harriet, its tireless paladin. Oh brother.

CAMMY FOLLOWED MINETTI back to Richmond to see who he talked to and to make sure Minetti was on the road back to Roads Port by noon.

The press had already made the Carey-Minetti-Shilla connection. Somebody blabbed to the press, Cammy reckoned. Maybe it was Buzz, maybe somebody in Minetti's entourage, maybe somebody else with a big fucking mouth.

BY ONE O'CLOCK the next afternoon, the courtroom was packed. To Bari's dismay, word had spread that Minetti's testimony would be explosive if he testified. Reporters speculated that since Stubby was a bookie, he might refuse to testify. Contempt citation be damned. In either case, the media and regular court spectators lived for these moments of high courtroom drama. But Bari knew that unless they could get Stubby's testimony, they were screwed.

The defense and prosecution teams were in place and standing when Judge Jones swept in and took his seat, motioning for the lawyers to do the same.

"Is there anything before I send for the jury?"

Bari took the question. "Your Honor, our witness hasn't arrived yet. We called his phone number at noon, but there was no answer. He must be on his way."

"All right, I'll give him a few minutes. In the meantime, let's take care of some housekeeping. Minetti is your final witness, correct? Okay. When he finishes his testimony, we'll go over the jury instructions. After that, I'll charge the jury and then hear closing arguments. As of now, I can see no reason to sequester the jury during deliberations, but if either side wants to argue for sequestration, I'll hear that argument now."

Bari and Louis eyed Harriet and Mimms who eyed them back. Neither side had anything to gain by sequestration at this point, and they knew it. Each prayed nonetheless that their opponents would request sequestration so that they could find a way to blame them for causing the jurors the pain-in-the-ass inconvenience of being cooped up in a hotel with cardboard food and no privacy.

"No, Your Honor," both sides said in unison.

"All right; we're in recess till two."

"Do you think Minetti would stiff the trial? I mean shit, this is serious," said Louis, standing up and looking toward the rear of the courtroom.

"What will you do Joe? I mean if he doesn't show up?" asked Paul, who up until now had been a rock.

"I'll move for a material witness warrant to have him picked up and brought here," said Bari. "The thing is that the judge probably won't grant it. Harriet will argue that Minetti's testimony isn't really material, and she would be legally right. But let's not borrow trouble."

The courtroom phone rang so softly that only the clerk could hear it. She motioned to Bari with the receiver that the call was for him.

"Hello, Bari speaking."

"Fifteen minutes ago, the cops pulled Stubby Minetti out of the James River with a bullet hole in his head. Also, we have your PI. Leave Manny Shilla's name out of the trial, Counselor, or we'll give him the same treatment."

Before Bari could ask any questions, there was a click, and the line went dead.

CHAPTER TWENTY-ONE

"MR. BARI, MR. BARI," SCREAMED the reporters. "The prosecutor said maybe you had something to do with the missing witness."

"Ms. Atkins knows that we received a phone call in court saying that Mr. Minetti was murdered, probably to keep him from testifying," said Bari in his gravest voice. "The Richmond PD pulled him out of the James River an hour ago, shot in the head, just like Detective Carey. Also our investigator, Cammy Brown, has been kidnapped and is being held. That's all we can say at the moment. Mr. Louis and I will be doing all we can to find out more about this shocking turn of events."

The media became hysterical. This was a perfect story. The defendant was rich and his cheating wife was gorgeous. And, the wife's murdered boyfriend was a cop. Could anything be better than this? YES! A key defense witness, an underworld figure, had just been murdered before he could testify. Shot! In the head. Could it get any better than this? YES, YES, YES! The defense investigator had been kidnapped!

The judge had given Bari and Louis the remainder of the week off. Three days to find another witness. If they couldn't find a replacement, they would be forced to rest their case on Monday morning.

"Held by who?" one voice shouted. "Have they asked for ransom?" bawled another. "Did you know this would happen?" The press continued to spew out questions as Bari and Louis ducked out a side door and trotted down the street.

"It was Shilla, that murderous fuck," said Bari to Louis on their way back to the firm. "And now they've got Cammy."

"I'm scared, Joe. Do you think we should send Sally and Ann out of town until the trial's over?"

"As long as his men have Cammy, Shilla has all the insurance he needs and he knows it. I'll call the chief anyway and ask him to put extra patrols on our homes."

BEFORE YOU COULD say "tabloid journalism," the media interest went national. At least twenty white trucks displaying multicolored channel logos had gathered across the street from the courthouse. The trucks were packed with electronics and bristled with antennas and satellite dishes.

A dozen reporters camped out in front of Bari and Louis's law firm. When the two lawyers came and went, it was the same thing. "Mr. Bari, is it true that . . . ?" "Mr. Louis, it has been reported that . . ."

"Let's be civil, Art. If we hear anything for certain, we'll tell them. Otherwise, *nada*. Agreed?" asked Bari.

"Agreed. I could kick myself for telling Minetti to see a lawyer," said Louis, sick with regret, throwing up his hands and shaking his head. "If it hadn't been for that, Minetti would still be alive and they wouldn't have kidnapped Cammy."

"Forget it, Art. I was dead wrong. It was the right thing to do. Who, but another fucking thug, could have foreseen that Shilla would pull a stunt like this," said Bari, picking up Louis's phone. "Helen, I'm in Art's office. Please get Sidney Foxe on the phone. He's a lawyer in Richmond." To Louis he said, "Let's put this on the speaker."

"Jones warned them not to watch TV news or read the paper, but I hope like hell the jury hears about this. Can you fucking believe it? Another bullet in the head!"

The phone rang and Louis pushed the speaker button. "Mr. Foxe, this is Joe Bari in Roads Port. I suppose you heard the news about Stubby Minetti and Cammy Brown."

"Yes, I did hear about Mr. Minetti. I recognize the other name, but that's all. Very unfortunate about Minetti. I knew him only slightly, and I'm sorry. How can I be of service?"

"First, Shilla and his gorillas have kidnapped Cammy," said Bari. "I want him released immediately. We advised Minetti to talk to a lawyer before he gave testimony down here. Did he talk to you?"

"He did, actually. I told him that I couldn't represent him, that he'd have to talk to someone else."

"And did you pass that information on to Manny Shilla?"

"I'm sorry, Mr. Bari. I can't tell you about any conversation that I did or did not have with my client."

"I understand, Mr. Foxe. Tell Shilla that I know that he had old man Minetti murdered and that if Cammy is harmed in any way, I'll come after him myself." said Bari, slamming the phone down and shaking with rage.

"I gotta call Cammy's dad and tell him, Art. He lives over in Smithfield and he's Cammy's only living relative."

AS IN MOST state capitals, the organs of government in Richmond, Virginia all hover near the statehouse. On the street that ran along one side of a lovely ten-acre expanse called Capitol Square, were City Hall and the state's lower courts. On the adjacent street was the state supreme court, and moving around to the side opposite city hall was the federal court building. This territory was the native environment of politicians, lobbyists, hangers-on and other tawdry types such as Manny Shilla's attorney, who was walking on the sidewalk beside a line of parked cars on his way to lunch.

"Mr. Foxe, get in the car or I'll blow your fucking dick off right here on the street."

The two men got in the back and the black Lincoln Town Car with tinted glass murmured away from the curb and slipped into traffic. The big car deftly made its way through the thickening early afternoon traffic and after negotiating a few turns was soon in a neighborhood as alien to Sidney Foxe as Alpha Centauri.

In less than fifteen minutes after leaving East Main Street in downtown Richmond, the black Lincoln pulled in beside a dilapidated old wood frame house with signs in the windows saying, "Condemned! Do not enter." The Lincoln deposited three men near the back of the house, backed out onto the street and was gone.

"Who are you people? I demand to be released at once!"

"Well Sidney, old boy, my name is Zack Brown and you're going to tell me where my boy is."

ZACK BROWN AND his burley associate had escorted Sidney Foxe inside the creaking old house to a room that had blackout ceiling-to-floor curtains around the inside walls and a six foot rebar cube in the center, wired into a cage. They had taken Sidney's clothes and shoes at gunpoint and shoved him in the cage with an empty plastic bucket in the corner.

"What is it you want?" asked Sidney, scared and humiliated. "Don't you realize that kidnapping is a capital offense in Virginia?"

"I want to know where my boy is, Sidney."

"What boy? What are you talking about?"

"My boy's name is Cammy Brown, and don't play stupid with me again." *I'd like to cap this motherfucker right now,* thought Zack.

"I know of your son. He's a private investigator. But I've never met him. I certainly don't know where he is."

"You don't know it, Sidney, but you're a lost ball in tall grass. Well, maybe your memory will improve in an hour or two."

They returned well after dark with flashlights and arranged them on top of an old chest of drawers to light the cage. Zack had a bag of sandwiches and a large bag of barbeque potato chips for Sidney.

"Well, well Sidney. Has a couple hours in the dark helped your memory any?"

"Please let me out of here. I'm hungry and I can't breathe."

"Here are some Smithfield ham sandwiches and a bag of potato chips," said Zack. "I don't want you to go hungry, I just want to know what that *A*-rab has done with my boy."

Eat those salty ham sandwiches, fool. Enjoy that good food.

Foxe wolfed down the sandwiches and tore open the potato chips, which in normal circumstances, he would scorn to eat.

"Could I have some water, please?"

"Of course, Sidney, of course. Just as soon as you tell me where Cammy is," said Zack grabbing the flashlights and parting the curtains to leave.

"What?" asked Foxe. "Are you going to leave me here? "

"I'll be back tomorrow," said Zack to his associate loud enough for Foxe to hear. "If he starts yelling and won't stop, whip the shit out him with your belt. Don't hit him in the face. Save his face for me."

Except for Cammy, Zack Brown didn't have much he could point to with pride. Every dime he'd ever made was illegal, which he personally didn't care about. It had been fun out-smarting The Man. The problem was Cammy. Cammy knew what he was. He could picture Cammy at a party or with a nice woman making up some story about him. My father is a retired carpenter, or a retired mailman. Something respectable. That was a killer, knowing that your son had to lie about you.

What was, was - and Zack had learned to live with that. The good part of the whole thing was that Cammy had turned out so well. By rights, Cammy should be in the penitentiary for interstate dope dealing or worse. How had he turned out to be such a good boy? Must have been on his mother's side.

That was another thing. Zack's wife, Cammy's mother . . . the memory was painful. He had never told anybody how she had died and he never would. If Cammy knew, that would be the end of Cammy. He'd never see him again. Some things are too much to swallow.

The key ingredient in bootleg whiskey is sugar. The U.S. Treasury Department requires merchants to report any sale over a hundred pounds. And unrecorded, unmarked sugar is almost impossible to come by.

Zack talked a big bootlegger in North Carolina into buying fifty thousand dollars worth of sugar in unmarked hundred pound bags. Zack had an in at a sugar cane processor near Sebring, Florida, or so he told the bootlegger. The bootlegger put up thirty-five thousand in cash as working capital, confident that no one but a fool would attempt anything funny.

The bootlegger didn't know Zack, and Zack wore a disguise anyway. Everything about the deal was phony, but Zack was so slick that the bootlegger never suspected a thing until Zack and his money came up missing. Not good.

The bootlegger put his entire bankroll to the service of finding Zack and Zack's confederates. A month went by, then two, and Zack had relaxed. In fact, he had gone out with some friends on a week-long drunk. When he got back home, he found his wife with her hands chopped off and her head missing. Baby Cammy was crying in his crib. He was covered in filth and flies and near death from dehydration.

Zack buried his wife - well, she wasn't really his wife - and never told a soul what had happened. He had arranged a marriage certificate and a death certificate and the authorities never inquired.

From that sickening, horrendous day on, he had never let Cammy out of his sight, except for that summer Cammy spent with Stubby Minetti when Zack was in jail. Oh, he had allowed Cammy to go to school when the time came, but he was always waiting for him when school let out. And when Cammy got old enough to ask about his momma, Zack had told him that she died of cancer.

ZACK SHOWED UP in late morning with a bag of ice, a gallon of water, and a tall glass.

"Good morning, Sidney . . . Did he behave last night?"

"Been drinking his own piss. Says he's thirsty."

"Please, some water. Please," said Sidney with tears in his eyes. It had been almost twenty-four hours since the sandwiches and potato chips.

"You know the rules, Sidney. Tell me where my boy is and I'll give you something to drink," said Zack putting ice cubes in the glass and pouring water over them until it ran on the floor. As the puddle reached the cage, Foxe tried to put his palm in it when a leather belt whipped across his knuckles. Foxe withdrew his hand with a scream.

"I DON'T KNOW!" Foxe wailed. "If Manny has your son, he would never tell me about it. I swear. Please give me something to drink, sir. I'm diabetic - I'll die if you don't give me some water."

"Okay, Sidney, you've touched me," said Zack opening the cage and handing Foxe the glass of water. Foxe greedily drained the glass. The water did a U-turn when it hit his stomach and Foxe spewed it all over the inside of his cage.

"It was salted, Sidney. Bad joke; I apologize," said Zack laughing at Foxe's misery. Foxe went into a heartbreaking, keening singsong.

"Now, let's get down to business, Sidney. This situation isn't going to improve. If I don't get what I want, I'll leave you here to die of thirst, and you will die a horrible death. I believe a bad man spends eternity in the same shape he died. Can you imagine roaming around hell forever as thirsty as you are now? Think, Sidney. If you don't know Cammy's location, I want to know where Shilla might stash him if he's still alive."

"I don't know," said Sidney in a high whine. Please, for the love of God, give me some water."

"No."

Foxe, near insanity, grabbed the top of his cage and kicked out toward Zack. "You black cocksucker! GIVE ME WATER!"

"Gee Sidney, I like it when you show some spunk . . . okay, give him half a glass."

Zack's partner filled a glass half with water from another container. He was about to open the cage door when Sidney threw himself toward the door, his blazing eyes fixed on the glass.

"Get back! Get back!" said Zack's enforcer, with his belt held over his head ready to strike. Foxe cowered on the opposite side of the cage, sly with madness. The partner came part way into the cage and put the glass down. Then, keeping his eyes on Foxe, he backed out.

Foxe leapt toward the glass, took it with both hands and brought it to his mouth quickly. The condensation caused the glass to slip his grasp and drop to the cage floor where it shattered. Foxe looked at the shards of glass in despair, heaving deep sobs and dropping to his knees. There was nothing left of Sidney Foxe. He was filthy and he stank. He could not reason and he could not resist. He would have murdered his mother for a glass of water.

Zack filled the glass and opened the cage door. "Easy, Sidney. Take the glass and be careful." Foxe listened to Zack's instructions with crazy, slavish attention shaking his head up and down. He took the glass and began to gulp down the water. Zack stopped him, and then let him resume. When he was finished, Zack refilled the glass and Foxe drank that too, but his thirst wasn't completely slaked. Foxe punctuated everything he said with blessings and thanks and begged for more water, which Zack gave him, knowing he would be thirsty again in twenty minutes.

"Manny Shilla leases a warehouse under a different name down by the river. That's the only place I can think of. He'll take a blowtorch to my face and kill my partner if he finds out I told you."

"I want the address of that warehouse, Sidney."

The second Foxe had given him the address, Zack was on his cell phone repeating it to an associate. "Okay Sidney, now we'll just have to see."

A tense hour passed, and finally Zack's cell phone rang. "We found him on the river bank in some bushes. He's broke up bad. They left him for dead."

"Get him to MCV hospital soon as you can, and I'll meet you there."

Before leaving, Zack told his hulking associate, "Stay here with the shyster. I'll be back soon as I see to Cammy."

CHAPTER TWENTY-TWO

"I WANT TO TESTIFY. JOE."

Oh Christ, another client who thinks his sincerity and pure heart will carry the day.

"We've got this thing won, Paul. The jury probably thinks it was a mob hit," said Bari. "We won't gain a thing with your testimony. What if Harriet gets lucky and makes you look bad? Don't do it, Paul."

"I agree," said Louis. "The jury knows your story by now. You left for the airport, you got sick, you drove home. What can you add to that?"

"I believe the jury has a right to hear it from me."

"The jury has no such right, Paul," said Bari. "You're the one with the right not to testify. It's called the Fifth Amendment."

"I know all that. I wasn't speaking about a legal right, and you know it. I think that before the jury deliberates, they should see me testify and hear my voice say that I'm innocent."

"Okay, okay," said Bari. "But first let me ask you a few questions. Ever been drunk?"

"Once or twice."

"Ever been arrested for driving while drunk?"

"Years ago when I was in graduate school."

"Did you try to get out of it?"

"Dad hired a lawyer for me.

"What was his name?"

"I don't remember now. Some attorney from out of state. DeFelice, I think his name was."

"What result?"

"We won. The breathalyzer was required by law to be calibrated weekly and it hadn't been calibrated in over a year."

"Ever go to a shrink?"

"Yes, I am in analysis now."

"What for?"

"Well that's private, actually. All right, I'll tell you. I've been anxious and depressed because I believed I was losing Marian."

"I didn't know any of that stuff, Paul, but if you think Harriet doesn't know all that and a lot more, you're crazy. I'm your lawyer and I'm your friend who loves you. Don't testify."

"DO YOU HAVE another witness, Mr. Bari?"

"No, Your Honor. The defense rests."

"Ladies and gentlemen, I will now read my instructions to you. Please pay close attention. Closing arguments will begin . . ."

"Your Honor, the Commonwealth has rebuttal witnesses."

Bari and Louis braced in their chairs. The hairy monster they dreaded had arrived. A rebuttal witness gives the last testimony a jury hears - testimony that can blow a winning case clean out of the water.

"The defense moves that we end here for today, and start with the issue of rebuttal witnesses first thing tomorrow," said Bari.

"Objection, Your Honor. This is a delaying tactic. The witnesses are here in court and ready to take the stand." Harriet was as pissed as Bari and Louis had ever seen her. Her anger was righteous for once, and even the spectators knew it.

"We're near the end of the day, Your Honor. We anticipate a protracted cross examination, in which case, the witnesses would have to return tomorrow anyway," said Bari.

Judge Jones was looked tired, and he was probably hungry. "Motion granted. The court will be in recess until tomorrow morning at nine."

While everyone was distracted in preparing to leave the courtroom, Joe mouthed the words "in my office" to Marian

"OKAY, MARIAN. IT looks like she's going to call Richard Kingman in rebuttal."

Marian looked desperate. "I thought the judge barred his testimony? How can she spring a witness on you like that, Joe?"

"Kingman will rebut your statement that you've never been unfaithful to Paul. It's allowed. Does Paul know you're here?" asked Bari.

"No, I told him I wanted some time alone. Poor guy. I think he was actually grateful."

Bari hesitated a moment. The trial had been an ordeal. Everybody looked it. Except Marian. Not a wrinkle in her clothes and not a hair out of place. Christ, she's supernatural, he thought. "We talked about Kingman before, Marian. Refresh my memory. Can he hurt us?"

"Not unless the jury believes him," Marian replied.

"Tell me about him."

"He's got a police record. He lives off horsey older women. He's a braggart and a phony. You should be able to make an ass of him on cross. Oh, I just thought of something. There was some gossip about him and his younger sister and incest. At the time, I thought it was probably bullshit, so I never bothered to run it down."

"What the hell did you see . . . never mind."

"See in him? God knows. When I look back, I can't believe it. It happened, and even though you'll never believe me, I'm sorry as hell it happened."

"Okay, Marian. Thanks for coming in. If you think of anything else, anything at all, give me a call."

MARIAN WALKED DIRECTLY to her car and got on I-64 to Richmond. There was no hurry. She wanted to miss the hellish late afternoon city traffic. When the signs said "Richmond 20 miles," she took an exit and stopped in a buffet restaurant for dinner.

When she emerged from the restaurant, daylight was waning. She drove to her and Paul's home and parked the car in the garage and closed the automatic garage doors.

There was still enough natural light coming in to see by. She took off every thing but her panties and snoozed on the sofa.

It was after midnight when she awoke. She felt her way upstairs, so as not to draw the neighbors' attention, and showered luxuriously in a marble shower with as much square footage as a small studio apartment. She dried off, brushed her hair and dressed. She felt her way downstairs, found the liquor cabinet, and polished off a half pint of vodka.

Marian phoned Kingman's condo. No answer. Then she tried Stoney's

"Hello, is Rich Kingman at the bar?"

"Yeah, I'll get him for you," replied the bartender.

"Hello, this is Rich."

"Rich, this is Marian. I'm calling to beg you not to testify in my husband's trial."

"Sorry, Marian, the prosecutor threatened to charge me with an old assault if I don't. Besides, you have it coming the way you treated me."

"For Christ sake, Rich, be reasonable. We weren't really getting along, and you know it."

"Yeah, well you might have had something to do with that, you bitch. I haven't had any trouble since."

"Look, you might be right - you probably are. In fact, I'm sure you are. I'm sorry, I really am. Here's a proposition. You blow town for the trial and I'll make you a rich man. Plus, I'll see you have the best lawyer on the Eastern Seaboard to defend you on the assault."

"No dice, Marian. I'll end up in prison if I leave town."

"At least meet me and let's talk about it."

"Toodle-oo."

Marian looked at the phone. It vibrated with Richard Kingman's hatred, and she realized with a sick, sinking feeling, that left her momentarily dizzy, that all further approaches would be useless. Nonetheless, she had to talk to him face to face. He was a dumb shit, and she just might be able to persuade him. It had always worked before.

Marian got in her car and drove to a small strip mall across the street from Stoney's. All the stores were closed by this time, and Marian found a parking space that gave her a clear view of Stoney's entrance and parking lot.

There it was: Kingman's blood-red Ferrari. He couldn't bear to be away from his buddies and his watering trough for one night, even if it meant driving all the way up to Richmond from Roads Port and back tomorrow morning, 140 miles round trip.

Marian knew that Kingman would mock her in front of his friends if she went in, but if she followed him back to his condo there would be just the two of them. She'd go down on him, if necessary. Maybe then she could get him to listen to reason.

At closing time, a group of customers, maybe ten, loudly exited Stoney's, waking Marian from her nodding snooze. The Ferrari's lights came on as it fishtailed out of the parking lot.

Marian eased out of the strip mall and got behind the Ferrari thirty yards back. To get to his condo, Kingman would stay on Ravenna Parkway until he got to the far side of a concrete bridge that spanned a deep ravine. Then he would turn right and drive for a half mile. His condo was cantilevered, and had a wonderful, terrifying view across and straight down into the ravine.

As the Ferrari approached the bridge, Marian floored it until she came abreast to signal Kingman. After waving, she pulled ahead to pass and lead them to the condo, but instead accidentally cut off the now accelerating Ferrari. The Ferrari swerved sharply to miss her and drove to the right of the bridge's stone railing, becoming airborne out over the ravine.

Marian saw the whole thing in her rear view mirror in hideous, sickening slow-motion. She prayed that no one else saw or heard anything. In fact, the ravine was so deep, that standing on the bridge, you could have barely heard the car crash into smithereens at the bottom. Of course, you would have seen the car's lights crazily making their way down, but the occupants of the condos and other houses that sat along the rim of the ravine had been asleep for hours and saw nothing.

Marian sped to the nearest public phone and called 911 in a high falsetto voice to disguise her own. She was shaking badly, but she managed to drive across town and find US 64. She didn't stop again until she pulled up in front of the beach cottage in Grand View.

When Marian arrived, Paul was up reading. "Oh, Sweetheart, you're back. I was beginning to worry," said Feldman.

"I shouldn't have driven around so long. I'm totally exhausted," said Marian, kissing her husband on his head and heading for the bedroom.

CHAPTER TWENTY-THREE

"THE COMMONWEALTH CALLS RICHARD KINGMAN to the stand."

Kingman was duded out in an olive Armani double breasted suit and low cut loafers with moccasin flaps. As he walked to the stand, Kingman looked around nervously, like something was tracking him.

It took every ounce of discipline that Marian possessed to keep herself from passing out. Lights danced before her eyes and her breathing became noisy enough to cause Mr. and Mrs. Feldman to inquire. Inside, Marian was screaming.

OH MY GOD! WHO WAS IN THE FERRARI?

"It will pass. I'm a little hypoglycemic. Happens when I eat preserves in the morning," said Marian, grateful for not blithering.

MOTHER OF GOD. I CAUSED THE DEATH OF SOMEONE I DIDN'T EVEN KNOW!

Hoping to shield Paul, his parents, but mainly herself from Kingman's salacious testimony, she had killed a stranger. It was an accident, but the poor guy was just as dead. Maybe there was a convent that would take her in, she thought, or maybe she should just take a header off the Ravenna Bridge and be done with it.

Harriet took Kingman through the preliminaries after he was sworn in. He had lived in Richmond all his life except for a short hitch in the Army. He trained horses and was currently unemployed.

"Mr. Kingman, do you know Marian Feldman?"

"Yes, I do."

"For how long?"

"Over a year. A year and a half, maybe."

"Describe your relationship with Mrs. Feldman."

Kingman mumbled something and straightened his tie, obviously avoiding Marian's unblinking stare, even while now and then stealing a furtive peek.

"Would you speak up, Mr. Kingman?"

"It was intimate."

"You had sexual relations with Mrs. Feldman?"

"Yes."

And with that answer, Kingman dealt his social life a mortal blow. *Now mark me how I will undo myself.*

"Was the defendant aware of your affair with his wife?"

"Objection. This witness can't know what someone else is aware of," said Bari.

"Overruled. I'll allow it. The witness may answer if he knows."

What the hell is wrong with Jones? He knows that a question calling for speculation is objectionable, Bari thought.

"He had to be. We weren't all that careful about it," Kingman replied.

"You honor, move to strike. The witness is engaging in speculation."

"Overruled."

Jesus Christ! Kingman is speculating about his speculation.

"How long did your affair with Marian Feldman last?"

"Eight or nine months."

"Why did it end?"

"I told my lawyer - name's Dave Harrison - about it and he told her. She got angry and . . ."

"Objection, hearsay."

"Sustained."

About fucking time.

"Was there also another reason why she called it off with you?"

"Objection. Calls for a hearsay response."

"Yeah. She said she was seeing that Detective Ca . . ."

"Sustained. The jury will disregard. Wait for my ruling on objections before answering, Mr. Kingman," the judge said.

"Thank you, Mr. Kingman," said Harriet. "No further questions."

This was what they had feared: a witness who would flatly contradict a key defense witness. The manifest danger with Kingman, Bari knew, was that even if he annihilated the S.O.B.'s character, the jury might believe him anyway. A New York jury believed "Sammy the Bull" Gravano, when he testified against John Gotti, even though Gravano owned up - on the witness stand under oath - to nineteen murders. Nineteen!

"You were coerced into testifying here today, weren't you?" asked Bari.

"Objection, Your Honor. May we approach?" The courtroom became a hive of curiosity, as four lawyers left their seats and stood before Judge Jones. This was a move by Harriet to take the sting out of the question that she knew was coming, and to rattle Bari.

"Your Honor, the Commonwealth agreed not to prosecute this witness for a felony in exchange for his truthful testimony," Harriet explained.

"Sounds like coercion to me, Ms. Atkins. Stand back, everyone. Objection overruled."

"Let me ask you again, Mr. Kingman. Were you threatened or coerced to come in here today and testify as you have?"

Kingman tried to look around Bari at Harriet, but Bari stepped in closer and blocked his line of sight. "Please answer the question, Mr. Kingman."

"I got a call on the phone. She said that if I didn't testify, I'd be prosecuted for an old assault charge against me."

"By 'she' you mean Ms. Atkins?"

"Yeah, the prosecutor."

"Do you have an old assault charge against you?"

"Yes."

"What is it?"

"Malicious wounding."

"That's a class two felony, isn't it?"

"Yes."

"You could go to prison for ten years or more if you were convicted of that crime, couldn't you?"

"I don't know. I'm innocent, I can tell you that."

"Who called you with that threat of prosecution, Mr. Kingman?"

"Ms. Atkins."

"Before you received the phone call threatening prosecution, you had decided not to testify. Correct?"

"That's right."

"And had you told Ms. Atkins that you were not going to testify?"

"Yes, I had."

"You were also charged with felonious assault in North Carolina three years ago, weren't you?"

"It was dismissed."

"Let's go back a few years, Mr. Kingman. You were kicked out of the University of Virginia, were you not?"

"Yeah, and so was Edgar Allen Poe," answered Kingman with a snigger, and the courtroom joined in the fun. Bari smiled good-naturedly, and let the laughter subside.

"I believe Mr. Poe left the University in good standing. You were kicked out for dishonesty, weren't you?" Score one for Cammy. *If that garbage Shilla kills Cammy, I'll hire Last Rites to kill Shilla. I swear to God I will,* Bari vowed silently.

"It was on a test."

"It was on a final exam and you cheated, didn't you?"

"Yes."

"And you were caught?"

"Yes."

"And you were kicked out of the University of Virginia."

"Yeah, that's right.

"I see that you're wearing a ring. Please identify it for the jury, Mr. Kingman."

"It's a college ring."

"From the University of Virginia, correct?"

"Yeah."

"Isn't that ring reserved for graduates?"

"Anybody can wear one."

"And in this case, anybody does."

"Objection, counsel is testifying."

"Sustained."

I'm not through with you yet, asshole. "You enlisted in the United States Air Force ten years ago?" asked Bari.

"Yeah."

"And you were discharged a year later under less than honorable conditions?" That early discharge had been because of Kingman and the base commander's wife, but Bari wouldn't bring that up, and Kingman certainly wouldn't.

Kingman smirked, "I received a general discharge."

Bari faced the jury. "Hmmm, a general discharge, a *general* discharge . . ."

The jury was beginning to squint at Richard Kingman.

Southerners are sensitive about duty and honor. Let the smart asses on TV joke about it, but below the Mason-Dixon Line, people take such matters seriously.

"You testified that you were unemployed?"

"Right now I am, yes. I train horses."

"When was the last time you held a job?"

"Objection. This is irrelevant."

"These are basic, biographical facts, you honor. I think the jury would like to know who's giving sworn testimony before this court."

"Overruled. You may answer, Mr. Kingman."

"Three years ago."

"You have a trust that pays you fifteen hundred dollars a month, correct?"

Kingman's forehead began to glisten with perspiration and he pulled at the knot in his tie.

"Correct."

"And the balance of your considerable living expenses is paid by assorted wealthy women years older than you are. Isn't that correct?"

"No, it is not correct."

"Then please tell the jury who makes up the difference between the fifteen hundred dollars your trust fund pays you and the seventy-five hundred dollars a month you spend."

"Your Honor, this is too much," said Harriet, affecting exasperation.

"Yes," agreed the judge. "Move on, Mr. Bari."

"I believe I'm finished with this witness, Your Honor."

Richard Kingman hurried from the courtroom and headed straight into the media buzz saw with its blinding camera flashes and nonstop questions.

Bari knew that Kingman would be tough for the jury to reconcile. Would a man, even a worthless man, under coercion from the Commonwealth, come into court and make up a lie about a married woman out of whole cloth? Surely *something* had happened between them. And even if that something was nothing more than a few stolen kisses, might not that be enough to make the defendant insanely jealous? Even if he had perhaps seen the tail end of only one of those kisses?

"THE   PROSECUTION   CALLS   Mr.   David
Harrison."

Bari and Louis stood, "Your Honor, may we
approach?"

The judge motioned them to come forward.

"Your Honor, the defense would like to know what
testimony Harrison will rebut," whispered Louis.

"Tell them, Ms. Atkins," said the judge.

"Mr. Harrison will rebut Mrs. Feldman's testimony
that she has never been unfaithful to her husband."

"Are you saying that Harrison will testify that he has
had sexual relations with Mrs. Feldman - is that what
you're saying?" asked Louis.

"No, Mr. Harrison is Kingman's attorney. He will
corroborate Kingman testimony that he told Mr. Harrison
about his affair with the Feldman woman and that she
threw him over for Detective Carey."

"That's all hearsay, Ms. Atkins, and it also involves
attorney-client privilege," said the judge.

"Mr. Kingman waives attorney-client privilege, Your
Honor," Harriet replied.

"It's still hearsay. If that's all he'll testify to, then it's
no go."

"There's more, Your Honor. Harrison will also testify
that Mrs. Feldman approached him about an affair and he
turned her down," said Harriet.

Judge Jones laughed, and said, "Okay, put him on."

"Testimony about Mrs. Feldman's out of court
statements is hearsay too, Your Honor, and highly
prejudicial," said Louis.

"I'm going to allow it, Mr. Louis. You can recall
Mrs. Feldman afterward if you want," replied the judge.

Louis was shocked and horrified that Jones had
decided to play fast and loose with the rules of evidence

this late in the trial. But he got his hearsay objection on the record and Harrison took the stand.

As a lawyer, Harrison had no business testifying in this case. Furthermore, Harrison knew it.

Harrison wore a light gray, summer weight suit, blue Egyptian cotton shirt and yellow silk tie. He was freshly barbered and manicured. Louis sat back admiringly. *So this is what a highly-paid corporate attorney wears to court when he is about to perjure himself*, he thought.

Harriet got right to the point. "Please tell the jury if you know Marian Feldman."

"Yes, I do know Marian. Her husband Paul and I work for the same company."

"And what is your job with that company, Mr. Harrison?" Harriet had come into heat over Harrison. Bari signaled Louis to notice the jury. The women jurors had picked up on Harriet and were suppressing titters.

"I am chief legal counsel."

"And how many attorneys do you have under you?" asked Harriet. Her eyes closed as though she was visualizing herself under Harrison.

"About a hundred and fifty."

"You heard Mr. Kingman's testimony. Correct?"

"Yes."

"Did he tell you about his sexual relationship with Marian Feldman?"

"Objection, Your Honor. This is blatant hearsay," said Louis.

"Overruled, Mr. Louis. If you don't like my ruling, you are free to take it to the court of appeals," said Jones. "The witness may answer."

"Yes, he told me. He said that she broke it off with him to go with Detective Carey."

"Mr. Harrison, what, if anything, happened the last time you saw Marian Feldman socially?"

"It was at the annual company picnic a year ago. Marian was waiting to take her turn at bat when I walked up. We said hello and remarked about the weather, and suddenly Marian propositioned me."

What hogwash, thought Louis. It appeared that Harrison's story was utterly believable to Harriet. Harriet, you horny bitch, you'd give Harrison a blow job right here in court if he exposed himself.

"Propositioned? How?"

"She said 'I'd like to get together with you sometime.' I was confused. At first I thought she wanted to ask me a legal question. She said, 'No, I want to make love with you.'"

"And what did you say?" asked Harriet, her breasts heaving.

"I said that she was married to a man I respected, and that our 'getting together' was out of the question."

"What did she say in reply?"

"I don't know. I walked off."

Harriet paused, gazing at Harrison. Everyone was waiting. You could have heard a mouse sip water. "Ms. Atkins?" inquired the judge.

Harriet collected herself. "Oh, no further questions."

Louis reached across Paul and put his hand on Bari's arm. "I got him, Joe."

There were two things Louis lived for: the law and his family. The state and federal law reporters at the firm library - the bound volumes that lawyers and judges invariably pose in front of when photographed - contained a record of human folly from this country's earliest beginnings to the present. There were rancorous accounts of dishonored obligations, property disputes, bankruptcies, divorce, mayhem of every description, and murder. Taken all together, the reporters comprised Louis's Bible.

Louis was also a realist. Not for him the pointless daydreams about beautiful women and parallel universes. He had exactly what he wanted and he wanted exactly what he had. Because he did not regard life's occasional bonus as merely his due for a life well lived, he was as happy as a kid with a hot fudge sundae when one came along. Dave Harrison was one of those bonuses, and as he walked over to face him, Louis's smile lit up the courtroom.

"Mr. Harrison, you want this jury to accept three improbable propositions, don't you?"

"I'm sorry. Is that a question?"

"Proposition one is that Mrs. Marian Feldman asked you to make love to her, right?"

"Yes, that's right."

"Proposition two is that you refused?"

"That's what I said, Mr. Louis."

"Surely you told someone about Mrs. Feldman's solicitation of sex from you."

"The less said about it the better."

"Admirable. Which brings us to proposition three, namely, that you refused to have sex with Mrs. Feldman on the high-minded grounds that she was married to a man you hardly knew but nevertheless respected. Isn't that right?"

"I would have put it differently, but yes, that's right."

"Then how is it that your ex-wife's divorce complaint stated that you were an inveterate cheat, and named several women, some married, as corespondents? Have you gotten religion since then, Mr. Harrison?"

Louis knew Harrison slightly from a bar committee they both briefly served on. Louis was also very friendly with the lawyer who handled Harrison's ex's divorce. They had shared a few yuks over a self-important prick like Harrison getting skinned by his wife.

"Objection, counsel is trying to humiliate my witness," said Harriet, red faced, and trying her best to protect her new beau.

"Overruled,"

"Divorce complaints allege a lot of things that aren't true, Mr. Louis, and you know it," Harrison said. His scorn was that of a big shot corporate counsel toward a lowly criminal defense lawyer.

Louis hoped that the jury, unaware of the rigid legal caste system, would see only an asshole. For once, he was glad of his rotundity. Louis knew that juries trusted him and he wanted the maximum contrast between himself and Harrison. He chuckled to himself at what an unlikely pair of contestants they were: Harrison, perfectly turned out and as sleek as an Orca. And Louis, balding and stout, his round, trustworthy face always about to break into a smile.

"I can have a copy of your divorce complaint in this courtroom in fifteen minutes if you'd like to go through it point by point and explain which fact is true and which fact isn't."

"Objection.   Is there a question pending, Your Honor?"

"Sustained. Ask a question, Mr. Louis."

"Did you challenge the facts in the complaint, Mr. Harrison? You could have, you know?"

"No, it was better for all concerned not to fight about it."

"Better for all concerned; you mean you and your girlfriends?"

"No, I meant better for my wife and for me."

"Nevertheless, the unrebutted facts alleged in the complaint are now a matter of public record. Am I right?"

"Yes, Mr. Louis, you are right," sighed Harrison, as though he were indulging a tiresome child.

"Let's return to the company picnic, shall we? In fact, you approached Mrs. Feldman for an illicit meeting, didn't you?"

"No, I did not."

"And she told you what you could do with your vulgar insulting approach, didn't she?"

"No."

"And you've wanted to get even with her all this time, isn't that so?

"No, of course it isn't," answered Harrison with a smile and a dismissive wave of the hand.

You just lost this battle, Harrison, you ass.

"Well, Mr. Harrison, I trust that the jury will correctly decide which version of the picnic story is true."

"OBJECTION!" Your Honor, Mr. Louis has done nothing but harass Mr. Harrison."

"He's a lawyer, and he knows how to resist Mr. Louis's blandishments, but I'll sustain your objection. Ask a question, Mr. Louis," said the judge suppressing a smile.

"I have no further questions, Your Honor," said Louis.

CHAPTER TWENTY-FOUR

BARI WATCHED CAREFULLY AS THE jurors directed their earnest gazes toward the judge. Judge Jones read the jury instructions and went over legal concepts they had heard every night on TV crime shows and thought they knew. But now they would have to apply them in a real case: innocent until proven guilty, burden of proof, proof beyond a reasonable doubt and the jurors' duty to deliberate.

Bari had had the good fortune years ago to sit on a jury. Since then, he had talked to innumerable jurors at the end of his trials, and he knew the drill. The instructions would accompany the jurors to the jury room, where a few would read and reread them looking for guidance, as the heavy weight of their responsibility settled in upon them. Others wouldn't bother even to riffle through them.

The jurors who had already made up their minds would show their hands first. The other jurors would chide them for it. And then the wrangling would begin.

The jury would also receive one verdict form for capital murder and another form for the alternative crime of murder one and the lesser-included offense of murder two, which gave them the option of a compromise verdict. *Well, there's not enough here to convict him of capital murder, but what the hell - he's guilty of something. Let's get him for murder two.* Lesser included verdicts were the bane of criminal defense lawyers and Bari hated them.

"Now, I ask that you give Ms. Atkins your attention for her closing argument," said Judge Jones.

Harriet had come dressed for a different occasion, a cocktail party or some other after-six soiree where dramatic hair and makeup were perfectly acceptable. Harriet's contrast with her thoroughly abashed pin-striped assistant couldn't have been more striking.

"The defendant, Paul Feldman, is the older, workaholic husband of a beautiful younger woman who was attracted to the victim in this case, Detective Arnold Carey," she began.

"Marian Feldman testified that she heard scratching noises outside her bedroom window on the nights of February thirteenth and fourteenth. She *says* she woke the defendant who also heard the noises. She testified that on the morning of February fifteenth, she called Detective Carey, whom she had met socially. Detective Carey came to her home to investigate the noises and was murdered with his own gun from a distance of ten feet. Marian Feldman testified that she then collected herself and called 911.

"I submit that this is a fantastic tale and that it is pure fiction. You heard the testimony of the chief homicide detective, Sammy Ditsel, who said that the victim's body had been nude at the time of death and then redressed by Mrs. Feldman.

"Why is it important that Mrs. Feldman and Detective Carey were intimate? Because the defendant was driven by jealousy to fake a sickness at the airport and return home to verify his jealousy."

Bari stole a look at Paul beside him. Paul could have been listening to the engineering specs of one of the rockets his company manufactured. He was attentive, that's it. No shaking his head in disagreement and no frowns. Perfect, thought Bari.

"Dr. Mason testified that the time of death was between ten and eleven that morning," Harriet continued. "The defendant's parking receipt showed that he left the airport at 9:55 a.m., ample time to make the drive home."

"You heard Mr. Kingman testify that he and Marian Feldman had been reckless lovers for several months and you heard Mr. Harrison testify that she brazenly approached him to have sex at a company picnic. Does it stand to reason that her husband, the defendant in this trial, was ignorant of her sleeping around? Of course not."

Harriet went through the pathologist's testimony about the time of death and evidence of recent sexual activity, omitting the anal sex.

"But when Detective Ditsel asked her to have a pelvic exam, she refused."

Both Bari and Louis leaped from their seats with an objection. "Defense moves for a mistrial, Your Honor!"

"Approach!" All the lawyers marched heatedly to the bench. *Christ, she's loaded with perfume,* thought Bari.

"What the hell are you trying to pull, Atkins?" asked the judge. "That issue was ruled inadmissible. If this weren't a murder trial, I'd grant a mistrial in a heartbeat and dismiss this case with prejudice. And you know I would. So here's what we're going to do. I'm holding you in contempt and fining you five thousand dollars. Do it again and so help me God, I'll grant a defense motion for a mistrial and a dismissal *with prejudice,*" said Judge Jones, fighting for control.

If he dismissed the case with prejudice, it couldn't be retried because of the Fifth Amendment guarantee against double jeopardy. Jones's name would be mud in judicial circles, Bari knew, and the press would scream for his resignation. If it got bad enough, the state bar's committee on judicial fitness might step in and force his resignation. Despite all that, it was clear to Bari that Judge Jones had made up his mind. If Harriet forced his hand, he'd take her down with him.

"Get back . . . Ladies and Gentlemen of the jury, please ignore Ms. Atkins's previous statement about Detective Ditsel and Mrs. Feldman. That statement is not to be considered by you in any way . . . You may resume, Ms. Atkins."

Harriet didn't miss a beat. She took them through the ballistics testimony and insisted that Carey's gun was the murder weapon. On the slight chance that the jury might see it otherwise, she suggested that the defendant had ample time to dispose of any murder weapon of his own and to wash his hands of gun powder residue.

Harriet danced around Paul's sterling character by saying that when it comes to murderous jealousy, character didn't count for much. She came dangerously close to suggesting that Paul could have cleared up any lingering questions the jury might have by taking the stand, but that tactic would have ended the trial on the spot. The defendant has a constitutional right not to testify, and any suggestion by the prosecution that he should have testified is grounds for a mistrial. Bari could see that Judge Jones was poised to pound her through the courtroom floor, and she barely managed to escape his wrath.

"A police detective, who gave many years of his life in service to this community, was murdered by a much lesser man because he couldn't keep his pretty young wife away from other men. Detective Carey is gone from us forever, but his murder cries out for justice. Answer those cries, ladies and gentlemen of the jury, and return a unanimous verdict of guilty of capital murder. Thank you."

BARI HAD BEEN going over his closing argument since Paul had first walked into his office. Excluding a few adjustments, such as Stubby Minetti's absence from the stand, it was the same argument. As he stood to deliver it, he placed a yellow legal pad on the edge of the defense table so that he could glance at it from time to time. The pad didn't contain the complete argument, just the main points in large block letters.

Other lawyers got nervous stomachs and other symptoms of fear right before closing, not Bari. Not until now, with his friend's life on the line. He could feel the sweat droplets streaming from his armpits down his sides. He took a deep breath and began.

"Ladies and Gentlemen of the jury, the Commonwealth's case against Paul Feldman is purely one hundred percent circumstantial.

"Marian Feldman testified that she heard noises outside her and Paul's bedroom window on separate nights in the same week, and awakened her husband to report them. The following morning, Paul Feldman left on an important business trip. When Mrs. Feldman arose, she called Detective Carey, whom she knew, to report the noises.

"Detective Carey came by to investigate, and while he and Mrs. Feldman were trying to open the bedroom window, which had been painted shut, an intruder came into the room and shot the detective in the back of the head and left unseen." Bari made sure that during his closing argument, he made eye contact with each juror. Now he paused and scanned the jury before going on.

"Who was the intruder? Was it the person who had tried to break in the previous night and once before that? Was it a personal enemy of Carey's? When police detectives arrest people, they do make enemies. Or was it the work of a professional assassin?"

Harriet was on her feet. "Objection. There was no evidence of an assassin."

Quickly, before the judge could rule against him, Bari said: "Perhaps the Commonwealth has forgotten, Your Honor, but Detective Sammy Ditsel testified that Detective Carey's death looked like a professional hit."

"Overruled. Continue."

Thanks, Harriet, for letting me remind all those on the jury who might also have forgotten Ditsel's testimony, thought Bari.

"There is no physical evidence connecting Paul Feldman to the death of Detective Arnold Carey. The Commonwealth produced no witness who placed him at the scene when Carey was shot."

Bari moved over behind Paul and put his hand on Paul's shoulder. "And finally, Paul Feldman had no motive to shoot Detective Carey. The Commonwealth alleges that it was the violent act of a jealous husband, but has produced no proof that Paul Feldman was indeed jealous or that he was capable of such a deadly act if he had reason to be."

Bari now moved directly in front of the jury. He wanted to make damn sure they were awake for this most important part of his argument.

As he was about to speak, he spotted the two goons, that the Attorney General had sent to threatened him.

They were standing in back of the courtroom, grinning like jackals.

"Let's take these points one at a time. The Commonwealth has said that Detective Carey was shot with his own gun, a gun that had only Detective Carey's fingerprints on it," he said, ticking off the points with his fingers.

"The Commonwealth's ballistics expert admitted that the lead bullet retrieved from Detective Carey's skull was so badly deformed by the impact that a match with a test bullet fired from Carey's gun into a water tank was all but impossible. Yet, the shell casing, the piece of evidence that could have settled the question whether the bullet that killed Carey came from his gun, is mysteriously missing.

"But if Carey wasn't shot with his own gun, says the Commonwealth, then Mr. Feldman shot him with a gun of his own. Well that theory certainly covers all the bases, but the problem with it is that the Commonwealth has produced no such gun belonging to Paul Feldman. Why? Because no such gun exists.

"The defense witness from long-term parking at the airport was the cashier that Paul Feldman paid on his way home from the airport the morning of February fifteenth. Paul was on his way back home because he was as sick as a dog. The cashier saw him throw up as he struggled to pay her, and she offered her help.

"Mr. Feldman received a timed receipt upon leaving the Richmond airport at 9:55 a.m. That receipt clearly shows that he couldn't have driven home from the airport in time to shoot Detective Carey by ten o'clock or by ten-thirty or even by eleven! And remember, the Commonwealth's pathologist estimated the time of death at between ten and eleven o'clock." Bari was rocking now, and he prayed that the jury was with him.

"You heard Miss Bernice Early testify that she saw a big black car pull in to the Feldman driveway at ten thirty on the morning of February fifteen and leave ten or fifteen minutes later.

"You also heard that Paul and Marian Feldman's young neighbor from across the street saw a United Parcel delivery man go into the Feldman's home and come out a few minutes later on the morning of February fifteenth. The United Parcel shift manager that morning testified that there was no scheduled delivery to the Feldman home. He also testified that he had received reports of a UPS truck in the neighborhood that morning. Those very suspicious events were uncovered by police investigation, but they were never reported to us as required by law. Was that delivery man an assassin disguised as a UPS employee? We'll probably never know.

"The police had Paul Feldman in custody, and they simply ignored the evidence of a hit man who very well might have shot Detective Carey. Aside from the Richmond Police Department, the only other witness who could have shed light on that question was shot in the head two nights ago."

"OBJECTION! Approach, Your Honor?"

When they were assembled before him, Judge Jones fired a fusillade directly at Bari's head. "Okay Joe. Five grand before you leave the court today. Make another move like that and I'll make it fifty. Understood? Get back . . . The jury will ignore Mr. Bari's statement about a witness who did not make an appearance in this court. I order you not to consider it in your deliberations. You may continue, Mr. Bari."

"Thank you, Your Honor." *Thanks for nothing, you jerk.* "The entire basis of the Commonwealth's case is, 'the husband did it.' Why? Because statistics all point to the husband when there is a love triangle. So to make this whole thing fly, the Commonwealth first had to make an adulteress of Marian Feldman," said Bari looking over to Marian who cast her eyes down demurely, "a perfectly respectable married lady. To that end, Ms. Atkins called two disreputable witnesses: Richard Kingman and David Harrison. Kingman testified under threat of prosecution, and the womanizer Harrison testified because Mrs. Feldman rebuffed his sexual advances at a company picnic.

"Objection!"

"Overruled."

No surprise there. Bari knew that closing argument in a criminal trial was sacred. You can't misstate the evidence, but you can do damn near anything else, including cry, quote the Bible, drop to your knees, anything. "Then the Commonwealth constructed a cockamamie story about the victim being nude when shot, and redressed afterward. That created a time problem for the Commonwealth, because they had to allow for enough time for the victim to be redressed, but not so much time as to rule out the husband as perpetrator.

"That problem was never solved. The Richmond International Airport was at least an hour from the Feldmans' home, but under the Commonwealth's theory, Paul Feldman had all of twenty minutes to drive home from the airport, park, enter his house, shoot Detective Carey and leave; only to return an hour or so later when the body was being loaded into the hearse. They produced no witnesses to all that coming-and-going, mind you, just theory and supposition." Bari paused to walk over to the defense table for a sip from one of the small paper cups supplied by the court.

"In closing, I'll say only that to convict Paul Feldman of any crime, whether it be capital murder or murder in the second degree, you must buy into every Commonwealth supposition about this case, no matter how wild. To convict Paul Feldman, you must bend and squeeze the evidence into grotesque shapes." Bari made gestures to the jury that made it appear he was struggling to bend an imaginary piece of rebar.

"But no fair interpretation of the evidence in this case will permit you to find Paul Feldman guilty of anything beyond a reasonable doubt. The Commonwealth's case is riddled with doubt from beginning to end.

"After you carefully review the evidence, I am certain that you will come to the same conclusion and acquit Paul Feldman of any offense. Thank you."

HARRIET HAD THE last word in her rebuttal summation. She gamely attempted to reestablish her witnesses' credibility and put a Commonwealth spin on Ditsel's testimony, the testimony of her ballistics expert, and the pathologist. Her pitch in rebuttal was essentially the same as her closing argument: if Paul Feldman didn't do it, then who did? As asinine as that argument seemed, Bari had seen it carry in domestic homicides.

Bari held his breath as the clerk drew the names of the two alternates who would not deliberate with the remaining twelve. *Dear Heaven, please.* The clerk read the names aloud. Both ringers survived the cut! With two solid votes to acquit, the very worst they could do was a hung jury, which, meant a dismissal and a retrial. On the bright side, their ringers stood to gain thirty thousand dollar extra apiece for an outright acquittal, and that meant they'd both be fighting their hearts out for a not guilty verdict.

CHAPTER TWENTY-FIVE

THE CHOSEN TWELVE filed out of the courtroom in the company of the bailiff. The alternates were taken to a different room in case one of the twelve became ill or was otherwise unable to deliberate, due to a death in the family, or some other major calamity.

Now began the wait for the verdict, Joe Bari's purgatory. There was little chance that the jury would reach a unanimous verdict before five o'clock when they would be released for the day. The judge's clerk had the defense and prosecution's office and home numbers, and would call the minute the jury indicated they were hung, or had reached a unanimous verdict.

Five o'clock came and the jury was sent home until nine the following morning when they would resume deliberations. Still no word of Cammy. The Richmond Police Department said they'd look into it. But the chief, pissed because of Bari's cross of his cop witnesses, made it plain that they weren't going to bust their balls.

As the next day wore on, no one could get any work done. Bari and Louis took heart from the lurid headlines in the newspapers and on TV. "Shooting of Witness in

Murder Trial: a mob hit?" and "Witness Silenced!" were the headlines in the *Daily Journal* and the *Richmond Post,* the two local papers serving Richmond and the Lower Peninsula. The local TV stations served up mob documentaries and mob organizational charts.

Unbeknownst to Louis, Bari had made sure that both the print and TV media knew what Minetti's testimony would have been. But that was before Minetti was fished out of the James River and Cammy was snatched. Bari was sick now, because Shilla's name was all over the place in the articles. God only knew what Shilla would do to Cammy because of it.

"The jurors would have to be deaf and blind to miss this fucking story," said Louis rubbing his hands in satisfaction.

"Then why in hell have they been out a day and a half, Art?"

"I know what they say," Louis replied. "In northern jurisdictions, like Connecticut and Massachusetts, long deliberations are good for the prosecution and quick verdicts are good for the defense. But the South is well known for lightning guilty verdicts. Come right down to it, you can't generalize about the South. Why just last month there was a six-day guilty verdict in Baton Rouge."

As far as Louis was concerned, no news was good news. Bari was another story.

"You're driving me crazy, Joe. Go get drunk and pass out. I'll take the verdict when it comes," said Louis, his face mottled with weariness and agitation. *Please*, Louis prayed, *don't let this case do me in.*

MEANWHILE, PAUL, WHO had been bearing up well under the crushing pressure, sank deep into a black depression.

"Paul, look," said Marian. "If the worst happens, we'll post an appeal bond and then we'll skip to somewhere that doesn't have an extradition treaty with the United States. We'll go to Nicaragua or El Salvador. It doesn't matter where we go so long as we're together." It's the least I can do after causing all this goddamn grief, she thought.

"No," said Paul. "I'll be okay. It's the waiting that's got me down."

"MR. BARI? THIS is Zack Brown. Cammy's at MCV; he's in intensive care. They don't know if he's going to make it. I thought maybe you'd want to know."

Bari and Aaron set a new land speed record on the trip up the Peninsula to MCV Hospital in Richmond. Medical College of Virginia Hospital is a large medical complex just off I-64, the highway they scorched to get there.

Bari got into a shouting match with hospital staff in admitting about visitors seeing ICU patients. Aaron took over and secretly dragged Bari through an underground maintenance tunnel. The end seemed like a mile from the entrance lobby. They took an elevator up to the ICU, where Bari composed himself and asked to speak to the ICU doc.

"Mr. Brown has sustained multiple fractures to his ribs and arms. One of his lungs was punctured and he's lost a lot of blood, which is the main problem. He was in shock when he was brought in. We transfused him and got him stable. A chest tube was placed on arrival in the ER to reinflate his lung. We suspect he has sustained

contusions to his spleen, kidneys and liver. A CAT scan
of the spleen will be done today. If the scan suggests
impending rupture, surgery will be necessary. That's
where we are now. He's young and otherwise healthy,
so he has a fair chance of coming through this."

Zack saw Bari and Aaron talking to the doctor and
figured out who they were. They assured each other that
Cammy would make it through just fine. Bari explained
about the trial and gave Zack his card. "Call me Joe.
Please call the minute you know something, Mr. Brown -
Zack - and my secretary will find me if I'm not in the
office. Cammy and I are close friends. I don't know
what I'd do if . . ."

ON THE MORNING of the third day, the clerk called
to say the jury had a question. "Helen, get Paul on the
line." Bari called down the hall, "Art, there's a question
from the jury!"

The news spread like a grass fire in a high wind. A
local TV news outlet had a monitor screen in the hall just
outside the courtroom. The trial had not been televised,
but Judge Jones allowed a video feed to the hall monitor
for the sake of journalists and spectators that couldn't
squeeze into the courtroom. Now, the hall was full, and
all those who could physically manage crushed in around
the monitor.

Bari had informed Paul that the jury had a question.
Paul's presence wasn't strictly required for a jury
question, and he had elected to stay home.

"All rise, the Honorable Harley Jones presiding."

The judge took his seat, greeted the two teams and
announced that the jurors had a question. He picked up a
sheet of paper and read from it. "Dear Judge Jones. We
the jury have a question for you. Is premeditation

necessary in the charge of capital murder where the victim was a police officer?"

The jury's question quick-froze Bari's heart, and Louis staggered back a step. The jury's question could mean nothing good for the defense.

"I'll hear arguments on what the answer should be, but I'm inclined not to answer it. The elements of the crime were clearly set out in my charge, and the jury has printed definitions of capital murder, and the alternative offense of first degree murder and the lesser-included offense of second degree murder."

Bari looked over at Harriet. She and her henchman, Mimms, wore malicious smiles. "The defense requests that Your Honor clarify the elements of capital murder, and emphasize that premeditation is an element of capital murder and strictly required." said Bari.

"The Commonwealth's position is that the jury has the definitions," said Harriet. "They don't require clarification. Additional commentary by the court will only confuse the issue."

"Very well," said the judge, ignoring Bari. I'll send word to the jury that I will not answer their question."

The jury's deliberation continued. Bari and Louis met in Louis's office. "How could I have misread that jury so badly?" Louis was near tears. "If Paul is convicted, Joe, I don't know how I can live with it."

"Don't borrow trouble, Art. It was just a question. It could mean anything or nothing. Look, my heart wasn't gladdened either, but let's wait."

Bari was counting on his two ringers on the jury to think about the extra thirty thousand dollars each would receive if there were an acquittal, and then argue the other ten into the ground.

THE WAITING TOOK them from purgatory down into hell. A day and a half crept by. Bari and Louis were in agony. As they were getting ready to pack it in for the day and leave the office, Jones's clerk called.

"Joe, you and Art have to appear in Judge Jones's court right away."

"Is there a verdict, Helen? What's up?"

"She wouldn't say. Maybe it's another question."

"Call Paul. Tell him to get to court ASAP."

Bari went into a half run, but had to slow down for Louis who was winded after a block.

When they got in sight of the courthouse, the media were active and milling about. When they spotted Bari and Louis, they broke into a run. The first reporter to reach them yelled: "What's going on, Mr. Bari?"

"Please don't put that thing in my face," said Bari, parrying the microphone with his hand. "You're keeping us from court. Let us through, please."

The courtroom and the hall outside were packed with people, mostly media types.

"How in hell do they find out so fast?" asked Louis.

"God only knows," Bari answered.

Harriet and Mimms were in place and looking apprehensive, which told Bari that they didn't know any more than he did. Good.

Within minutes, Paul walked in and quickly took his place between Bari and Louis.

"All rise," called the bailiff.

Judge Jones ascended the bench, and with a brief glance to see if the parties were in court, said "Bring in the jury."

The jurors looked worn out as they filed in. The ladies were wearing no makeup and the older jurors had dark bags beneath their eyes.

"Ladies and gentlemen of the jury, I understand from the bailiff that you have been unable to reach a verdict. Is that true, Mrs. Forelady?"

"Yes, Your Honor."

"Without telling me what side is for or against, please tell me what the count is."

"It's eight to four, Your Honor."

"All right. I know you're tired. But this is a murder trial and there is a lot at stake. You really haven't deliberated very long, although I can appreciate that it *seems* a long time to you. It's late now, but I want you to return to deliberations first thing tomorrow and give it everything you've got.   Approach deliberations tomorrow with clear and receptive minds, and try to give this defendant and this court a unanimous verdict one way or the other. Okay, this court is adjourned."

"I never thought a 'dynamite charge' would be necessary in this case, Art – not really."

"Well Joe, I'm resigned to a hung jury," said Louis, stooped with exhaustion. "Actually, I think we're lucky to get a hung jury after that stupid-ass question they asked."

ANOTHER FULL DAY went by and at four thirty in the afternoon there was another phone call from the clerk.

"Helen, call everybody. There's a verdict," said Bari.

This time, he walked to Louis's office. "Art, there's a verdict," he said softly.

There was another mad media scene at the courthouse, only more so. They had heard there was a verdict. The affiliate reporters and station reporters arranged themselves in little groups that formed a broad semicircle on the front lawn of the court.

Make-up people were busily making last minute touchups and adjustments to the human mannequins who would report the verdict to a ravenous public hooked on murder trials. Station cameramen were focusing and fiddling with the settings on their formidable TV equipment.

Paul stood inside the rail and tried to cheer his parents and Marian, huddled together in their usual seats in the first row behind the defense table, stricken with anxiety.

Suddenly, Judge Jones entered to the sounds of a hundred people leaving their wooden benches to stand respectfully.

"Please remain standing for the jury," said the bailiff.

Louis was having sweats and stomach pain. He silently swore for the thousandth time that this was his last criminal trial. As the jury filed in looking as grim as ever, Bari stood as erect as a marine colonel facing an enemy firing squad.

Lawyers down through the years have asked themselves why jurors can't tip their hand when they enter. Why, Bari asked himself, couldn't they wear black robes with hoods if the verdict were guilty and clown costumes if the verdict were to acquit?

"Ladies and Gentlemen of the jury - have you reached a verdict?"

"Yes, we have, Your Honor."

The forewoman was the short business woman that Bari had his doubts about. His first impression was that she could vote to send someone to death row as coolly as signing an escrow document. The thing that sold him on her was her deep understanding of the presumption of innocence and reasonable doubt. When asked about them, she was able to go on at length. Bari could imagine her arguing for a pet project around a boardroom table, soothing the unreasonable doubts of more conservative directors.

"Madam foreperson, will you hand the verdict form to the bailiff."

In a ritual as old as recorded history, a man's fate was being decided. Was it to be life, in the bosom of his family, enjoying all the freedom and protection society affords? Or, death, ignominious and alone?

"To the offense of capital murder, how say you?"

"Not guilty."

There was a noisy stirring and scattered cheering among the spectators. "Silence!" ordered Jones.

"To the alternative offense of murder in the first degree, how say you?"

"Not guilty."

"To the lesser included offense of murder in the second degree, how say you?"

"Not guilty."

Pandemonium! The courtroom exploded in wild applause and shouts. Paul Feldman, his eyes streaming with tears, hugged Joe and Art. He turned to his parents and Marian. David and Rachel were at the end of their endurance, but their son was innocent and that's all that mattered. Marian had her arms around them both when the verdict was read, and now she reached for Paul. The Attorney General's men were not to be seen.

The gavel came down. "Order, order in the court." The courtroom immediately went silent. "I thank the jury for its attention and service," said Judge Jones with obvious sincerity. And then, smiling, "Mr. Feldman, you are free to go."

CHAPTER TWENTY-SIX

AFTER BEING KEYED UP FOR months, Bari and Louis were wrung out. Under different circumstances Bari might have felt differently. But now, he was glad that he'd made Ann a promise – a promise he couldn't get out of if he wanted to preserve his marriage - to take a vacation.

Louis knew that he was facing decisions he had put off for over two years when his cardiologist had told him he needed surgery to repair a heart valve, combined with a by-pass. He swore an oath, for the hundredth time since the verdict, that *Commonwealth v. Feldman* was his last criminal trial. As far as Louis was concerned, the only grace note in that whole ordeal, aside from the enormous fee the firm would receive from Paul Feldman, was the verdict.

THERE IS A pleasant loop you can take, and many tourists do, from Newport News over the James River Bridge to Smithfield, through a beautiful old neighborhood, and out past one smoked pork packing house after another. The road continues across the Pagan River, through the Civil War town of Surry, and down to the ferry. The ferry takes you back across the James River to Jamestown several miles north of the James River Bridge.

There is no charge to take the ferry. Just drive on and take the stairs to the upper deck for the twenty-minute ride across the river to the landing on the other side, a hundred yards west of where the first settlers got a taste of winter in the New World in 1607, and where the first slaves were brought into America in 1619.

On the night before the verdict was read, a black Lincoln Town Car had driven down a dark dirt road and stopped several yards from the river bank. Two men had pulled out a third from the trunk. The terrified man's mouth was stuffed with a face cloth and securely taped, and he wore handcuffs at his wrists and ankles. There were two hay hooks attached, hook-side up, to the bound man's back with wide electrician's tape wound several times around his back, chest and arms, and down through his belt and then several more times again. The hay hooks arched out like angel wings in an advanced state of molt.

There had been a fourth man waiting in a black rubber Zodiac powered by a 100 horse Mercury Phantom outboard. The air at the river's edge was sultry, and the crickets were deafening.

The Zodiac had held the four with room to spare. When all were aboard, the fourth man started the motor and backed them out into the river. The raft headed quietly upriver toward lights in the distance, the landing for the Jamestown ferry or "Surry Ferry," as the locals called it.

The ferry ran year round, bringing mainly tourists over to Jamestown from Surry across the river and back. Now, during tourist season, the ferry was always packed with its limit of sixty cars and two hundred people. The trip across took twenty minutes, plus ten or fifteen minutes to unload and reload, which meant the ferry docked at Jamestown hourly, give or take ten minutes.

The lights from the ferry on its way back to Surry were still in sight as the raft pulled under the unlit section of the pier leading out to the boarding ramp. The ferry would return to Jamestown in a little over a half hour.

There were several groups of creosoted pilings that made a V-shaped slip from the ferry landing out into the river. Each grouping was held together into one giant piling with steel cables. The cables were wrapped around them in a two-foot band near the top and another two-foot band of cables right above water level.

The Zodiac had hidden under the bridge that led to the landing until the ferry's return trip from Surry was well underway. It then made its way slowly around to the pilings directly under the steel diamond plate boarding ramp, which was raised several feet when the ferry docked.

Whenever the ferry approached the landing on its trip back to Jamestown and reversed its engines to dock, its bow made contact with the pilings under the boarding ramp; then it was made fast with rope hawsers tossed over cleats attached to the pier.

"You murdered my wife and you cut off her head and her hands. You left my baby in his crib to die of hunger and thirst. You murdered my good friend, Stubby, and you near beat my boy to death. And now you're going to pay for all that," Zack Brown said. Zack's face was illuminated by the lights on the landing above. The handcuffed man peered deeply into Zack's eyes. And with the creeping, growing, petrifying recognition of the man he had punished so many years ago in North Carolina, he began to shake his head violently back and forth in denial of Zack Brown's merciless bill of particulars.

As the raft pulled close to the ferry side of the pilings, one man held the raft in place while the other two hung the struggling, handcuffed man by his hay-hook wings from the top cables around the pilings. They slipped another hay hook through the steel cuffs on his ankles and onto the lower band of cables, a few feet above the water. With the hooks in place he was tight against the pilings with his midsection at the point where the ferry's bow would make contact in less than twenty minutes.

The raft backed away from the pilings. The three men watched as the hanging man's terrified eyes begged them not to leave him there. He wriggled furiously, but there was nothing he could do. Even if he somehow chewed through his gag, no one would have heard him down under the ramp, especially with all the cars and people shouting with high summer exuberance. Manny Shilla had exactly fifteen minutes remaining to review his past. He had no future.

CHAPTER TWENTY-SEVEN

WITHIN DAYS OF THE VERDICT, the defense team, for team is what they truly had become, received an invitation from Paul and Marian Feldman to attend a cocktail party and dinner at their home in Richmond whenever Cammy was well enough to make the trip.

Once again, doctors were astounded at how fast the body of a man in his thirties recovers from such extensive punishment. Within a month, Cammy was walking around. In another month, he was almost as good as new.

Cammy took care of his two jurors by simply calling them from a public phone and telling them - in the appropriate voice - where they could find the balance of their money.

Louis and his wife wanted to take their two teenage daughters to Paul and Marian's party. Cammy wanted Aaron and his girlfriend to be there, but he decided to go alone. Joe Bari suggested they rent a van so that they could all drive up together.

The Feldmans were thrilled at all the people who wanted to come. It was a catered affair and a few extra people made not a ripple. Nearly everyone there had contributed to the defense effort either directly or indirectly by supporting the team over a very long haul.

THE VAN ARRIVED amid great fanfare. The Feldmans came out to greet them and Joe Bari gave a rebel yell. Marian motioned to Cammy before everyone went inside. "I think there's someone inside that you just might want to see."

Cammy was mystified as Marian led him through the entry to the party room where a magnificent buffet awaited. Paul led the rest of the party behind them.

At the far end of the party room stood a knockout in a peach cocktail dress slit up the side.

"Kiki!" cried Cammy.

She ran to him and he lifted her easily and twirled around. "My real name is Nancy," she said. Cammy kissed her to wild applause from his friends.

HAD IT BEEN up to them, David and Rachel Feldman would have awarded Joe Bari and Art Louis Nobel Prizes. They would have felt the same way about Cammy and Aaron, for that matter, had they a glimmer of their critical contributions to Paul's victory.

Before setting off to the party, Bari had made a decision to take David Feldman aside at a convenient moment and tell him that Jackie Lupo hadn't killed Detective Carey after all. Bari's revelation wouldn't permit Mr. Feldman to remove himself from the furnace of guilt all together; he had conspired with Lupo to kill a man, it was true. It was consoling nonetheless that his efforts had failed, and that was no small thing to an old man bearing a burden that was too much for him.

Bari wouldn't presume to tell that intelligent older man how to analyze away the tangled mess he had created for himself. Instead he grasped both his hands. "Sir, I believe that very few of us go through life without blemish. For my part, I have done things for which there is no forgiveness, yet I have forgiven myself because I couldn't go on otherwise," he said. "I hope with all my heart that you do the same."

MARIAN HAD TASTEFULLY decorated her home with yellow ribbons for the party. She wanted her guests to know just how grateful she was.

From Paul's arrest onward, a profound Scrooge-like change had worked itself within Marian's heart for many reasons, not the least being the disclosure that the mob had killed Carey. His death had nothing at all to do with her philandering. That was on the plus side. But she still couldn't deal with the accident at the ravine quite yet.

During the cocktail party, Marian overheard a guest order a brandy and soda. "I'm very sorry, ma'am, we don't seem to have any brandy. We have some very special Canadian whiskey, if that's all right."

Marian, horrified, slipped out of the house and got into Paul's car, which blocked hers, and drove quickly to the state liquor store next to the new mega-supermarket on the edge of their enclave. Thinking of the stink she was going to raise with the caterers, she was about to go through a stop sign when a car crossed in front of her. She stood on her brakes and barely avoided hitting the car. As she regained her composure, she noticed that a small prescription bottle had slid out from under the driver's seat and had come to rest next to the accelerator pedal.

Marian bought the brandy and then sped through the vast supermarket next door. She dashed over to the pharmacy and placed the prescription bottle on the counter. "Can you tell what this prescription was for? I don't recognize the name."

"Yes," said the pharmacist, quizzically reading the label. "It's syrup of ipecac, an emetic. It induces vomiting."

"JOE, I'M COMING down to Roads Port this morning to go shopping with Ann. Mind if I stop by for a few minutes before I meet her?"

"Of course, Marian. Looking forward to it."

Bari expected that Marian wanted to come by and express her thanks privately and personally, and repair his opinion of her. It wasn't necessary. Since the trial, she and Paul had gotten along famously, and that's all he cared about. Her former screwing around was in the past and forgotten as far as he was concerned. Besides, he was a lawyer, and Marian's infidelity was a trifle compared to some white collar defendants, who had ruined thousands and stolen millions.

Helen showed Marian in, and she and Bari sat on the sofa. "It was Paul who killed Carey, Joe. I found a prescription bottle in his car the night of our party for the defense team. The bottle was empty. It had held a compound that causes vomiting."

"Syrup of ipecac?"

"Yes."

"Why are you telling me this, Marian?"

"I had to tell someone, and you were the only person I could trust."

"I knew it was Paul, Marian. I've known it since midway in the trial. Paul had the motive to kill. No one else did, not really. Also, his choosing me to represent him was a tip-off. I do criminal work, but I wasn't the best criminal lawyer he could have gotten. He chose me because he knew I'd stop at nothing to get him off, and he was right."

"What do you mean, Joe? Are you saying the fix was in?"

Bari ignored her question. "Back when we shared a house in college, Paul and I used to talk into the night about excusable and inexcusable behavior," said Joe. "We finally agreed that there was no telling how far a man might go to defend his home, his family or his friends from genuine and severe harm, but that almost anything he did was acceptable. I believe that to this day."

"You still trust him and love him as a friend?"

"With one or two small reservations. What about you?"

"I didn't love him at all until this happened," she said, looking away, color rising to her cheeks. "You knew that, of course. Now, I love him deeply."

"Then good has come from it after all."

"Yes, it has," said Marian softly, pausing several seconds and looking down at her hands. "Someday, Joe, I'll tell you another secret, but not now," she said, standing and extending her hand. Joe rose with her.

"Would it have anything to do with a Ferrari going off the Ravenna Bridge in Richmond three months ago during the trial?"

"It was an accident, a horrible accident. I wanted to talk to Richard, to plead with him not to testify."

Bari was about to stop Marian from going further, but changed his mind. He no longer represented Marian, and he didn't particularly want knowledge of a crime. But what did it matter? This was a private conversation, and besides, he was dying to hear what had happened.

"I called him on the phone and he hung up on me. I drove out to his favorite bar. I thought maybe if I saw him in person he might change his mind. Frankly, Joe, I was prepared to have sex with him. His car, or what I thought was his car, was in the bar parking lot. I mean, how many red Ferraris can there be in Richmond, for God's sake?"

Bari had seen dramatic, unbelievable coincidences crop up in a number of his cases. Mistaken identity was a classic example. It's dark. You see a guy where you expected to see someone else. You misidentify the innocent guy as the person you expected to see. Happens every day in criminal court. But this red Ferrari . . . parked at the very bar . . . Manischewitz!

"I nodded off, and then woke up just as the bar was closing. Cars were leaving the car lot. I saw Richard, or who I thought was Richard, get into this red Ferrari. Anyway, I followed him for some distance and then decided to drive around and signal that I would meet him at his condo. I pulled even with his car and waved. Then I continued around and ahead of him. There was plenty of room, believe me, but he made a sharp turn to the right like he was trying to avoid an accident. That's when he went into the ravine.

"I went to a phone, disguised my voice, and called 911. But no one could have survived. That ravine is almost two hundred feet deep. I didn't know until the following morning that it wasn't Richard."

Marian's story was just screwy enough to be true, and Bari was inclined to believe it.

"I'm sorry, Marian, I really am. Now that you've told me what happened, don't ever retell it. It was an accident, period. It happened, and there's not a damn thing you or anyone else can do to undo it. For the sake of your happiness and Paul's, say a prayer for the guy who died - then, put it the hell out of your mind forever."

Marian smiled sadly. She squeezed his hand with both of hers in the way people do when they want you to know just how very much they appreciate your keeping a confidence.

Marian leaned forward and kissed him lightly on the cheek. Then she turned and walked out of his office.

PAUL FELDMAN WAS presently basking in Marian's adoration and respect. Marian believed that Paul had deftly eradicated his rival and gotten away with it. Never mind that he had scared the living hell out of her while doing it. It added up to balls, and despite all that had happened, Marian still respected balls. Had she known the truth, she would have appreciated the irony, because the real killer had no balls at all.

Sometime after Paul Feldman had left for the airport on the morning of February fifteenth, his addled mother, Rachel, drove over to take her daughter-in-law shopping. Playing her piano and shopping with Marian were Rachel's favorite things. And although Rachel's driving worried her husband, Mr. Feldman couldn't bring himself to deprive his wife of the car for short neighborhood trips, her last claim to independence.

It wasn't Rachel's style at all to drop over without calling, but *she believed that she had called Marian.* When no one had answered the doorbell, Rachel tried the door and entered, thinking that Marian was probably in the shower.

After laboring upstairs, Rachel opened the bedroom door on a horrific scene that she could not endure. Dear God! Some man doing this awful THING to Marian in Paul's home. This scum couldn't take Paul's wife like that! It was an abomination and it was hideous. Rachel was shaking. She had to do something, NOW! She opened her mouth to scream, but there was no sound. She glanced quickly around the room. A gun was hanging right there, within arm's reach.

A professional assassin couldn't have improved on Rachel's performance. She hadn't been seen and she was in and out in ten minutes.

RACHEL'S NEXT CONSCIOUS stirring was a growing awareness of driving into her own driveway. She looked around the inside of the car. No packages, so she couldn't have gone shopping. Oh well, perhaps she had just driven around the block as she did more and more often. She liked the feeling of freedom that she got from driving. Freedom: that's what cars were really for after all.

It would be erroneous to say that Rachel didn't remember what she had done. People remember that which has been forgotten, and Rachel had forgotten nothing, because - thanks to her increasing senility - the shooting of Detective Carey hadn't been imprinted on her mind in the first place. There was no memory, and therefore no guilt, nothing, zero.

Rachel could have been subjected to hypnosis, to Pentothal, to the threat of harm to her son or her husband. Nothing could cause her to retrieve the memory of putting a lead slug in the back of Detective Carey's brain, because the memory simply wasn't there.

Rachel's adored son, Paul, would have been more shocked than anyone had he known the shooter's identity. Paul had long suspected that Marian had a lover and wanted to find out for himself by coming home unexpectedly. He had taken ipecac - accidentally overdosed was more like it - to give himself cover for missing his flight to Houston and passing up a golden opportunity.

Paul hadn't for a second bought Marian's story about the noise outside the house or Detective Carey, but he also hadn't an idea in hell who actually shot him. Paul was not alone. Nobody else had either, and no secret was ever safer.

MG